Greyla

SISTER ANNE RESIGNS

'Josephine Elder' was the pseudonym of Dr Olive Potter. She was born in Croydon in 1895 and educated at Croydon High School, where an inspirational Botany mistress helped her to win her scholarship to Girton. She completed her medical training at the London Hospital in Whitechapel, one of the first four women there. After a couple of years in hospital doctor posts, she set up as a GP in Surrey. Patients were slow to come to women doctors in the 1920s, so she turned to writing. Her first book, *Erica Wins Through* (1924) was followed by nine more school stories for girls, and six adult novels (two under the further pen-name 'Margaret Potter'), including *Lady of Letters* (1949), *The Encircled Heart* (1951) and *Doctor's Children* (1954). She didn't retire until she was eighty-eight, and died five years later, in 1988.

By the same author

Lady of Letters
The Encircled Heart
Doctor's Children
The Mystery of the Purple Bentley

SISTER ANNE RESIGNS

JOSEPHINE ELDER

Greyladies

Published by
Greyladies
an imprint of The Old Children's Bookshelf
175 Canongate, Edinburgh EH8 8BN

Originally published in 1931 by Selwyn Blount
under the pseudonym 'Margaret Potter'.
© The estate of Olive Potter

This edition first published 2012
Design and layout © Shirley Neilson 2012

ISBN   978-1-907503-20-7

Set in Sylfaen / Perpetua
Printed and bound by the MPG Books Group,
Bodmin and Kings Lynn,

SISTER ANNE RESIGNS

PART 1

SCHOOLGIRL

"Here lies a changeling love,
        who found me empty-hearted,
Left a warm home for later loves,
        and so, departed."

Time and Tide

CHAPTER 1

I

"NOT going back next term? But—*Father!*"

Anne stood gripping the table and staring in front of her.

John Lee removed his pipe. "That's what I said. That you'd better say goodbye to all your cronies because you won't be going back next term."

"But, Father, I'll be in the Upper Sixth and they're sure to make me a Prefect and—and we shan't have half such a good chance for the hockey cup if I'm not there . . ."

Words failed her. It flashed through her mind that it did not matter what happened to the hockey cup if she was not going to play in the school team. It did matter, of course . . . but . . . here it was, only two days before the end of term and she had this sprung on her.

"What am I to do, if I don't go back to school?" she asked.

"The same as most girls of sixteen do when they leave school. Help your mother with the house. There's plenty to do. She's on the run all day, I know. And your dresses and Violet's always look as though they could do with a little extra looking after." He tweaked at a three-cornered tear in Anne's gym tunic.

"Bunjie did that just now," Anne said absently. Her face was bleak. She tried once more. "Miss Fenton said I should easily get exemption from Matric on Senior Schools. And she thought I *might* have a chance for a Schol to Oxford

3

or Cambridge—"

John Lee banged his fist on his knee. "Do stop talking this rubbish to me! You've stayed at school longer than I'd have had you stay already, all because of a fad of your mother's, and what good's it done you? You play hockey and tennis, and you talk nonsense about Prefects and Oxford and Cambridge. I tell you, I'm not going to have any daughter of mine wasting her time and my money on books when she's over sixteen. You can't possibly understand one half of what they teach you, and even if you did understand it, where does it lead to? Nowhere. There's no sense in book-learning for a woman."

"Lots of people from school go in for teaching," Anne ventured.

"And turn into hags—"

"Well—there are plenty of other things you can do if you've got a degree—"

John replaced his pipe between his teeth. "Don't argue with me. You're not going back to school next term. You're going to stay at home and help your mother. She's slaved for you for sixteen years—"

Anne, after a glance at him, turned blindly from the room.

Once outside, she paused. It was no good going to her mother. Emily Lee was a capable little body enough in the house. She thought of nothing but her home. That was why she had not wanted Anne to leave school before. A half-grown girl in the house was nothing but a nuisance. A grown-up one might perhaps be made into a help. She fed, dressed and housed her children excellently, she was busy all day long mending and making for them, and she talked incessantly about her neighbours and her maids and her aunts and uncles and cousins and about nothing else. Anne realised dimly that her father's opinion of women was based entirely on her mother. He had no sisters and he worked with men. He *liked* women to be like that. If he had had a son, he would have spent his last ha'penny on educating him. But he had only four daughters.

Anne wondered which of her sisters she had better talk to, for talk to somebody she must. Violet was not a bit fond of school, she was always at the bottom of her form and would not have minded leaving in the least. Well, her time would come, she was fifteen now. Edith loved helping mother with housework; it wasn't any good expecting sympathy from her. Anne climbed wearily up to the attic floor where they had their bedrooms and looked for Angela—pretty, twelve-year-old Angela, who was the youngest in her form and already in the Second Eleven. She would understand. It would help a little, to talk to Angela. But not very much. What *did* one do, at sixteen, if one was not at school?

2

Anne, at twenty-one, was growing out of her young leggy plainness. She was at least interesting, and gave promise almost of beauty. In her schooldays, her hair had been dragged back from her high, square brow and tied in a tuft on the top of her head, as if it were meant to balance her jutting, bulldog chin. Now she had defied her parents so far as to have the hair cut short, and the forehead, bugbear of her youth, was covered with a fringe. Below it were finely arched brows and deepset eyes which were brown in the dusk and gold-flecked in sunlight. Her lips were thin, but beautifully curved, with quaintly tucked-in corners. It was her smile which made people say she would one day be beautiful. Her rather grim young countenance would break up into curves and dimples and the eyes would twinkle, all suddenly, and the smile be gone, as it had come, in an instant.

Her face expressed her personality well; good health and Lancashire common sense in its rosy squareness; humour and quickness in the glint of the eyes; in the curly, tucked-in lips, restraint and the possibility of a passionate tenderness which at present expended itself in pity for hurt things and small things, and sometimes laid the common sense in ruins; and in the tilt of the chin, a gallant courage and a hint of the rebelliousness which would always fight quietly for its own way and never sulk.

She was walking home with a basket, having been into Manchester to shop. She did not mind shopping; it did at least take her out of the house. Shopping and cooking were the only two branches of housekeeping which she could bear. How she envied Angela—pretty, sparkling Angela, who could turn their father round with a look, who had announced, on her sixteenth birthday, that she was going to learn shorthand and typing, and had done so and immediately afterwards got herself a job in a shipping office. But then, Angela had known for years that she would have to leave school at sixteen, not had it sprung upon her as Anne had done. Anne hardly ever saw Angela, these days. She seemed to despise her stay-at-home eldest sister who spent all her spare time with her nose in a book and behaved as though education were the only thing in the world which mattered. Even Edith, who had no pretensions towards brains, seemed to be more use in the world than Anne. She really did help their mother, while Anne just as often hindered because she was so often thinking about things in books. She was a failure, really, with her books, too. She did not know anything thoroughly, because she was always being dragged away to mend stockings or make scones or take Bunjie, the dog, for a walk. She was ignorant, untidy—and not very mannerly—how could she be anything else, when her education had been cut short when it had hardly begun and her social life had never begun at all? Her father would not even let them join the local tennis club.

As she turned the corner into the road in which the Lees lived, Anne saw that Edith was leaning over the gate of their house watching for someone. She came out quickly and walked towards her sister. Anne wondered what had happened. People did not lean over gates in that particular suburb of Manchester, and nothing ever happened of such importance that it could not wait the length of the road to be imparted.

She called to Edith when she came within earshot:

"What's up?"

Edith was breathless and her eyes had an amazed, unbelieving look in them.

"It's Father. He's been taken ill at the mill. It's a stroke, they said. Mother wants you to go and see him—"

"*Me* go and see him?"

"He's too ill to be moved. A man came and told us."

"But why *me?* I can't do anything, if I do go."

"Someone's got to. Mother can't, she's crying and shivering so that she can't keep still. I can't leave her. And Vi's gone over to help Aunt Polly with some sewing. I haven't tried to get her, it's such miles away. Besides, you're the eldest." Edith had their mother's garrulously practical nature.

Anne was taking in, slowly, that she really had got to do this revolting thing. She pushed past Edith into the house.

3

When she arrived at her father's mill, she walked straight in as though the place belonged to her. It was only at the door of John Lee's room that she stopped, suddenly frightened by the sound of men's hushed voices behind it. She knocked, and her father's foreman opened the door and stuck his head through the crack.

"Oh—it's Miss Anne." He turned and spoke over his shoulder. "Shall she come in, Doctor?"

A young man whom she did not know came and looked at her. She stood very straight, staring at him. He saw her strong young figure and the good-looking face which was resolute yet shy, and came out, shutting the door behind him. "You're his daughter?"

Anne nodded. "Yes. What's happened?" She was not

8

used to dealing with strangers, and she was too much agitated to be polite.

"He's had a stroke. Tried to lift something heavy directly after a big dinner, and fell down unconscious."

"Is he dead?" Anne asked.

The Doctor glanced at her, appraisingly, and told her the truth. "No. He might go on for weeks, in a paralysed condition. But I don't think, myself, that he'll last very long."

"How long?" she insisted.

"Perhaps—an hour? I don't think more."

"I'd better go and fetch Mother."

"Do you want to see him?" he suggested.

Anne hesitated. She did not want to see him. But she had an uneasy feeling that to do so was her duty, that her mother would expect it. "I'd better," she said, and the Doctor turned and she followed him into the office.

John Lee was lying on the camp bed which he had taken to the mill once during a strike when he had had to be there all night. His usually red face was livid, his lips were blue, and he was breathing slowly and snoring. His teeth were showing in a sort of snarl. He looked as though he was very angry, and asleep. The Doctor lifted one of his hands and let it fall again, quite limp. "He's paralysed like that all over," he said.

Anne wondered whether she ought to kiss him. He had never encouraged demonstration from any of them, except from Angela. Why should he expect it now? She stood looking down at him gravely, suddenly terribly sorry for him. She hoped he would not go on for weeks, like that. He would simply hate it. It was a new and painful sensation, to be sorry for her father.

Outside again, she asked the Doctor: "What is a stroke? What makes him like that?"

"He's broken a blood-vessel inside his brain," he told her. "If it stops bleeding very soon, he may live. If it doesn't, he'll die."

"And there's nothing you can do?"

"I've done all I can. And I'm afraid it isn't going to be any good."

She thanked him and set off home. When she returned, in a cab, with her mother and Edith, John Lee was dead. Anne's dominant feelings were, relief that, once begun, it was over so soon; that new, painful pity for him; and a great reverence for the young doctor who appeared hardly older than herself and who yet knew so much that he could tell by looking at a man how long he had to live.

4

When they had comforted their mother and put her to bed, Anne realised with a thrill which took away her breath that now she would be able to do as she liked. She need not stay in this horrible house any longer, wasting herself over unnecessary housework which she hated. She could get away and do something.

She brought her mind to grips with the practical side of the situation, always a difficult matter for her. She would need some training, and that would need money. Her mother, she supposed, would have all her father's money. The mill would belong to her, now, and the income from it would go on as before. There should not be any great difficulty in getting money for training out of her mother. Edith would very soon learn to do the cooking. There would not be very much cooking now, with no father, and herself and probably Angela away. Anne began to whistle with excitement, then noticed the drawn blinds and was quiet. She began, with an effort, to try to decide what she would be trained for. She saw herself as an efficient confidential secretary, exquisitely dressed and highly paid. Later on, as a Member of Parliament, a Labour member, because her father had been rabidly Conservative. There was no end to the possibilities before her.

5

John Lee's will had been read. The few guests at his funeral had left, and with them the old solicitor who had interviewed his family. Emily Lee and the four girls, and Aunt Polly and Aunt Alice, Emily's elderly sisters, were gathered round the dining-room table.

"But what will you *do,* Emmie? What will you *do?*" Aunt Polly was querying.

Emily, for all the narrowness of her outlook, was a sturdy little woman. She faced this new crisis with determination. Perhaps, Anne thought, watching her, she had not been entirely ignorant of the state of her husband's affairs. She must, of course, have known about the heavy losses after the war. And she must have known, as the girls had not, that the mill was not John Lee's property but only rented. She had probably not known that, when all John's debts were paid off and the goodwill of the mill sold, there would only be left the house and just enough for his wife to live on very, very quietly.

"What'll I do? Well—" Emily stated her decision. "We've been talking it over, Edith and I."

"She ought to have talked it over with all of us," Anne thought dully.

"And we've come to the conclusion that she and I together could be very happy staying on in this house and taking two or three guests. We're well known here, and I must have something to do, I can't be idle. Edith agrees with me, don't you, dear?"

Edith assented, and her mother chattered on, as she always did, and Anne's thoughts wandered. Edith could do as she liked, of course.

"The others will have to get something to do. There wouldn't be room for us all here," Mrs. Lee was saying.

Angela, fidgeting with the tablecloth, began to speak. "I ought to have told you before, only it never seemed to be the right minute. I'm engaged. I shall stay on at the office, of course, until we're married—"

At any other time, she would have made a sensation. As it was, only Anne showed any excitement.

"Angela! Engaged? Who is he? What's he like? Tell us about it."

Mrs. Lee just said calmly: "Well, then you'll be off my hands. That's a good thing."

Angela grinned at Anne. They could talk afterwards. Anne could see that she was relieved at having got the confession over. Violet was taking up the thread:

"I knew I should probably have to find something to do. I went to see Mrs. French yesterday. She wants a companion, now that Miss French is going to be married. She's a dear old lady. I think we shall get on very well. She wants me at the beginning of next week."

Mrs. Lee nodded. That was two of them settled. The eyes of the whole party slewed round and fixed themselves on Anne.

Anne experienced a sensation of horror. They had been quietly arranging matters—while she had been dreaming that she would be rich and independent.

"I've been thinking about you, Anne," her mother said. "And it seems to me that there are only two or three possible openings. You might perhaps go into one of the larger houses as nursery governess. You were good at your books, at school, and you could easily look it up again—"

Anne had a vision of a tired, rusty-black and grey lady with frizzed hair who had taught her how to make pot-hooks and hangers. She shook her head irritably. "I couldn't possibly do that!"

"You don't seem to like old people, or you could get a post like Violet's. The only other thing I can think of is hospital nursing."

Remembering her father lying still on that camp-bed, Anne was going to shake her head again. Angela broke in sharply: "Well, you must do something, unless you want to stay here and help with the P.G.'s!"

Edith was eyeing her solemnly. "I saw a bus conductor the other day. He pushed off a whole crowd of people so that a nurse in uniform could have the only place. It wasn't her turn at all. They're awfully—sort of respected, hospital nurses."

"And you're strong. You'd want to be strong," Violet put in.

"It's a wonderfully noble profession," Aunt Alice intoned. "Utter renunciation of self. Iron discipline. A life of service."

Anne hunched her shoulders. It sounded awful.

"It *is* a form of service," Emily Lee said quietly. "And, as such, worth doing. Far more worth doing than copying out letters or even looking after old ladies so that their daughters can go gadding about. I've known some very fine women who were trained nurses."

It was that, and the memory of the young doctor who knew so much, which made up Anne's mind for her. Nurses had to pass exams nowadays, and that meant learning out of books. Perhaps it would not be such a bad life after all.

A fortnight later, she was disembarking from a cab in a slum street, then following a trim, starched woman shaped like Mrs. Noah, upstairs and along a gloomy but scrupulously clean passage, to a green cell of a room. Mrs. Noah turned, at the door, and said, "Supper at eight. There's no need to put on uniform, but please be quite punctual."

Anne grinned at the wooden, machine-like back. This, as an end to her dreams!

CHAPTER 2

1

THE newest probationer in Southcliffe ward, not as
spruce as she had been before a devastating morning spent
in cleaning things and being hunted from bed to bed by
her seniors, seemed to herself for a moment to have
nothing to do. It was almost impossible. It was quite
impossible. The Staff-nurse caught her eye.

"Nurse! Don't stand there wasting time! Go and change
Baby Browning, and don't forget to powder her tail!"

The newest probationer was startled, but pleased. It was
only two days since she had come out of the "Paddock"
into the real hospital. She had spent the last six weeks in
the company of a houseful of greenhorns like herself, who
had attended lectures and read books and practised,
solemnly, washing, bandaging, and bed-making for papier
mâché models who suffered, transiently, from this disease
or that. It was, she had found, very much like being at
school. The learners were very much like schoolgirls, and
she herself had felt younger, in the Paddock under the
stern eye of Sister-tutor, than at any time during the last
five years.

This command from the Staff-nurse represented the
first time she had been allowed to touch a real patient.
The two days had been taken up with beds and brass
knobs and utensils of all sorts of odd shapes and uses. She
approached the cot of Baby Browning. She had heard that
there were babies who were born with tails, but she had

never seen one. She visualised it, upcurled, pink and bony, like the tail of a skinned rabbit. She supposed that they would cut it off, and no one except that baby's parents would ever know about it until the baby produced tailed babies of its own.

She found a napkin and some powder and began, a little nervously, for she was not used to very young babies, to unpin the small kicking creature. Baby Browning was so downy as to be almost furry, very much like a monkey. Perhaps she really was a monkey. The Pro lifted her up by her ankles in the deft way which she had seen and admired in the Staff-nurse, and peered, and peered again. There was not the faintest semblance of a tail. Nothing but a dimple.

The Pro let her down again and turned a guilty eye over her shoulder. She was learning not to ask questions unless she was driven to it.

"What's the matter?" the Staff-nurse inquired.

"You did say Baby Browning?"

"I did. Why?"

"She hasn't got a tail."

"Hasn't got one? Oh, my goodness! Anderson, Nurse Lee says Baby Browning hasn't got a tail!"

The Senior Probationer joined the group, and doubled up with silent laughter.

"But—but you did tell me to powder her tail!"

"Bless the woman," the Staff-nurse said blandly. "What did you want me to call it?"

Anne flushed, dimpled, and bent again over the cot, and the three of them giggled quietly. The story would go all round the ward to enliven the tedious routine work of the nurses. She flushed again when she thought of it. Well, she did not really mind being laughed at.

2

That was Anne's last job before lunch. It was her first half-day off duty, and when lunch was finished she crossed the court to the Nurses' Home, averting her eyes, according to rule, from the strolling pairs of students and Resident Medical Officers who met and passed her. She wished she could have looked at them. She might have found one like that young doctor at the mill.

She was a little lonely, now that the novelty of the life was wearing off. She missed her sisters very much. There was simply no time to make friends in this rushing, bustling place. In the Paddock, she had felt herself much older than most of the people of her year; older, if not in days then in experience. Some of them had come straight from school, most of them from happy, normal homes where they had spent their spare time dancing and playing tennis. Hearing snatches of their talk, she understood how hemmed in had been the life which she and her sisters had led. She could not talk these girls' language. Her shyness sat on her like a spell and made it impossible for her to join the chattering groups in the Common Room. Instead, she would sit alone with a book and comfort herself by thinking that they talked of nothing but rubbishy hospital gossip. That was true. But Anne did not realise, yet, that one way of making bearable this conventual life, which had none of the central inspiration of a real convent, was to make mountains out of molehills, jokes from the scantiest material, true stories out of the flimsiest rumour. They all did it. Those who had been long at the hospital had made a fine art of it and took it for what it was worth. To a newcomer it was nothing short of scandalous.

When she had time, she would go off alone on a bus to explore this much-talked-of town of London. It fascinated her. She would brood over its shops, or penetrate into old parts of it which most people had never heard of, and come back refreshed by these glimpses of the larger world in which she had not yet lost all interest.

When she was at work, she was perfectly happy. St. Edmunds is one of the largest hospitals and its training one of the best in the whole of London. Anne found the work of absorbing interest.

Every morning she walked along arched, cloister-like passages to her ward. The ward was very high and light, with shining green and white walls and glass tables which reflected the green, and rows of cots all white and tidy. Small, quiet children sat up in bright red coats, and babies made whimpering, wriggling lumps under the bedclothes. It seemed at first a most inhuman place, full of bright, hard people, some in grey, some in bright blue, some in little caps and some in big. Anne had very soon learnt which denoted a Sister, which a Staff-nurse and which a mere probationer like herself. It was more than life was worth, not to know these things.

She was expected to do innumerable jobs in what

seemed at first an incredibly short time, many of them unpleasant and most of them apparently petty. There was none at all of the high nobility which she had been led to expect about the business. The triviality of her duties oppressed her for a while. Then, one day, she heard a Visiting Physician teaching his following of students— "Treatment is a matter of detail. It's no good ordering the right medicine if the patient's not comfortable in bed and having the right sort of nourishment in a way that he can take it" and realised that even trivialities are important in the mass.

As the days went on, definite individuals began to crystallise out from the crowd of hurrying people. Sister, for instance, was recognisable not only by her bright blue and her goffered strings, but by her sweet, tired face and her patient explanations, round the table in the evenings, of everything which her nurses chose to ask her about the happenings of the day. Anne gathered, from the talk which went on round her, that Sister Southcliffe was a gem of her kind. Most of the Sisters at St. Edmunds were not in the least like her. "The Probationers' Paradise," she heard the ward called.

The Staff-nurse, too, was a happy, cheery soul who had been trained by Sister Southcliffe and had absorbed some of her graciousness of bearing. Anne liked her. But she was too far above the newest Pro to be thought of as a friend.

Anne herself, too, began to be recognised as a personality. Her good looks, her strength, her quickness in absorbing what she was told, her very aloofness, all

19

combined to make her noticeable. There were other things about her, too—

"There's that untidy Susie with the crooked cap!" a senior nurse would call. "Nurse! Put your cap straight!"

And Anne would dimple, quite good-humouredly, because she only lost her temper when she was unhappy, and set her cap in the middle of her head, where it would stay, until next time. The senior who had admonished her would be pleased, really by Anne's smile, although she would have said it was because the "Susie" could take a rebuke without turning sulky; and would give her an extra job to do as a reward. Anne accepted the extra jobs for the compliments they were, and performed them very well. Sister and the Staff-nurse realised that they had, for once, got hold of a promising probationer.

Then, just as Anne was beginning to jog along on greased wheels in her new groove, the Staff-nurse was moved to another ward. Her successor was a thin, hard-eyed young woman to whom Anne took an instant dislike. She was quick to take dislikes, and not in the least successful in disguising her feelings. She was not rude, and she did as she was told at once and exactly. But she looked down from her greater height on Nurse Paley as a polite child might look at a maggot in her cabbage—a look of hurt incredulity that such a thing should have power to move her. Nurse Paley could not avoid seeing the look, and knowing that it indicated an enemy. A Junior Pro who was, in some indefinable way, her superior, was a person to be bullied into submission. Nothing else could be done.

She snapped at Anne and sneered at her and gave her the most horrible things to do over and over again, and there was no way in which Anne could retaliate. A row with the Staff-nurse, or a complaint about her, would only mean removal to another ward and perhaps a report to the Matron. Getting on with unpleasant people was one of the things which had to be learnt.

After one particularly busy morning, the nurses were hurrying round the ward with plates of almost liquid mince for the patients' dinners. There was one child in the ward just then of whom Anne was specially fond—a little coster girl called Gertie, skinny and strident and very affectionate. Anne was making for her with a plate, her eye on the child's grinning face rather than on what she was carrying. She never knew exactly what happened. It seemed as if Nurse Paley had felt that she must at all costs divert that grin from Anne to herself. Anne felt an impact on her elbow, side-stepped and lost her balance, and both her plates went crashing to the floor. She looked up to see the Staff-nurse settling Gertie's dinner on her bed-table. The grin had vanished and Gertie was proclaiming shrilly: " 'Twasn't 'er fault! 'Twasn't 'er fault!"

Nurse Paley's thin voice rebuked Anne in front of them all. "You really must try to be less clumsy, Nurse Lee. Clean that up now at once. I shall have to do the rest of your dinners myself."

"What the dickens made you cut in like that—"Anne was indignantly demanding. But Nurse Paley had preserved her dignity and returned to the kitchen.

When the pieces were picked up and the floor clean

21

again, and the nurses were lined up in the kitchen waiting to start off on a round of puddings, Anne stepped elaborately in front. "I'd better go first, then I shan't trip over you again," she said.

Everyone giggled. It was the difference in size between them which made the remark so funny; that and the contrast between Anne's twinkling eyes and Nurse Paley's look of fury. It was an obvious breach of hospital etiquette for a Pro to walk into the ward in front of the Staff-nurse.

Although Anne twinkled, she felt very angry. Nurse Paley was so petty and horrible. As soon as the patients' dinners were cleared away, she raced along the passage to her own, almost chattering with rage, thinking of nothing but how she hated the pernickety little senior. She was brought up short suddenly at a corner by a shorter, fatter person who was nearly flattened against the wall by the impact of her head with Anne's chest. For an awful instant Anne was sure she had collided with the Matron. It was, she felt, the sort of thing that she would do on that sort of a day. Then she heard a chuckle and a pleasant voice which asked: "What on earth's the matter with you?"

Bringing her eyes back to earth, she recognised a girl only a few months senior to herself, a rosy, laughing person whose face had often attracted her. She forgot that she was shy. She gnashed her teeth comically and said, "I'm in a rage." She was of half a mind to be in more of a rage when the other opened her mouth and laughed aloud.

"That's obvious. Why, though?"

Anne laughed too, suddenly ashamed of her fury.

"Oh, just everything," she said.

The other nurse fell into step beside her. "Sounds awful. Oh, but you've got Paley in Southcliffe now, haven't you? She's enough to send an angel into a rage."

Anne was surprised that anyone outside the ward should know that she was in Southcliffe. She was glad that she had laughed. "She's a fiend. But I expect I deserve it. She's got her knife into me most frightfully—I don't know why."

"I bet you don't deserve it. She's a devil. She hates anyone who's got any guts. She and I used to have some terrific fights. Well, you're going and I'm coming away. Dinner, I mean. And if either of us is late in this clockwork place there'll be a row. See you sometime."

She turned along another corridor and Anne went on. She felt better. She was glad that person thought she had guts. And "see you sometime" had sounded almost friendly. She was tired of being so much by herself.

After lunch, she kept herself out of Nurse Paley's way. She would have liked a "terrific fight" with her, but she felt she did not know how to begin.

She was looking forward to the report round Sister's table, because she had noticed something odd about one of the babies and was all agog to find out about it. She wished she could have been a doctor and learnt all about disease. A nurse's knowledge always seemed to stop short, as her schooldays had done, just when she knew enough to be hungry for more. But the family would never have consented to that. It disapproved of unfeminine occupations. Although why it was more feminine to wash bedpans and dirty feet than to write prescriptions and listen through a stethoscope she never could see. Anyway, she told herself, a doctor's career was an expensive one, and she was poor.

She handed in her list of unsavoury details, asked her question eagerly and was given the usual only half-satisfying reply. She was hurrying off duty to look up some more about it in a book, when Sister called her back.

"Nurse Lee, I want to speak to you."

She stood before the older woman and thought how much she liked her sweet, tired eyes and firm mouth, her grey hair and her trim dignity. Why did her face wear that almost wistful look when she thought no one was watching her? Was nursing so thankless a profession to grow old in, even if you were the nicest Sister of the best ward in the hospital? It must surely be very pleasant, to have the gratitude of your patients and the adoration of your nurses. Of course, each short generation of both left you very quickly, and perhaps they forgot and then you were alone

She was interrupted by Sister's slow voice. "I had thought you were promising, Nurse. Now I'm afraid you were only a new broom. Your report from Staff-nurse this week had been anything but good."

Anne blinked at her. Staff-nurse? That was Paley. She would not have expected exactly a good report from Paley. But she would not have expected one bad enough for Sister to comment upon. She had done her work just as thoroughly as usual.

Sister went on. "Staff-nurse tells me she's always having to clear up after you. And she's complained about your manners. We like our nurses to have specially good manners, you know."

"My—manners?" Anne could think of nothing better to say.

"I'm told that you don't let her finish speaking when she's giving you an order. You rush away in the middle of a sentence. And sometimes you answer her back rudely. And then, of course, there's the untidiness."

Anne smiled. There was no indignation in Sister's voice, only kindness and weariness. How tired she must get of ticking people off for these idiotic little faults.

"I—I know I'm untidy," she said. "My head simply doesn't seem the right shape for a cap, and I've always forgotten where I've put my cuffs. It's as though they'd got a demon in them."

Sister thawed a little. "I had thought you were getting better."

Anne said vindictively, "So had I, Sister."

"Well, what about the other things?"

Anne deliberated. She could have said quite a lot about Nurse Paley. It *was* like being back at school. She said simply, "I'll try to be better about them, Sister."

Sister surveyed her silently. "You mustn't *do* these things," she said. "We don't like our nurses to be untidy and have bad manners. It isn't *Ed*-munds!" She spoke with a peculiar plaintive drawl. Anne never forgot dear gentle Sister Southcliffe and her "It isn't *Ed*-munds!" If she said that to you, you never did the offending thing again. You couldn't, somehow.

Sister became suddenly brisk. "Nurse," she said. "Did ye know Nurse Paley had been having to clear up after you?"

Anne met her eye. "No," she said. "And I don't believe there was anything to clear even if she did."

Sister was scribbling on her blotting paper. The night nurses were coming into the ward. "You can go now, Nurse," she said.

3

Anne took her *Handbook of Practical Nursing* into the Common Room with her to finish looking up her question. She had only just opened it when she was hailed by her friend of the morning.

"Are you safe now? Or still in a rage?"

Anne laughed. "Better now, thank you. But that devil went and reported me to Sister for being rude."

"The dog! Paley'll do anything to get her own back."

"It's all so silly and babyish," Anne exploded. "Why should she hate me just because one of the kids happens to like me—after all, the kid's more used to me than to her, I've been in the ward longer. And even if she does hate me, why on earth take it out on me in a thing that really matters like a report? Spoiling my whole record just because she doesn't happen to like my face! That's all it boils down to!"

She had not made so long a speech since she had come to the hospital.

"Well, I don't suppose Sister payed much attention to it," the other soothed her. "She's a lamb, is Sister Southcliffe."

"She is. No, I think she understood."

"You're lucky, starting there. I had Paley right at the beginning. I nearly left. What's your name?"

Anne told her.

"Mine's Belsize. Jewish. I suppose you can see that." Their eyes met in a smile. They liked each other. Nurse Belsize beckoned to another girl.

"Here, March! Here's another of Paley's victims. March was under Paley just now in Huxley," she explained to Anne.

"Paley's noted for it, then?" Anne said.

"Oh yes. If you want to get on with her, you must pretend you admire her. Bring her presents now and then—bananas, cakes of soap, any old thing. She'll be awfully nice to you then."

Anne made a face, but the others looked serious. "She's a bad enemy, you know," they warned her.

"She can't do one any real damage, can she?"

"Not with Sister Southcliffe, perhaps. Sister sees through her. But other people often don't. She's clever."

Several other nurses joined the three, and Anne found herself in the middle of one of the groups which she had half envied, half despised. The talk was certainly nothing but hospital gossip; but not so uninteresting when one realised its ins and outs. She felt almost grateful to Paley.

4

The barrier of her shyness once broken down, the Common Room lost its terrors for Anne. Belsize was a popular member of it, and Anne's shrewd Northern comments soon made her a welcome member of any group into which she drifted. She learned the customs and catchwords of hospital life and found the nurses' language becoming intelligible. In the ward, she avoided open warfare with the Staff-nurse and continued to work hard. Her time was always completely filled up. She lived in a whirl of duties always too many for the time allotted, in a crowd of uniformed women known and unknown. House surgeons and students drifted in and out of the ward, but she had no personal contact with them. The Honorary Staff made pompous rounds, but she as Junior Pro hardly ever saw them. Presently a Pro more junior than she appeared, and Anne subjected her to the same kindly raillery with which she herself had been licked into shape. One day the newcomer was told to clean the bath with soda-water because it was more than usually dirty, and Anne, attracted by a strange noise, found her with all the ward syphons collected round her, squirting for dear life. She felt that her mistake over Baby Browning's tail had been wiped out. She seemed to have belonged to St. Edmunds for years.

CHAPTER 3

1

AFTER three months Anne was moved into another ward. Her report had been good in spite of Nurse Paley, and she had signed on for four years of training. She was put on night-duty in a women's surgical ward. In the morning she went to bed and spent some restless hours tossing to the sound of trams and lorries far below. She wondered if she would ever be able to sleep, and, if not, how she would ever be able to work. Then she must have dozed, for she woke to find it seven o'clock in the evening. She ate with distaste her second breakfast that day, and went on duty.

Each ward at night is managed by a Staff-nurse and two probationers, superintended by a Night-sister who visits them at intervals. Neither the Staff-nurse nor the other Pro was known to Anne. The one appeared fat and amiable, the other pale and nondescript. They pounced on Anne the minute the day-report had been read.

"Can you cook?"

Anne grinned. "I've cooked for a houseful since I was seventeen. Why?"

The Senior Pro expressed relief. "I've had to do it, and I can't cook for toffee. It's made her so cross—" She nodded towards the Staff-nurse, who sniffed good-humouredly.

"Well, one must eat. You'd better take it over, Nurse Lee. Our dinners, and the breakfasts. The stuff for the dinners is up now. Sardines and bread and cheese, I think it is. Someone's got to make a two-course dinner out of that. You can swap with the other wards sometimes, and there's generally something or other left over from the day. And tomorrow when you're out you can get some extras. I shall want mine at half-past twelve. You get yours when I've done. Come along and do some work now or we shall have Flannelfeet on us. There are these two splints to be padded, and some plaster bandages to make—I'll show you how to do that—"

The hurry of small duties began again, much the same as during the day. Then darkness began to creep into the corners of the ward, and the bare, shining place turned into a world of shadows. The shaded lamps brought down the high, unfriendly ceiling. The red shades on them gave a warm and rosy glow. Little grunting, whimpering sounds came from the sleeping patients, and now and then one would cry out suddenly. The bright bustle of the day gave place to peace.

The nurses echoed the change in their movements. They moved slowly, on hushed feet, and spoke in whispers, coaxing, instead of cheerfully, crisply giving orders.

From eleven until twelve the several House-surgeons came, talked in low tones to Night-sister or to the Staff-nurse by the table, looked at anyone who was very ill, and went away. The Night-rounds over, the nurses settled down. Collars and cuffs were taken off, the Staff-nurse and the other probationer sat by the fire to make swabs, and Anne went to the kitchen to cook.

To make a dinner from the material provided needed

thought. In the end she produced a savoury compound of sardines, cheese and a tomato, and an appetisingly browned bread-and-butter pudding. The first would be tasty, the second solid. Just as she was going to serve it, the other probationer rushed into the room. "It smelt so good I thought I simply must warn you! If Nurse likes it, she'll eat the whole lot!"

Anne chuckled. "She'd have a job!"

"She'd do it! She's the greediest pig!"

So Anne, a little nervous lest her boasted skill should be despised, set the Staff-nurse's share before her on a plate.

"Might have put some flowers on the table," was that lady's only comment when the second course appeared. But she was licking her lips appreciatively and Anne noticed that her eyes fixed themselves at once on the new plate as it was carried in. Both the plates were scraped clean.

At half-past five they woke the sleepy, grumbling patients and washed them in the cold light. At seven the Staff-nurse beckoned to Anne.

"Go and call Sister Housekeeper. On this floor, at the end of the passage. Take her a Seidlitz powder, and stay there till she's had it, or she'll go to sleep again."

Anne knocked at the door and went boldly in. Sister Housekeeper, acid and terrifying by day, lay snoring, her grey hair in curl-pins, her window tight shut. Anne spoke to her, approached her, shook her by the shoulder.

"A—ooah? ye—nur—?" She had no teeth.

"Here's your Seidlitz powder, Sister."

"Thankye. Pu' i' down there—" She jerked her head at

31

the table and snuggled down again.

Anne added the fizzy powder to the quiet one. "It'll stop fizzing if you don't drink it now, Sister."

"Oo— pu' i' down, Nurse."

"Here you are, Sister. It's nearly stopped."

Sister Housekeeper heaved herself upright, and seized the glass.

"Aw-right, Nurse. Awake now."

She drained the glass and handed it back, and Anne slipped away. Well, she would never be afraid of Sister Housekeeper again.

2

So night followed night. Sleep came, uneasily, but enough to rest her, by day. She saw little of her friends, for they were seldom off duty when she was free, but she was too tired to wish much for company. She went for sleepy bus-rides and took to reading silly books because she could not, for the present, grasp the sense of more solid ones. During the night, she became an automaton. One night a woman died in the ward, and she helped the Staff-nurse with the gruesome task of laying her out and was not greatly moved. Her unpleasant tasks were almost outside her consciousness. The occupants of the beds changed before they were more than strangers. She sat for hours making dressings and padding splints and did not think at all. The only matter over which her brain did rouse itself, and that probably as the result rather of the habit of years than of present needs, was the ward cooking. She bartered flour for chicken legs and mince for sugar, bought sponge cakes and almonds when she was out, and fed the Staff-nurse into the contentment which spelt peace for herself and Nurse Grey.

One night, a woman was brought in, very ill, at two o'clock in the morning. Night-sister looked at her, helped them to get her to bed, and went off to call the House-surgeon.

Staff-nurse, torpid after a good dinner, yawned. "Who's 'taking in'? Oh, Mr. Dalloway. Look here, I'm busy. You chaperon him, Nurse Lee, will you?"

Anne made herself tidy, and when a dressing-gowned young man slouched into the ward, marched discreetly before him to the woman's bed.

"I want to examine her," he said.

"Yes, Mr. Dalloway, she's all ready."

He went off for a screen and Anne stood by the woman.

Ronald Dalloway was House-surgeon to Sir Roland Spurge and Mr. Terrington. He was very young, very keen on his work and very clever at it, and very ambitious. He knew that he was a very important person and that the lives of many depended on his skill. He realised that his future advancement depended on it too. The reputation of the hospital was mixed up with it in some way, and the good names of Sir Roland Spurge and Mr. Terrington, and the proficiency of the six students who shambled after him when he visited his patients by day. A House-surgeon at St. Edmunds might be "A Tsar for six months and then lost in the crowd", but at present he was revelling in the six months, and he did not intend ever to be lost in the crowd again. He knew the value of goodwill—everybody's goodwill—to the young person who would rise in the medical world, and so he was very careful to keep on the right side of everybody, chiefs, fellow-residents, students, sisters, nurses, patients and even porters and lab-boys.

He arranged his screen carefully, so as not to make a noise, and looked at the woman in the bed. She was grey and drawn, gasping a little, evidently exhausted. Dalloway glanced round for information.

"Anyone with her, Nurse? Or do you know about her?"

"Her husband's in the kitchen. But I heard what he told Sister."

"Right-o. Fire away."

"She had a sudden very bad pain the day before yesterday—" Anne plunged into the recital. It was lucky that she had paid attention to the talkative husband. The woman had been so awfully ill that she had wanted to know about her.

Dalloway nodded at intervals, and looked up at her with some interest when she stopped speaking. A jolly well-told history, he thought, and an unusually nice voice. Northern, somewhere. Was it Highland? Soft, and sort of lilting. He was not at all a susceptible young man, certainly not to the charms of nurses. But nurses didn't generally have voices like that. She looked so slim and trim, too, standing there waiting for him to get on with it. He felt suddenly horribly unwashed. He hunched his shoulders more firmly into his dressing gown, passed a hand over his upstanding hair, and began to examine the woman's abdomen.

After a few minutes he straightened himself and

motioned Anne away from the bed.

"She'll have to go up to the Theatre pretty quick," he said. "She's shocked now, but she'll be over that soon if we're careful. Will you tell Night-sister, please? Give her some saline and some atropine and have her ready in half an hour. I'll go and call Hilton. Thank you, Nurse."

He stood aside with lazy politeness to let her pass. But she was intent on getting things done, and, having seen him away from the patient, she sped across to the Staff-nurse and took no further notice of him.

He saw her once again, standing under the light, when he brought in the Registrar who was to operate on the woman. The Staff-nurse rather liked the Registrar and attended on him herself. Dalloway pleasantly confirmed his impression of tall, slim coolness. Anne met his eyes, but was evidently not thinking of him at all. He made a ridiculous gesture indicating that Hilton and the Staff-nurse had left him out in the cold. She smiled at his absurdity, and the smile made him blink like an owl. He had never been interested in nurses' smiles. But this one looked as though she was really a person, inside her stiff uniform and her shell of officialdom. He watched her until Hilton and he left the ward together, and hoped that he would see more of her.

3

He did see more of her, though not by design. He was much too busy all the next day even to remember her. The "take in" of a Surgical Unit in a great hospital is no joke, either for the House-surgeon or for the nursing staff.

Every surgical case which comes into the hospital for three days and three nights—sometimes six come, sometimes thirty—is nursed, watched, operated upon and treated by the members of the unit. The nurses are run off their legs, the House-surgeon is on duty all the days and all the nights.

The following evening Dalloway was visible striding from ward to ward, writing belated notes, putting fractures into splints, opening abscesses—dealing with all those cases which were too bad to be sent home and not bad enough to be taken to the Theatre. The night staff, as a rule, detested them, because of the flurry and the mess which they made in the quiet ward. After a ward anaesthetic there was always a burst of excitement among the other patients, eyes and ears cocked to find out what was being done behind the barricade of screens, complaints at the noise, at the smell of the ether, little groans of pity, or laughter, as the anaesthetised patient wept or swore during the process of waking up.

It was expected of the House-surgeon to get these disturbances over as quickly as might be. So it was that Anne, intent on collecting a good supper for her Staff-nurse, came out of a ward kitchen and ran full-tilt into Dalloway and a friend whom he had collared to give his anaesthetics. They were bolting round a corner, white coats flapping, with never a thought for whom they might meet. There was a surprised scramble, a hollow plop, and the three stood away from each other and looked at a mound of jelly on the floor and a pink and slimy stain on the anaesthetist's coat.

"Damn!" said Anne and the anaesthetist both at once, and then laughed.

"Sorry, Nurse!"

Anne bent over the mound and tried to buttress it with a spoon. It wobbled and heaved, and when she tried to pick it up it split in two. Dalloway chuckled.

"Let me try—" He tried to slide the plate under the jelly while Anne pushed with the spoon. The anaesthetist stopped dabbing at his coat and came to help. Their muffled laughter was broken into by a voice as cold and piercing as a pin.

"Nurse! May I ask what you are doing?"

Anne straightened herself and tried to straighten her cap and her face before she answered. The anaesthetist was before her.

"Our fault, Sister. We were haring round the corner and butted into Nurse and spilled her pudding."

Sister ignored him. "What are you doing out of your ward, Nurse?"

"I was swap—exchanging some food for supper, Sister."

Sister inclined her head. "Go back to your ward at once. No, leave that. I'll send the Night-porter to clear it up."

Anne's ward was only round the corner. She went into the kitchen. Presently she heard the two men chatting in the testing-room next door.

"Nice lass." That was Pedley, the anaesthetist. He spent as much thought on such matters as Dalloway did on his work. "Nice voice. Nice shape."

Anne grinned. Now what would Mr. Dalloway say?

Dalloway's voice was annoyed, and his opinion

disappointing. "Didn't notice. There's a navvy in there with a fractured femur. I expect he's had steak and onions for tea. They always do. For God's sake don't make him sick—"

Anne laughed outright. The two men went into the men's ward next door.

Back in her own ward, she received a warning from Night-sister.

"You know, Nurse, we don't expect you to talk to the Residents in any circumstances. You have your work and they have theirs. Don't let it happen again."

Anne bore the rebuke in silence. Excuses, however valid, were of no account at St. Edmunds. When Dalloway came into Annie Zunz later, they exchanged reminiscent grins behind Sister's back.

Later still, each was visited by a vision which intruded on thoughts of symptoms and treatment. Dalloway saw a slim girl, very clean and trim and smelling faintly of soap, with sweet eyes and an obstinate jaw, who smiled a glorious smile at him over her shoulder. Anne came face to face with a sleek-haired young man whose dark eyes met hers in a second's comical apprehension over a mound of shivering jelly.

4

It was after this incident that Anne began to live. Before it, she had moved in a half-dreaming state of fatigue and routine. Now she began to enjoy her work again, as she had done on day duty. She became interested, too, in the patients. Hitherto, they had seemed only dull, colourless occupants of beds. She had pitied them at first, terribly. But they had taken their ills so calmly that she had been ashamed of her pity and thrust it away. Now she realised that it was not pity but friendliness which they needed. She talked to them and smiled as she washed them, and remembered their family histories and their fads, and a little wave of liking followed her as she went about the ward.

She loved the hospital at night so much, too. Every evening, when she left the ward the first time for the quiet, dark passages, she would catch her breath and stand for a minute, lips parted, eyes expectant, awaiting some great adventure. After the minute had passed, she would walk crisply away, on some errand or other, Nurse Lee again, capable, observant, well balanced.

Sometimes she would meet Dalloway, and pass him, if no one was about, with her frank smile. She did not speak to him again after Night-sister's hint. She had a suspicion that Sister Southcliffe would have said, "It isn't *Edmunds!*" In other hospitals queer, silly flirtations might take place in the passages by night—she had heard that they did—but not here, and not with Mr. Dalloway.

Every night he would stalk in to do his night-round. Sometimes she would chaperone him, if Staff-nurse felt lazy. Then she would ply him, quite lawfully, with questions about the cases—why that happened, why this was done—and he, flattered, took trouble to answer her concisely and simply.

"Nurses don't need to know why," he teased her one night.

"If they don't know why, they won't remember," she retorted.

"They only need to do as they're told."

She laughed. "With reservations. Tell me, please, Mr. Dalloway, how much glucose solution, what percentage and what temperature, you'd like Joan Harling to have for that rectal feed you've just ordered."

He scratched his head. "Oh lor'. You have me there, Nurse. That's Sister's business. *I* just order a rectal feed of glucose and go away!"

"And Sister does as she's told—dear, dear!"

She wagged her head at him and they both laughed.

But it rankled a little—nurses this and nurses that, always with the smallest inflection of patronage. What was the matter with nurses? Were they a class apart, not persons, certainly not women, to be despised? Was it because they did dirty jobs which no one else would look at, did them with an air, as though they gloried in them, to disguise the fact that they were within an inch of running away and being sick? "Utter renunciation of self," Aunt Alice had said. Anne had not realised what Aunt Alice had meant, or how true the words were. Probably Aunt Alice had not realised herself. Anne did not feel at all, yet, that her self had disappeared. It was a very vital self, particularly when she was with Mr. Dalloway.

On other nights, the Staff-nurse would herself escort Mr. Dalloway round the ward. Anne would suffer aching disappointment and follow them round with her eyes; and Dalloway would throw over his shoulder a look of resignation, and she would gurgle with laughter and feel happy again. The two had never yet strayed from matters of work in those talks, and always her raillery was tinged with respect and his with authority. Even though she was only a probationer in her first year, no one could have complained that their talk was unprofessional. Their communications did not last for more than ten minutes at any time, but that ten minutes became the pivot of Anne's whole day. She wanted knowledge so much, and he could give it her. It was as a teacher, not particularly as a man, that she thought of him. A woman doctor, equally willing to instruct, would have done just as well. "I must ask Mr. Dalloway that," she would remind herself several times a day. The very shortness of their time together made it the more eagerly awaited.

5

There were several incidents which stayed in her memory, framed like pictures in the routine work and the soft, dark night.

In one of them, Dalloway was transformed from the earnest, ambitious young teacher into a teasing schoolboy. He had come in one night in the wildest spirits, as if the nightly lessons were reacting on him as well as on Anne. He had been taken round the ward solemnly by the Staff-nurse, and he had made her giggle and had winked at Anne over his shoulder. When he left the ward, Anne went as usual into the ward kitchen to cook. The Staff-nurse came in to fetch something, and the two of them stood chatting in low voices. Suddenly, soundlessly, Dalloway's face appeared round the door. Anne saw it from the first, and fancied that a shade of disappointment passed over it when he saw the Staff-nurse. But it was gone at once, and he tiptoed in and gently shut the door.

The Staff-nurse whirled round. "Mr. Dalloway You know the Residents aren't allowed in here! And we never shut the kitchen door—how can I hear what's going on in the ward—"

Dalloway, his finger to his lips, gently prevented her from opening it. "Ssh! The ghost's outside!" he whispered.

Anne noticed that he was shaking. What could be the matter?

"Ghost?" the Staff-nurse echoed. "What? The Grey Lady?"

Every hospital has its ghost. Probably each really has many, but one is generally legendary. The St. Edmunds ghost was a nun who had succumbed to the efforts of an early apothecary who wished to learn the surgery of the brain. She walked, by night, in her grey robes, and carried her brains on a silver dish.

Dalloway nodded. "I heard a noise," he croaked hoarsely. "Swish—swish—like that. And then I saw her, sweeping down the corridor after me with her dish in her hand. I ran. I wouldn't have minded a thug—but a ghost, no."

He shuddered, and the nurses shivered in sympathy. Anne wanted to laugh. She was sure this matter-of-fact young man did not really believe he had seen a ghost. He was trying to frighten them. He stood upright, his head on one side.

"I say—I do believe she's coming this way!"

They all stood rigid, listening.

"Yes—don't you hear? Swish—swish!"

They could all hear it. They really could. The Staff-nurse snorted nervously.

Anne took hold of the door-handle. "I must see her! I must."

"Be careful!" Dalloway warned. "Remember, you're a dead girl if she touches you!"

She shot a teasing look at him as she stepped out. The Staff-nurse cowered into a corner.

Swish—swish—there was no doubt about the soft sound which was coming nearer. A grey form came into view.

"There she is!" Dalloway whispered. The Staff-nurse squeaked and tried to pull Anne back, but Anne only leaned out farther. Suddenly she choked with laughter. "Swee—sweeping down the corridor!" she hiccoughed.

Dalloway met her eye, pinched her elbow, and darted out and away, his fingers cocked puck-like behind his ears.

The Staff-nurse's reproachful wail followed him. *"Oh, Mr. Dalloway!"*

The night-cleaner, an old woman like a beetle, skirts bunched up to show flat feet in elastic-side boots, doggedly swept the day's dust into mounds and collected them in the dust-pan which she held in her left hand.

"I wonder," Anne said as they returned to the kitchen, "if he'll try that on Flannelfeet."

Judging by Night-sister's grim face when she slid silently into Annie Zunz ward, he had, and successfully.

"I wonder," said Anne to herself, "if he was *really* disappointed that there wasn't only me. And if he meant to play that joke when he first came in. And if he always pinches people's elbows. And if he's just as nice to everyone he meets. I expect he is, everyone seems to like him."

"I hope," she thought, "that he isn't going to start coming into the ward kitchens. If he does, I shall have to squash him."

The second incident was just a talk with a patient, and had nothing to do with Dalloway at all except that she told him about it afterwards.

The patient was a governess, old, withered and worn out, but more intelligent than most of the women in the ward. She had cancer of the breast, and was to have the big operation for its removal the next day. She was very quiet about it, asked no questions as so many of them did. But Anne, attending to her in the night, thought she caught a look of dread in the tired eyes. She tried to reassure her.

"It's not so bad, you know, Miss Simmons. You won't feel anything, and you'll be so relieved when it's all over in the evening. Everybody says it's not nearly as bad as they expect."

Miss Simmons smiled her tired little smile, and said:

"That's kind of you, Nurse. I know you can't understand, any of you, that's why I try not to make a fuss. It's just part of your daily work to you. To me, it's the greatest adventure I've ever had."

Anne had thought about that afterwards. The sentence

was so intensely personal. The greatest adventure I've ever had. Even the most selfless, the most insignificant of persons was so completely the centre of his own universe. It mattered enormously to Miss Simmons how she behaved before the operation, whether she was brave or craven, how she bore the pain. Those things mattered to her more than whether she died or lived, whether the operation was successful or not. And they didn't matter to anyone else. Anne realised suddenly the terror of being alone, and then its satisfaction. To be entirely dependent on oneself—oneself, self-made, in a great space, moving forward to meet the doom one had earned. It was splendid. Terrifying, but splendid. She supposed people depended on God at such times. She hoped she wouldn't. "Oh, God," she remembered reading somewhere, "give me strength not to call upon Thee." It was the glorious mixture of humility and arrogance which appealed to her.

She turned to Miss Simmons again and patted her and tucked her in. "You're jolly plucky, Miss Simmons," she said.

The little woman gave her a smile of shy pleasure as she settled down.

One couldn't help being dependent on other people, just a little. If they said one was plucky, one was. It was only when one died that one was alone in that great white space.

She told Dalloway of the incident that night as they passed Miss Simmons' bed. He paused and looked at her, asleep.

"Poor beggar! Had a dull life, I expect, if she has to

make an adventure out of an operation," he said.

Ridiculously, Anne was disappointed. But then, he hadn't heard Miss Simmons say it.

The third incident was just a silly schoolgirl trick which Anne herself played. It was one evening when she had gone into the kitchen to inspect the provisions sent up for their supper. A Pro from a neighbouring ward burst in upon her, complaining—"I say, we've got those *horrible* sausages again! It's the third time this week, it's too bad! Oh, you've got them too. I thought we might have got yours by mistake."

The sausages were fat, chocolate-coloured things, flabby and tasteless. Everyone grumbled about them. Sometimes the nurses made them into rissoles to disguise them. More often they were simply left.

The Pro went on: "Well, I'd hoped you might swap them for something. I s'pose you won't. I don't know what to do with them! Make something cheesy and ignore them, I think."

Anne looked at the three fat things, like sleeping pigs laid side by side. "If you're really not going to use them, put them here," she said.

"I'll be glad to be rid of them. Sister Housekeeper makes such a fuss when they're sent down again. What'll you use them for?"

"I'm going to abolish them," Anne said grimly. To the Staff-nurse she said, "Just going borrowing."

She sped round all the wards. Everywhere she met the same response. "Sausages? You *want* them? Take them, and burn 'em, if you like"

At the end of the tour she had thirty-three sausages bundled into her apron. She had to hurry into a doorway once, to avoid Night-sister on her silent round. She reflected that if she had been Night-sister she would have been sporting enough to carry at least a jingling chain. She reached Annie Zunz safely and hid her load in the splint-cupboard. She made cheese straws for supper, wonderful flaky ones which lingered on the Staff-nurse's tongue; and when she and Nurse Grey came to have their supper and Staff-nurse was safely in charge of the ward, she turned the sausages out on the floor.

Nurse Grey gasped, listened, giggled helplessly and then set to work. The two of them stole matches and stuck them into the sausages, four for legs, two halves for ears and one for a tail. They drew evil little eyes in black ink and made a paper banner which read "We are not popular. Please let us go home." They laid the regiment of pigs on their backs in the splint-cupboard, washed up the supper things and went on with their work.

In the cold morning, Anne waited restlessly to hear the day-nurses go to breakfast. Once they were safely in the dining room, Night-sister with them to serve the meal, she left Nurse Grey in earnest conversation with the Staff-nurse and set out, her apron bulging. She stood the pigs in a long line in the middle of the passage, the foremost, with the banner stuck into the top of his head, just outside Sister Housekeeper's door.

It was Fate who arranged that Ronald Dalloway should be called at that uncomfortable hour to see a case in Casualty just round the corner. Anne saw him with a gasp of delight. She could not resist taking him just the few steps along the passage to show him the procession. It was Fate also who made Nurse Paley oversleep, most unusually, on that morning and be very late for breakfast, and made Dalloway's gust of laughter cause her to look over the banisters. No one ever asked her who was the culprit over the matter of the pigs, so she had no chance to tell. But the sight of a Night-Pro and a Resident in conversation in a corridor so early in the morning was a juicy morsel for her to chew. She chewed it in solitude, waiting for more.

Squeaks of laughter echoed among the day-nurses when they came out of the dining-room and were confronted by the pigs, and conversation hovered, chuckling, over the subject all day. Sister Housekeeper was a woman of understanding, and opinion upon that particular type of sausage was undivided. No inquiries were made, pig sausage disappeared from the hospital menu, and Anne became something of a heroine for a few days.

Two nights later, her three months on night-duty came to an end and, whether by accident or design she never knew, it was not renewed.

CHAPTER 4

1

ANNE was proud of herself. She had been appointed Theatre Pro, a position recognised as a reward of efficiency and seldom filled by one who had not been in the hospital at least a year.

At breakfast, she caught Belsize looking at her with a twinkle in her eye.

"What's the matter? What are you grinning at?"

"You. You're so cock-a-hoop. You won't be, for long."

"Pig. Why not?"

"Well, Sister Theatre's a cow, for one thing. You'll hate her. Matron's awfully good at that. She finds out all the most horrible, dirty, hard-worked jobs, calls them 'responsible' and pretends they're prizes. If she didn't, no one would do them. It's rather like nursing itself. Everyone who isn't a nurse says it's such wonderful work and praises up the people who do it and talks about 'born nurses' and vocations. Really, it's sweated labour. Only they get us young and make us feel noble, and we like that. So we do it, instead of office work—or nursemaiding or dressmaking or whatnot. We're idiots, of course. We'll either wear ourselves out and die when we're thirty, or end in almshouses. They'll never pay us enough for us to save. The people who work in offices marry, and the nursemaids at least get comfortable homes. Why do we do it, Lee? I bet someone told you it was noble work!"

"Someone did," Anne acknowledged, laughing. "I don't

care, it's fun."

Belsize looked at her sideways. "That's because you're pleased with yourself. Why d'you think you got that job?"

"I don't know. I suppose because there wasn't anyone better than me who was due to change."

"Oh, you're not bad at the work," Belsize said. "I grant you, you're not bad. I should think you're jolly good. But that wasn't why you got that job. You got it on your Staff's report."

"Well," Anne said, puzzled to know what the fuss was about, "I suppose she only reported on what I did."

Belsize seized her hand and swung it up and down. "You're an old innocent, aren't you? What about your cooking? Didn't you make such dinners as that Staff had never tasted in her life? And do most Pros make dinners like that? That's why she gave you such a topping report. For one thing, it's easier to write a good report than a bad one when you're full of good food. And for another, she hopes the office will say, 'Those two seem to work together very well,' and then she'll get you again. See? Tummy, not brains. Her tummy, not your brains."

Anne was laughing in spite of herself at this cheerful cynicism. "Really and truly?" she asked.

"Truth and honour. Oh, you'll see, it's the little, silly things that don't really matter a straw which get you on in this life. It's because we're such a henhouse, I expect. But you watch out for Sister Theatre, she'll give you a dog's life, no, a cat's, if you let her."

So Anne, a little chastened but not really fearful, climbed up to the long stone corridor under the roof and peered into the square, tiled rooms like pale green swimming-baths, with queer, shining things in them standing silent, expectant. A cupboard of an anaesthetising room opened off each theatre. There were rooms to change in, rooms for dirty linen, rooms for Chiefs, for students, for nurses, for theatre-swabs, each sacred to its own purpose; and two rooms separated by a great Moloch with a mouth which opened into each, one to put in and one to take out by—the steriliser.

The Theatre was a place utterly different from the wards. Instead of suffering mortals, needing treatment with differing degrees of sympathy and hardness, there were these shining mechanisms, to be kept spotless and lifted with gentle, reverent hands; and still, quietly breathing things on trolleys, things without feelings, with only a square of skin left uncovered by the white sheets, and that painted so yellow as to be quite unrecognisable; chaff and swearing among the surgeons, because the patient could not hear them and the nurses were all masked and shrouded and nobody but Sister knew really who was who; a ritual of spotless cleanliness governing everything. A curious, impersonal place, full of wonders and excitements.

2

She found Sister Theatre exactly suited to this kingdom over which she ruled. She was tall and stiff, straight as a ramrod, her cap and strings, dress and apron starched and immaculate. Dark, hostile eyes stared out of a still, white face, seeking for faults. Her mouth cut a thin line between a sharp nose, red and drawn at the tip, and, unexpectedly, a chin that faded away into her neck. She should not be blamed for her faults, which were many. Once she had been like Anne, full of ambition and enthusiasm, though without Anne's well-balanced strength and humour. She had realised early, as Anne had, the importance of trivialities, but only their importance to herself. From a means of education and treatment, they had become to her an end. She could not see round them. The Matron, with an unerring eye for fitting pegs to holes, had given her the Theatre to control, and she had become as sharp and efficient as one of her own scalpels. The God of Hospital Etiquette, whom she worshipped, moulded her into a priestess after his own heart. She tried loyally to proselytise all those who came under her. Rarely, she succeeded, and then she made, after her own fashion, a friend. She had more enemies than friends.

On this first morning, she looked Anne up and down.

"Can't think why they sent you here. Much too junior. You won't be the slightest use."

"I'm a good learner, Sister," Anne put in hopefully.

"Don't be impertinent, Nurse. Go and clean those waders of Mr. Terrington's. You'll find the things in the cupboard just above. Then there are the tables and stools to keep clean, the taps and switches, and all the dirty mackintoshes and gloves, and the floors after operations. You will be responsible for the anaesthetic tables, keep them clean and the bottles filled, and see that Mr. Thornton doesn't knock the bottles over during operations. And anything else that wants doing."

"Am I in the Theatre during operations"? Anne asked, full of excitement. She had never seen an operation. Would it be very horrible?

"Of course you are. Where else would you be? In my room in an armchair? You stand behind the anaesthetist, and keep your eyes fixed on my face. If you see that I want anything done, you go and do it, without asking questions. And no fainting or nonsense like that, it's quite unnecessary and I don't allow it. Come to me here at half-past one, Nurse, and I'll show you how to scrub yourself up."

She swept out, leaving Anne to an apprehensive vision of herself, stripped to the skin, and Sister scrubbing her with a scrubbing brush and hissing.

She pulled herself together and tackled the boots.

Her days were taken up with matters of cleanliness again. Not the personal scouring of her dream—a wash for five minutes by the clock from fingertips to elbows was all that Sister demanded—but spotless sterility of the Theatre and all that was in it. No germ had a chance to live, much less to multiply, in St. Edmunds' theatres while Sister had charge of them.

The cleanliness was punctuated incessantly by Sister's nagging. Did Anne dust, Sister followed her round with a piece of cotton-wool, rubbing it on every ledge and in every cranny; and if that cotton-wool showed on its whiteness the slightest smudge of grey, Sister would hold forth until Anne either wept or ran away biting her lips with rage. Sister's arrows of criticism were always barbed with just that germ of truth that her victims would rather have kept hidden from her. There was no hiding anything from Sister. The particular label which she attached to Anne was "superior." Perhaps it was because the girl still held a little aloof from the hospital tittle-tattle; perhaps Sister had sensed her ambition to be good at everything she did.

"Ho!" she would snort. "You'd better get those mackintoshes cleaner than that, my girl! You won't be so above yourself when the Matron comes and asks me who did disgraceful work like that. Don't like bloody things, don't you? Well, you shouldn't have pushed your way up here till you'd learnt to."

Anne would scrub doggedly then at some old mackintosh that had not been white for months and never would be again, and Sister would swoop upon her.

"Nurse! Nurse! Whatever are you wasting time on that old thing for? I said get the blood off, not the rubber! Cleanliness and whiteness are not the same thing, you know. *We* can't afford to throw things away directly they've got a little stain on them. Put that away and get on with the gloves."

The talks with Dalloway had ceased abruptly. Anne saw him often, assisting his chief in the Theatre, but they never spoke, hardly even exchanged smiles, so surrounded were they by their superiors. If she had not seen him at all, perhaps she would not have missed him so much. As it was, she had time to notice about him all sorts of things that she had not seen in the dimly lit ward at night. She saw how slim and long-legged he was, how broad-shouldered and how clean; what long, delicate fingers he had and how gently and accurately he used them; how his diagnoses were generally right; what good anaesthetics he gave how careful he was for the comfort of the patients; and how popular he was with everyone. She admired him more and more. And, somehow, her heart sank.

Sister taught her nothing but the ritual of the Theatre, and she told herself that her brain was getting rusty and that was why she was so gloomy. She read Surgery books, but she did not know enough yet to digest them. She thought of scores of questions, and there was no one to answer them for her. She noticed how Dalloway's eyes twinkled over his mask at the little funny things that happened in the Theatre, things that she found laughable too, but that no one else appeared to see. She saw other funny things too, lots of them, when Dalloway was not there, and longed to tell him them and see him throw back his head and hoot as he had done over the procession of pigs. She was ever so much more lonely than she had been on night-duty. There was no one human to talk to at all. Sister was a mechanism, the Staff-nurse a faithful disciple, and her off-duty time did not correspond with Nurse Belsize's, though of course she met her and her other friends at meals and in the evening.

Then she found George.

3

George was round and red and solemn. His grey hair made a ring round the shiny dome of his head. No one knew how old George was. He had always been and would always be the same, never young and never very old. He took care of the instruments, sharpened them, repaired them, knew what they were all for and put out those that were wanted for each operation. He lived on the Theatre floor, in a room lined with boxes and cupboards, cut off from the outer world by a polished counter over which he was addressed and behind which no one but George had ever been seen.

Anne was sent hurrying to him in the middle of preparations for the afternoon's operating, to fetch a guillotine. She had never been to the Instrument Room before, and she felt a little frightened. Who was this George? Did one call him Mister? There were so many pitfalls, and one had to find them all out for oneself, without any warnings.

George's solemn face bobbed up from behind the counter.

"Yes, Nurse? What do you want, all in a hurry?"

He looked so clean and sleek and friendly that Anne smiled.

"A guillotine, please."

"*Now,* Nurse! A guillotine, she says. What sort of guillotine—Mackenzie's, Heath's, O'Malley's, Hasting's? And what size guillotine? Large one, small one, medium?"

Anne opened bewildered eyes.

"How would I know? I've never even heard of a guillotine before, except the French Revolution kind."

He clucked his disapproval.

"And you a theatre nurse! Well, *I* don't know what you

want. You'd better go and see."

She turned away dolefully. "Without asking questions," Sister had said.

George was regarding her. Perhaps he was remembering her smile, for he called her back suddenly.

"Well, p'raps we can manage something. Who's it for?"

"Mr. Terrington."

"He likes a Mackenzie. Always remember people's fads, Nurse. Flatters 'em. *They* don't know you remember everyone else's too. Surgeons' fads in instruments, Physicians' fads in words, husbands' fads in puddings, Sisters' fads in how to do things you could do just as well some other way. How's Sister got 'er hair done today, Nurse?"

"Got her *hair* done?"

"Yes. Pulled back tight off 'er ears, or parted in the middle and smoothed down like a Dutch doll, or Mar-cel waved?"

Anne considered, her mouth twitching.

"I think it's pulled back tight."

George lifted the instrument he wanted out from under some others.

"That means a bad day for us, that does. Pulled straight back—thou shalt do all things well. If thee doesn't, thee'll get my tongue across thee, an' if thee answers back, a report to the Matron. The martin-*ette* touch, pulled straight back is. Sergeant-major. Child or adult, Nurse?"

Anne took her mind off Sister's hair with an effort.

"Child of three."

"Smallest size, then. Lucky you noticed 'is age, wasn't it

Nurse? Always notice things, even the way Sister does her hair."

"What do the other ways mean?" she asked.

"The Madonna—*she* doesn't think it's like a Dutch doll—and the Fluffy Bit? I'll tell you about them another day, Nurse. If she's the Martin-ette today you'd better get back with that guillotine."

Anne thought Sister looked suspiciously at her when she presented the instrument. Perhaps she had been expected to come back with a question. Yes, her hair was dragged back tight. And she was in her most acid and fault-finding mood. Anne chuckled. That funny little man!

She managed to take the guillotine back to him when the afternoon's operations were over. He was unpacking a box of new knives, and seemed disposed to talk.

"Thank you, Nurse. And *what* kind of guillotine was that?"

"Mackenzie's. Smallest size," Anne told him meekly.

"That's right. Never forget things you've been told. It flatters the person that told you. You better come along here tomorrow and learn the names of some more of them. If you don't know them, you'll find yerself in the soup one day. An' if you do know them, Sister'll be surprised and nag you more'n ever. Sister don't like bein' surprised, 've you noticed that? No, you can't stay here now, Nurse, you haven't cleared up the Theatre yet, I'm sure."

She went back to her work, lighter hearted than she had been for days. He was a dear funny little man, seeing that she didn't get into rows.

She slipped along to him again the next day, and he spread out instruments for her and told her all about them as he cleaned them and adjusted them. He told her stories, too, of the early days of Surgery, when the theatres were sprayed incessantly with carbolic and the theatre staff were always on the watch for the green stain which meant carboluria and the beginning of carbolic acid poisoning.

"There was always one or other of us off with it. I was a swab then, running round with a squeegee and a dirty white coat."

He talked of the Surgeons of that time, and how they behaved before the days of asepsis.

"They each had an old frock coat," he said. "The coats used to hang up behind the door in the Chief's room downstairs, and they'd put them on there and go up and do all their operations in them. Filthy? Filthy isn't the word! The more begrimed they were with blood and pus, the more they stank, the better the men liked it. It showed they were young an' inexperienced to have a clean coat. But they didn't do many operations then. It was almost sending a man to 'is death to send 'im to an operation. They used to ring a big bell when there was going to be one, an' everybody went to watch."

"No place for Sister Theatre, then," Anne said, thinking of the fury let loose if even a newly washed finger touched one of Sister's sterile theatre gowns.

"That's a fact!" George chuckled grimly. "Oh, there was Sister's hair I was goin' to tell you about. Well, you just watch. I saw it before she'd been up 'ere a month. If she comes down in the morning ar lar martin-ette, nothing you can do's right, so you don't need to worry how you do things. No, that's risky, because if you do 'em really badly she'll blab to the Matron about it, on Martinette days. On Madonna days, she's resigned. She knows you're hopeless. She'll try to teach you, those days, because it's 'er duty. But she won't bother to tick you off. They're not bad, those days; trying, but not bad. You got to do yer best, but you won't get nagged for it. Not ter say *nagged*. And on Fluffy Bit days—they don't come very frequent, not now she's getting older—you needn't even do yer best. She won't notice. She feels young. She even makes eyes at the Chiefs. Everythin' is peaches. If you see a Fluffy Bit day, with Mar-cel waves, you can do just as you like an' no harm'll come. But you may not see one."

Anne was chuckling.

"It's still the Martinette today," she said.

"I know. Don't I know? Not that I mind, really. She may nag, but I goes my own way."

"I believe," Anne said, her eyes dancing, "you've got the whole Theatre staff under your thumb, Sister and all."

George looked at her under his bushy brows. "I remember Sister when she was a little frightened Pro," he said. "I taught 'er instruments. An' I still know more about instruments nor she does. That makes a difference. But" —he tilted his glasses and looked sternly at Anne over the rims—"she's a very good Theatre Sister. I know. I taught 'er. I'll teach you, if you like. But you won't find 'er equal, not in any hospital in London."

"I know," Anne said. "I try to be like her, in the Theatre. But I don't want to be that sort of *person*."

He winked, and moved away in his deliberate fashion. George was never in a hurry.

He made a great difference to Anne. He was the only person she saw at all often who was really friendly. He taught her a lot, too, as much as she could take in at a time. But still there was a load on her heart for which she could find no reason.

4

It was Anne's half-day off. Sister had been very much the Martinette all the morning, poking and prying and nagging. Anne had become nearly beside herself with rage, had bitten her lips till they were sore to prevent herself answering back and putting an end to her career in the Theatre.

Once she was off duty, she felt that she must get right away from it all. She took off her uniform and dressed herself carefully. She had not many clothes. It was no good having them; there was nowhere to keep them and very little opportunity to wear them. But the few she had were still left over from more prosperous days, and they were good and well cut.

It was only on half-days that she took much notice of the weather. The days seemed all alike when she spent them in the hospital. Today the sun shone and the sky was a pale blue dome over London in fine spring weather. Anne was glad that her nicest hat was a straw one, a little brown thing with a turned-up brim and a golden buckle on it. It went well with her only coat and skirt. That was brown too, with a short, straight coat which made her look very slim. She pulled on some silk stockings and smiled over her low-heeled strap shoes. They had been hoarded from her schooldays, since the time when she had discarded them as babyish and taken to Court shoes with high heels. Now they were in the fashion again, and really they did not look so very old. Angela, in a moment of generosity, had given her a little brown umbrella. It was not going to rain, but the umbrella seemed to give a finishing touch. Anne seized it and ran downstairs, and out into the sunshine.

Across the road a bus was just going to start. She made a dash for it and climbed up to the top. There was a front seat free, and she sat down on it with a sigh of satisfaction. Now she would ride west in luxury, away from squalor and smells, fried-fish shops and stalls with flaring lights, little rules and voices that were sharp like pins.

Someone had sat down on the other front seat. Anne looked across, rejoicing half-consciously in the sight of people who were neither encased in uniforms nor made unreal by fear or suffering. She started with pleasure, and smiled at Ronald Dalloway.

For a second the young man stared. Then he leaped up. "Why, Nurse, I didn't recognise you in that get-up! I haven't seen you for ages, anyway. May I sit here?"

She made room for him and he sat down. She tried to think of the scores of questions she had meant to ask him, and could think of none of them. With her uniform she had shed some armour of good-fellowship. What could she say? What did young men like to talk about?

"How's the Martin-*ette?*" he inquired easily.

She turned to him, laughing. "Do you know about that, too?"

He laughed with her. "George tells that tale to all his chosen. He's rather proud of it, really. I guessed you'd be a chosen."

"Have you ever seen a Fluffy Bit day?" she asked him.

"Once. The day after Armistice Day. It was awful. Simply awful."

"It would be," Anne said thoughtfully. "She'd look a hag. She's dignified, as she is now. Respectable. I mean, one can respect her."

He smiled approval at her turn of phrase. "D'you get on with her?"

"Not so badly. I don't mind her, now. I was terrified at first. The first operation—" She stopped. He must have heard scores of people's impressions of their first operation.

"Go on," he said.

"I had to stand behind Mr. Thornton and whisk the table out of his way when he moved his arm. You know how he threshes about and sends all the bottles flying—"

Dalloway nodded, still smiling.

"And yet she'd told me I must keep my eyes on her face. I couldn't remember which *was* her face at first, they all looked the same in their caps and masks. I stared and stared at someone who didn't take any notice of me at all. Then I felt a most awful gimlet feeling in my left cheek. I stood it for a bit, and then I looked round—and there were Sister's little piggy black eyes on me and her head jerking, trying to make me go and fetch something or other. It was awful. I hadn't a chance to think about the operation at all, and I'd thought I was going to be so thrilled and so self-controlled."

He laughed outright, at that. "Are you still thrilled?"

"No," she confessed. "I'm never allowed near enough to see."

"Pity. You should see old Terry. He's a picture to watch—the neatest, gentlest way he manipulates things—"

This was pure shop. Eagerly her questions came thronging back to her. "Oh, Mr. Dalloway, do tell me—"

The "shop" continued until they had reached the heavy building of the Tivoli. Dalloway had answered her, painstakingly, with a little pause before each sentence, in the old pleased, rather pompous way. Then he broke off. "I say, I don't know your name. Tell me."

She told him, suddenly shy again.

"Can't we see each other again? When d'you have another half-day?"

"In a fortnight."

"Let's go out somewhere. Kew, or somewhere open, if the weather's like this. Will you? Or are you doing something else?"

"I should like to very much," Anne said demurely.

"Right. Same time, same bus? I've got to get off here. Charing Cross. Goodbye."

He waved his gloves at her and was gone, balancing

himself to the lurching of the bus.

She sat still, tingling with pleasure. She was honest with herself. She knew now why she had been gloomy and why she was gloomy no longer. She went over the whole conversation in her mind, then thought of the look of him, his puzzled face when he had first seen her, his friendly eyes, his slim figure swaying between the seats.

"He really did look pleased to see me," she told herself. "What a mercy I'd got on some decent clothes!"

5

By the end of the fortnight which elapsed before Anne's next half-day, the friendship between her and Dalloway seemed to her to be secure. Hurried greetings in corridors, eye meeting eye across the Theatre, jokes shared by half-smiles, these were the cement which bound them. And so pleasant and so engrossing were these small diversions that it never occurred to either of them that notice might be taken by persons who should not have been concerned with their private interests at all. They were not themselves of the type which scents a love affair whenever a boy and a girl exchange a word with each other. They were much too busy living their own lives to bother. They did not realise that many whose own lives have lost all semblance of adventure must, for sheer self-preservation, concoct scandals and romances all round them and pass them from ear to ear as gospel truth. There are innumerable such people in a hospital.

The half-day came, and they were on the front seat of

the bus again. Anne wondered again, panic-stricken for a second, what they should talk about. She reassured herself. They had got on excellently last time, why shouldn't they now? She looked silently over the edge of the bus at the people loitering round the stalls.

Quite suddenly, she heard her thoughts spoken aloud beside her. "I like this heaps better than the other side of the river, don't you? These Jewesses—they're jolly nice to look at. And they bother about themselves—look how they do their hair, and the bright colours they wear."

She took up the thread instantly. "Yes. Have you ever been in Bermondsey? It's about the same level, only Christian. Or p'raps one ought to say, British. They're sluts, the women over there. Filthy clothes and rats' tails and cloth caps."

"It's a bit difficult," Dalloway said, "to tell the level of these people. They may have been quite different—in class, I mean—in Poland or wherever they come from."

"That's true. Some of them can't speak a work of English, though they've lived here ten years or more."

"Queer, isn't it? Though I've met English people abroad like that, who've never bothered to learn. But these Jews live in a world of their own. Look at the names—Levitsky, Grunbaum, Petroff—all sorts. It isn't England at all. They don't hate us, either. Despise us a bit, perhaps. But mostly they're just remote from us, although we're all round them."

"It's partly the Sabbath."

"And the way everything they do—eating, washing, all the ordinary things—is part of their religion."

"While ours—if we have any—hasn't any part in our ordinary lives at all. How can we understand each other?"

"And yet," he said, "the people they simply can't get on with are the Irish Catholics, whose religion is even more a part of them than the Jews' is. The Irish have driven every Jew out of Wapping, down by the docks there, except one."

"Why the one?" she asked.

"Oh, his grandfather saved an Irishman's life years ago when Jack the Killer used to live in Wapping."

Anne pointed to a girl on the pavement below them.

"Look at that one! Those lovely black curls, perfectly done, and the little green shoes matching her dress. And yet I dare say she lives in one room."

Dalloway leaned over in front of Anne to see her.

"And I expect she's not more than fourteen," he said. "She looks thirty. At forty, that's what she'll be like." He nodded towards a tiny wizened woman, her greasy wig a little sideways, her body a draped cone with the apex above.

"Even she's got a bright shawl on. And the Bermondsey ones get old almost as quickly. The Jewish children are lovely, anyway."

"Pampered little brats! Full of tummy-aches and pickled cucumbers. Yes, they're lovely kids. What I was going to say is, these people are artists, mostly, one way and another—music, for instance, brings them right out of themselves. Our own, those living under the same conditions, are just animals, even though they may have a pretty high sort of herd instinct which makes them help

67

each other."

"The half-breeds ought to be rather splendid," she said.

"They are, some of them. But you can't have a well-balanced artist, it's not possible."

"Isn't it? I'm not sure." Anne was loving this. They were serious and thought they were being deep. They were both consciously pleased to find someone with whom they could be serious and deep. Anne, silent for a moment, went off at a tangent. "Look at the jellied eels! And I always think that vulgar lemonade looks so good and cool in its glass pans—"

"What *are* jellied eels, I wonder? "Dalloway said idly.

"Petticoat Lane on Sunday—making meals off jellied eels—the taste will last till Monday!" Anne quoted, and wondered if she had been coarse.

But he was as drunk as she was with the wine of spring and youth, and he just blew out gusts of laughter into the sour, sharp air that was heavy with fumes of frying oil.

They came into the City, through crowds of bareheaded, well-dressed young men.

"They have an easy life—seem to do nothing but stroll about and talk and make money!"

"Oh, look at the flowers!" she cried. "Violets and snowdrops! I can almost smell them!"

Then, Fleet Street.

"I was almost a newspaper man," he told her. "Only I went and got a scholarship to Edmunds. That settled me, the Pater not being a millionaire. I'm jolly glad it did, now."

Now, what did he mean by that?

They came to the Griffin, rampant on his tower.

"I love the Law Courts, don't you? I had a fairy tale once, all about them and the Griffin and London. The Two-Eyed Griffin."

"You'd like fairy tales," he said soberly. "You're rather like a fairy-queen yourself."

She threw him a little smile.

"Rather a solid one. Look at her feet!"

She stuck out the size seven schoolgirl slipper, and they laughed together.

The crowd was growing better dressed. They raced along Piccadilly, exclaiming at the shops and the sky-signs as if they had never seen them before.

Just before Hyde Park Corner he turned to her.

"What about getting off here for some tea? It's half-past three and I had lunch early. I hope you did too."

"I did. I feel awfully tea-ish."

They clambered down and Dalloway guided her into a little teashop, daintily set. Over tea they chatted of books. She had a Boots' ticket when her finances ran to it, he read when he had to sit up late at night. This talking, she thought to herself, was easy enough really. You just had to say whatever came into your head, not thinking modestly that it was too insignificant to give words to. Of course, you had to use your eyes, or things wouldn't come into your head. It was great fun. She thought perhaps Dalloway was enjoying himself too. He seemed very cheerful.

They strolled out and looked round for a bus. Dalloway suddenly fixed his eyes on a tall girl who stood with her back to them.

"Hullo, that's my sister! H'lo, Dora!"

The girl turned round to them, and the man with her raised his hat.

"My sister, Miss Lee. Miss Lee, this is Mr. Drew, Dora's fiancé."

They shook hands. The girl threw Anne a friendly smile, accepting her at once. Anne had a comfortable feeling that her clothes were all right, anyway, for the girl was most daintily dressed, pretty and sure of herself. Anne smiled back and Mr. Drew looked at her with veiled admiration.

"Where going, Ronnie?"

Ronald looked vague.

"Oh—Kew or somewhere."

"Come to Roehampton. We're going. There's some polo."

Ronald's eyes lighted.

"Can we?"

"Course. We can take you."

"Would you like to?" Ronald asked Anne.

She nodded, struck dumb by a sudden sense of inferiority, then realised that she must mind her manners.

"I should like it."

"I love watching polo, don't you?" Miss Dalloway said.

Anne smiled again and said that she did, and prayed that no one would ask her any questions that involved a knowledge of the game.

"D'you ride a lot?" the fiancé asked, noticing Anne's supple length of limb.

"I did when I was small. I haven't since I came to town."

She could not disgrace Ronald by allowing that she had never sat on even a donkey in all her life.

"One day," Ronald said vaguely, "you must come and renew it at home. I expect we could rake up some sort of a nag for you."

They were all climbing on to a bus again. The top was crowded, and Anne found herself perched on the end of a seat, with Dora Dalloway on another at her side.

The girl smiled across at her lazily.

"Are you a medico too?" she said.

"Well—not quite. I'm a nurse."

She said it lightly, unthinking, just glancing at the other's face. Then she flushed crimson, for she saw drawn there an expression of surprise, amusement, and finally, delicate disdain.

"Oh," she heard Miss Dalloway say slowly. "A nurse!" Then, as if she had collected her shattered social sense: "It's a very hard life, isn't it?"

"Very," said Anne.

It is easy to be on separate seats on a bus without talking. The two did not exchange another word, and presently Ronald signalled to them to get off, and they separated into couples for the short walk up the road.

Anne was happy again with Ronald, exchanging comments with him as they passed through the terrace where tea is set, and walked by the tennis courts and the ground where the maimed and the middle-aged play earnestly at croquet. They came out opposite the undulating golf course, set about with little trees, and made for a seat alongside the boards. Several men and ponies stood about, one galloped by himself on the ground behind them.

"Begin in a minute," Mr. Drew explained.

Dora Dalloway addressed the company in languid tones.

"I don't believe Miss Lee has ever been here before. Have you? And isn't it exciting to come for the first time?"

How on earth did she know that, Anne wondered. She laughed easily.

"Not since I've been in hospital, certainly," she allowed. "I'd been several times before I began to train."

She wouldn't be inferior. She probably wasn't, really, at all, except that these people were rich and hers were so much poorer since the War.

Dora looked at her curiously. She seemed puzzled by her. After all, she was probably saying doubtfully to herself, quite nice people did take up nursing sometimes; but generally not till they were middle-aged and disappointed and had to pay a premium for their training, and not as a rule in a great grubby hospital like St. Edmunds.

Anne saw that she was being covertly watched during the game that began. She lost herself entirely in the excitement of it. It was exciting to see polo for the first time. Once she woke sufficiently to wonder whether her squeaks had given away her utter ignorance, then forgot everything and squeaked again. Ronald chuckled softly at her, pleased at her obvious enjoyment.

During a pause in the game, Dora turned to her again,

as she followed with her eye a group on the golf course.

"Do you play golf?" she asked, with an air of one who makes plans for the future.

Anne, still in the magic of padding hoofs and quick turns, looked up. "What? No, I've never played."

Dora turned to Ronald with a pretty affectation of regret.

"Ronnie, Miss Lee doesn't play golf, isn't it a pity. I'd thought we might arrange something. Ronnie's so keen on it," she added to Anne.

Anne gnashed her teeth. Why had she let out that she didn't play golf, or do *any*thing that these people thought was the proper thing to do?

"What?" Ronald looked up with just the same preoccupation that she had felt herself. "Not play? Oh well, everyone's got to begin sometime."

Anne shot a look of gratitude at him and they both returned to breathless contemplation of the polo.

Presently two ponies were racing, neck and neck, after the ball. One gained a little, and his rider, leaning out, made a tremendous lunge at it. He missed by inches and the pony slid along for ten yards. His opponent, turning in an instant, had driven hard and straight towards the other end of the ground.

"Oo—oh!" Anne breathed.

"Miscue! Bad one!" Ronald said lazily.

"Mis-what?" Anne asked, laughing.

Dora turned to her.

"Miscue. Billiards, you know," she said sweetly.

"I think," she said a little later, "Phil and I will have to be going. We're doing a theatre and we want to go back to Hampstead first."

"We'll have to go too then, shan't we?" Ronald asked. "Being visitors?"

"Oh—well, you don't want to stay, do you"

Ronald laughed. "No, not really. Come along."

"Are you going to a show, too?" Drew asked.

Anne nodded. "Yes. I've got theatre leave."

"Good heavens!" Dora gasped. "Do you have to get permission, like a schoolgirl?"

"Yes," Anne told her shortly. "Once a month, we're allowed it. You see, we have to work pretty hard. We couldn't, if we were gadding about every night."

"I don't know," Dora commented, "how you can possibly bear nursing. Can you?"

Anne having decided that she hated this woman, was perversely moved to annoy.

"I like most of it," she said. "The operations are most awfully interesting. Sir Roland was doing one yesterday, on a tiny baby who'd got—"

Dora turned hastily to Drew.

"Is this the best way to get out, Phil?" she asked.

"You must forgive me," she told Anne gently the next minute, "I simply can't bear even to hear about ugly things. I think we've got to keep a hold on beauty; we lucky people who have it round us, to pass it on to the less lucky ones. We must keep as far away from mud as we possibly can, or it'll soil us and never wash off. Don't you agree?"

"No," Anne said grimly, "I don't. I want to—to wallow

74

in it, until I know all about it. Then perhaps I may be able to help people out of it, or even wash it all away and prevent there ever being any more. I don't in the least want to go away while other people are being sucked in, and then boast how clean I am."

Dora's eyebrows had risen higher and higher.

Anne stopped suddenly, aghast at herself. Why had she blown off like that? And however loud had her voice been? Now she would have set Miss Dalloway against her forever.

On the bus again, Anne and Ronald were several seats ahead of the others. Sometimes snatches of their conversation rose above the hum of the traffic, clear to Anne's ears.

"—shouldn't have expected it of Ronnie!" she heard Dora's voice say.

A grumble in Drew's deep tones followed.

"What was it they wouldn't have expected?"

"Oh, yes, pretty," was the next audible comment. "Knows how to use her eyes, and *you* get taken in at once. I don't exactly blame her, it's the poor thing's only hope of escape from the filthy life. It's their one ambition, I expect."

Uncomfortably, Anne knew what that ambition must be. But it wasn't true, not of her, and not of anyone else that she knew well. Of course, it was of a few of them. But not of the best, not for an instant.

"—half-educated people like that!" she heard.

That was true. She was. But it wasn't her fault. She'd a good enough head, if only her father had let the right things be put into it. Now it was too late, and she would always feel ashamed and afraid before the very people who attracted her.

At Charing Cross they changed buses, and Anne and Dalloway went on by themselves.

"My sister," Ronald said, staring into the sky, "is sometimes a bit of a cat. I ought to have remembered. It's only since she got engaged to that chap Drew. His people are the most awful snobs."

"She was damned rude!" Anne stormed, from out of her hurt pride.

Then she laughed.

"I'm awfully sorry—didn't mean to say that. I don't mind tuppence, as long—"

"As long as what?"

"As you're not like it too. I *am* rather ignorant, I know. I've never had a chance to be anything else."

"Ignorance doesn't matter a hoot. You're—" Ronald was labouring again; it was not quite his nature to pay a compliment which was sincere, and he was trying to— "you're a jolly sight better looking than Dora, and you're—you're goin' to be a jolly fine person. She was only pretending to herself that she wasn't feeling inferior."

Anne chortled. "*She* feeling inferior! That's absurd, because I was, all the time."

"Absurd of *you!* "Ronald grinned. "No, none of the rest of us are snobs. I expect Dora will grow out of it."

They went on to *No, No, Nanette!* and choked with laughter. Education was not a necessity there. They both laughed at the same things, and their eyes, crinkled with enjoyment, were continually meeting and drawing reluctantly apart. Once their hands touched on the arm of a seat. Anne knew that she hoped that would happen again.

CHAPTER 5

1

ANNE was back at her old task of cleaning Mr. Terrington's white Wellingtons. She did not approve of Mr. Terrington. He was the most conceited man she had ever met. He liked to be different from everybody else, so he wore Wellingtons in the Theatre instead of the white things like pillowcases which everyone always had worn and which simply went to the laundry with the gowns. He used different tools, too, and if anyone forgot to hand him his own particular needle or pair of forceps, or to stand in the exact position which he and no one else demanded, he would swear most profanely and never apologise. After an operation, he would swagger to the middle of the Theatre, his legs apart, a bland smile on his face, and skin off his rubber gloves. Then he would look round, the corners of his sardonic mouth twitching, and hurl the gloves, all wet and slimy, to one of the nurses, who would bear them away and wash them. It was just Mr. Terrington's little way and no one seemed to mind. He certainly had the most wonderful results to his operations.

Anne did not think of him for more than a minute as she rubbed at his boots. She saw again the blue sky and the green turf at Roehampton, and the little dark trees standing out against it; the eager swoops and swift turns of the wise little ponies; Ronald's earnest, friendly face; and felt his long, slender little finger as it brushed against her wrist.

She supposed she ought not to be thinking of these things when she was on duty, but really, boot-cleaning did not call for much concentration. When she was busy with things that mattered, instruments, or standing at attention throughout an operation, she thought about nothing but the matter in hand.

There was Sister, coming back from her daily interview with Matron. What was the hair going to be like today?

Instead of staying for a minute or two in her room as she usually did, Sister came straight to the little cupboard where Anne was. Anne glanced at her. The hair was simply straining back from the tight forehead. The very eyebrows seemed to be struggling to escape from the pull of it.

"Nurse!" she said, and her voice was so thin and penetrating that Anne seemed to feel it coming out at the back of her, between her shoulder-blades, having transfixed her heart on the way and stopped its beating,

"Nurse! Leave those now. Go and put on a clean apron and clean cuffs, and go down to Matron's Office at once."

Her eyes snapped and shone like the lamps of a lighthouse.

Anne searched her conscience as she hurried. There was nothing that she had done, no prank at all that she had played, since the procession of pigs, and that was weeks ago. Then she clucked with her tongue against her teeth. Were they going to make a fuss about her outing with Ronald? It couldn't be that. It had all happened when she was off duty, away from the hospital altogether.

She settled her cap straight on her head, tucked in a curl that would stray out over her ear, and ran downstairs to the dreaded door, behind which sat the inhuman, tight-waisted goddess who could make or mar Anne's career and seven hundred others. Really, she was just an elderly single woman, with no adventure behind her save that of years of nursing; no tradition to guide her save the narrow one of hospital custom; very little learning to broaden her; and the awful isolation of absolute power to rob her of any wisdom which she might once have possessed.

A worn little Assistant Matron ushered Anne into the presence.

"Nurse Lee, Matron," she said in a little grey voice, and went away.

Anne stood in an attitude of respectful attention behind the mahogany desk, watching the still, stern face before her. She did command respect, this woman of steel who ruled them all. Perhaps Sister Theatre would be a Matron one day. She would make just such another as this.

The Matron looked up, her mouth set in a thin line.

"I have had complaints about you, Nurse, of a very serious nature. I shall be glad to hear what you have to say."

Anne stood silent, waiting for more.

"Don't sulk, Nurse. I am waiting."

Anne found her tongue with an effort.

"I—don't know what—what the complaints were, Matron, please."

The corners of Matron's mouth almost disappeared.

"Don't be ridiculous, Nurse. Of course you know quite well. You don't mean to tell me that you think it proper behaviour for a St. Edmunds nurse to be seen on an omnibus with one of the House-surgeons, to have tea with him in a tea-shop, and later actually to go to the theatre with him?

"I couldn't help it," Anne said lamely, "if he sat down next to me on the bus."

"A right-minded nurse," Matron snapped, "would instantly have made an excuse to leave the bus. Or, if that were quite impossible, have travelled inside."

Anne's dimples showed for one awful, irresistible second. Then she controlled herself.

"Please, Matron," she ventured, "it was my half-day."

"Thank you, I am quite aware of that. You don't deny having been out with Mr. Dalloway?"

Anne opened wide eyes.

"Of course I don't."

"I'm glad you're honest. Or that you used frequently to talk to him when you were on night-duty?"

"I—" Anne stopped. Damn, that would mean giving away the Night Staff, who had been too lazy to take the House-surgeon round the ward herself. "I did speak to him sometimes," she acknowledged. "Not every night."

"I should hope not, indeed. You were seen with him in the corridor, I may tell you. He was in his dressing-gown!"

She glared under horrified brows, and Anne bit her lip. She knew now that she was probably going to get the sack and be returned, disgraced, to her family. But really, the whole thing was so funny! As if the House-men didn't always come down in their dressing-gowns when they were called at night!

"Have you any excuse for this disgraceful behaviour?

"No. Except that Mr. Dalloway was teaching me Surgery."

"Don't be impertinent, Nurse. The Sister-tutor will teach you all the Surgery you need to know. Don't you realise that it is a rule of the hospital—one of the very strictest rules—that nurses shall never even speak to the Residents or the students?"

"Yes, Matron. I suppose I did. But I never thought—"

"It is your business to think of these things—"

"That it mattered what I did in my off-duty time," Anne finished intrepidly.

The Matron appeared to be about to burst.

"Is it *nothing* to you that you've disgraced the hospital? Do you think I will allow my nurses to be described as common flirts? Don't you see that it's *dishonourable* to break the rules when you've signed on and promised to obey them?"

Anne lost her temper. If she was going to get the sack she might as well do so in a flare of blue flame. "I'm not dishonourable! And anyone who describes me as a common flirt is a liar!"

She saw the white, amazed face before her growing even more still and remote.

"I can't agree with you, Nurse. I'm told that you spend a great deal of your time on the Theatre floor talking to George." Her chin sank on her stiff collar. She had proved her point.

Anne looked round her with a sense of terror. George? Flirting with dear, ninety-year-old George? What on earth would they say next? She often gave good morning to Dicky, the grubby little Theatre-swab, who had just left school. Would they bring that up against her?

"George has been teaching me instruments," she said.

"Don't attempt to argue, Nurse."

She bit her lip and stood silent. After all, Matron could twist her excuses any way she pleased. It was no use offering them.

"Nurses have been dismissed for one such offence as yours," Matron was saying. "Have you ever done such a thing before? This going out with Residents?"

"No, Matron. At least, Mr. Dalloway spoke to me once before on a bus, but that was quite by chance!"

"Is that the truth, Nurse Lee?" Anne felt the hot, suspicious eyes trying to pierce her skin.

"Of course it's true!" she said.

"I only hope so."

The accusing voice droned on. Anne thought suddenly about black caps. Would the Matron solemnly remove her wig—no, her goffered frill—or would the black cap be perched on top of her own?

"I am not going to dismiss you, Nurse."

"Dear me, how sad," Anne thought. "Now I shall never know!"

"Your record in your first ward was good, in your second of unusual excellence. Sister Theatre tells me you are shaping well up there—"

Good old Martin-ette. And blessed, blessed cooking.

"You must give me your word that such a thing will never happen again with any Resident or student. You will leave the Theatre tomorrow and go into the Gynaecological Block. You see, I can't even put you into a men's ward now. That will do, Nurse."

Anne escaped. She was thankful that she was to be allowed another chance. But it rankled—a common flirt, not to be trusted in a men's ward, or—she chuckled—to be left alone with George. Her dark brows met. It was all so silly. She was not in the least that sort of person. They ought to have seen that she was not. Who could possibly have sneaked? And why? Were they all jealous, because she had attracted the attention of clever, popular Ronald Dalloway? How had they dared to interfere with what she did when she was away from the hospital, in mufti, not a nurse at all? Why had she let them interfere? She hated them, for having the power to spoil either her enjoyment or her career. Telling her she was hardly respectable and treating her like a schoolgirl, when she was a responsible woman of twenty-two, responsible enough to have the care of people who might die if she neglected them, of horrible poisons and virulent microbes. How dared they?

By the time she regained the Theatre, she had worked herself up into a great rage. Sister met her with a melancholy stare. Anne returned the stare. What had happened to Sister? Anne stared again and almost exploded. Sister had had her few minutes' "lunch-time" while Anne had been away. She had been to her room and returned, the Martinette no longer. The occasion merited the Madonna, all sleek and parted and resigned.

84

2

By the afternoon, Anne had simmered into a state of prickly irritability. The Theatre was so hot, and she was so interested in the routine and hated so much the thought of leaving it. Everyone seemed to know of her disgrace, so quickly does news travel where news is rare. Some of the nurses passed her with pursed lips. Some leered at her, jealous of her success and glad at her downfall. Belsize and her other friends laughed good-humouredly as at a joke.

She stormed at them after lunch in the Common Room. "Dogs! I don't know how they've the face to treat anyone like that!"

"Well, you old silly," they said, "you knew what you were laying yourself open to!"

"I didn't, I didn't! I hadn't the slightest idea I mightn't do exactly as I liked with my off-duty time. And even if I'd thought of it, I should never have suspected them of prying like that! How could they?"

"We're always under St. Edmunds' paternal eye," Belsize told her lightly, "even when we're on a holiday bathing in the sea. It isn't only here, it's the same at all hospitals. In the old days, nurses weren't allowed ever to go to a dance or a theatre, however much off duty they were. They weren't allowed to go out except in uniform. If they did, they got the boot. It was worse than being a nun, they worked harder."

"Of course," Anne said, "they all were nuns, once. I suppose that's how it all originated. This silly supervision."

"I suppose so. All the same, you really are an old loon. A whole lot greener than I thought. Didn't you really know the risk?"

"I swear I didn't!"

"What about the cuddling on night-duty?"

"It *wasn't!*" Anne shouted at her. "You've got a dirty, beastly mind!"

Belsize laughed.

"I haven't, really. I was only trying to show you what general opinion's like. What did you really do?"

"Lawson was so lazy that she never—or hardly ever—went round with him herself, so I had to. That was all. And I used to ask him questions about the patients, just because I was interested."

"Honest truth?"

"Of course it's honest truth! First Matron says I'm a liar, and now you!"

Belsize looked at her curiously.

"I don't. I only say you're an innocent. So you are. You take my advice. Think of the meanest, cattiest, dirtiest-minded old hag you can imagine, and realise that you've got people like that all round you, every minute, hating you because you're not like them, trying their best to nose out faults to prove to themselves that you're not really any better than they are, and blabbing them to people who can punish you. They can't help it, they've grown like that. We all shall, if we stay here long enough. There are jolly few who've escaped. Sister Southcliffe's one, and she's as near a saint as I've ever met. But—remember they're watching you. Then you learn discretion." Anne almost believed her.

"They're not as bad as that," she said feebly.

"No. It's pretty difficult to find a person who's all bad. Most of them have some silly failing or other that makes you forgive them. Sister Theatre, for instance—the joke about her hair makes her just human, and you can't help respecting her because she's so good at her job."

"She said—I wasn't so bad at it," Anne said.

Belsize nodded.

"That's it. She's just, as a machine is just. She's never merciful. She'll simply hate you for this, because you've offended against Hospital Law. But she gives you your due for your work all the same."

Anne felt that she almost loved Sister Theatre for only being hard, not meanly bad.

"What's Sister Gynae like?" she asked.

"Lord! Are you going there? My poor child! Oh, my poor child"

Belsize walked away, wagging her black head. And Anne, still feeling ready to run away and bang the door if anything annoyed her, went back to the Theatre.

3

Mr. Terrington was operating. Sister was not quite as efficient as the Madonna as she was on the Martinette days. Her movements were the tiniest bit slower, and the Theatre Staff not quite so much in awe of her. So the theatre routine did not flow quite as smoothly as usual, and the Surgeon's irascible temper needed frequent vent in blasphemy.

"God! What have you given me?" he would say

whenever anything was handed to him.

Sister, always recognising without any trouble that she was the person so addressed, would turn up her softened, chastened eyes and hand him something else.

"Damn you, Thornton, why can't you keep the patient under the anaesthetic? D'ye think I like him to wobble like a jelly every time 'e breathes? He's goin' to be sick, man, and then where'll my stitches be?"

Thornton would whirl round, scattering everything about him, whisk the mask off the patient's face, and glare through his big glasses.

"I'm givin' this anesthetic, Sir, or are you?"

"You are—or think you are, blast your eyes!"

"This patient's in the third stage of anaesthesia. Surgical anaesthesia. If I take 'im deeper 'e'll die. You know that very well."

They would subside into a rumble of grumbles, and the House-surgeon or the clean dresser would be the next object of abuse.

Generally Anne was immensely tickled by these electrical afternoons. They were so different from the operating days of the other surgeons, who worked quietly and methodically and got done in half the time, who sometimes diverted the Theatre with jokes and funny stories and never abused anybody. But today she hated it all. In the morning she had seen the furtive, envious spirit which worked among the nursing staff. Now it seemed that Surgery, which she had almost come to worship, produced other qualities in its devotees than quiet strength and dexterity; greed, conceit and uncontrol were what this man reeked of. She hated him.

The operation was nearly over. The patient's abdomen was being sewn up, and the floor becoming strewn with little bundles of gauze that had been used to swab the wound dry.

"Count, one of you!" Mr. Terrington directed sourly.

Anne felt Sister's eye on her.

"Count the sponges, Nurse."

She bent and picked up the soiled mops, dropping them in the pail and counting them as she went. There was a little mound of them under the table, and she could not see how many of them were there. She clucked and stretched out for them, brushing the Surgeon's leg with her shoulder as she did so.

"Christ! Is there a dog in the Theatre?" She touched him again accidentally as she came out.

"Damn and blast it! This stitch has pulled out now What the bleedin' hell are you doin', Nurse?"

Anne separated the last mop from its neighbours. Then she stood up and glared straight into Mr. Terrington's eye.

"I was picking up the bloody sponges," she announced.

The whole Theatre stared. A dresser sniggered. Mr. Terrington looked her up and down, gave a deep grunt, and went on with his stitching up.

He did not swear any more during that operation. When it was over and the patient was wheeled out, he stood in the middle of the floor and held forth to the students on what he had just been doing. He talked well and the students hung on his words. He was soothed by the time he had finished.

He skinned off his gloves one after the other, and rolled them into a ball. He twirled round on his heels, deciding who should have the honour of catching them. In a second, Anne, standing, against the wall by the sinks, received them full in her chest.

She was furious. How dared he, the swearing, stuck-up pig! Without a second's thought she hurled them back, straight at the red, perspiring, arrogant face of their owner.

Mr. Terrington spluttered.

The Theatre was filled with a terrible silence.

Now, thought Anne, *I shall get fired*.

Mr. Terrington gave a little deep laugh, and his sardonic mouth opened in a real enjoyable smile. "Good shot, Nurse," he said pleasantly.

The spell was broken.

One of the dressers picked up the gloves. Anne, scarlet-faced, washed them, the Staff-nurse untied the Surgeon's gown, Sister jangled trays of instruments.

A little later Sister took Anne aside.

"Please control yourself, Nurse."

"I'm sorry, Sister. I don't know what happened. Had I better go?"

"Go? And leave me a nurse short? On Mr. Terrington's afternoon?"

"I only thought I should be sent away. Shall I, Sister?"

Sister looked more resigned than ever.

"It's nothing to do with me, Nurse."

"But—you'll have to report it?"

"Mr. Terrington has taken the whole thing out of my

hands. He spoke directly to you. If *he* reports it, I can do nothing. Come along, Nurse, be quick with those drums."

Blessed be the God of Hospital Etiquette.

4

The afternoon dragged on. Anne was quiet and decorous now. Religiously she kept her eyes off Dalloway. It was not so very difficult, when one was on the go all the time like this. She wondered what he thought of the afternoon's fracas. She had seen his shoulders shaking after the incident of the sponges, but she had not dared to look at him after the trouble with the gloves. He thought the world of Terrington. Probably he thought she was awful.

Another operation was nearly over. The last case for the afternoon had come up into the anaesthetic room. The nurse who had brought the patient from the ward had opened the double doors quietly and was peeping through, trying to attract someone's attention. Anne went noiselessly over to her.

"Sister wants me to go down again at once. Somebody's haemorrhaging and there's an awful rush. Can you manage here?"

"I'll ask Sister," Anne replied. Why on earth couldn't the woman say bleeding? Lot of twaddle they did learn to talk.

She repeated the message and saw Sister's glance move round the Theatre and light on Dalloway. With her newly opened eye for the inner affairs of hospitals, she read

Sister's thought. "Mr. Dalloway's safe here where I can see him. She's the only one I can spare. She'd better go, even though Matron did tell me to keep her under strict observation. It's the only thing to do." Sister might have said it aloud.

"Go into the anaesthetic-room, Nurse, and help with the patient. Now at once."

The time was getting late. The Honorary Anaesthetist had packed up his engines and gone home, and one of the House-surgeons was carrying on in his place. Anne heard Mr. Terrington speak to him as she went out.

"Go and start the next one, will you? I've just on done here. He won't want any more." Mr. Terrington hated to be kept late.

The patient to be anaesthetised was a lusty navvy, who twisted and turned as he began to lose consciousness. Anne had much ado to hold him down.

"He'll get worse," the anaesthetist said laconically. "Better get someone in. George! George! "

They heard the deliberate footsteps of George coming along the passage and saw him look through the little window. "Send a man, George!"

George came in himself. "You want someone now, you do. No time to send for men. Carry on, Doctor!"

He took up his stand beside Anne, and together they threw themselves on the heavy, struggling body. The anaesthetist was using all his strength to keep the mask on the man's face as he swung it to and fro on his great bull neck. "Lord, he's simply drinking the stuff!" he gasped. Anne and George did nothing but grunt and hang on tight.

"Keep him on the table," the anaesthetist warned, he'll fall off the other side, George, in a second!"

"You get 'im under, Doctor!" George was retorting, when the doors opened again and Dalloway strolled in.

"Ready? Terry wants me to wash out the chap's stomach before he comes in. Oh, not ready, I see!"

The man had given a great lurch. Dalloway rushed to help on the other side of the table. Under the continued onslaught, the anaesthetist at his head, Anne, George and Dalloway gripping various parts of his body under the blankets, the patient's activity waned. He lay still and began to breathe stertorously. The struggle was over.

Then it was that George brought Anne's world tumbling about her ears. He had for some minutes been regarding Dalloway with a quizzical stare. Then he broke out:

"Well, young man, an' how long are you goin' on squeezin' my 'and lovin'ly like this? S'pose you think it's Nurse's 'ere. Well, it isn't, not this time. *Your* mistake, Mr. Dalloway, sir."

Anne's eyes met Dalloway's in a horrified glance. Then Dalloway stood up straight.

"Can I get on with the wash now, John?" he asked the anaesthetist. The anaesthetist, shaking with laughter, nodded.

INTERLUDE

1

RONALD DALLOWAY and his friend John Pedley, the anaesthetist of the afternoon before and of a previous occasion, strode together round the brownish, lumpy plot of ground known as the grass tennis courts.

Ronald's hands were deep in his pockets, his shoulders hunched, his brows drawn over angry eyes. Pedley was talking very fast.

"Yes, I know all about that. There's nobody like her, never has been and never will be. It happens to all of us at least once while we're here. Sometimes oftener."

"You don't seem to realise that it's not just a flirtation," Ronald objected. "I'm not that sort. Nor's Miss Lee."

"So much the worse," Pedley explained patiently, "For both of you."

"I don't see why."

"You can't have thought about it, then. You know what happens if a man and a nurse get muckin' about together."

"I don't."

"Well, she gets the sack, if there's anything definite about it. Sometimes he does too. If it's only a suspicion, she gets the most filthy time from the Matron and everybody else, and he gets on the wrong side of all the Sisters. You know what that means. If the H.S. doesn't get on with the Sisters, he can't even see a dressing, much less do one. His patients are all spirited away whenever he wants to see them. Sister never tells him a thing about anyone—and, mind you, she has a jolly sight better chance of knowing all about them than we do—and then looks pained when the Chief doesn't know things, and butts in with some vital bit of information herself. The Chief thinks you're a rotten House-surgeon and reads you a lecture about trusting entirely to Sister. And, if it goes on, you get a bad mark against you in the Matron's book—which is more important than the Bible in this place—an' you never get another job, an' you're surprised."

"Rot!" Dalloway said incredulously. "Is it true, though?"

"Gospel, my dear lad. The nursing side rules this hospital. The Matron's word is law, and all the Chiefs and all the lay Committee obey her. Everyone knows that if she takes a dislike to a nurse, that nurse goes. But it's true about students, too. It's not worth anyone's while to get up against her, even for the sake of the most promising student. And they don't. The student—or resident—quietly goes, directly the job he's doing at the moment is done. I don't blame 'em. She's here forever and we're only birds of passage. We can't cramp their style like she can. And I expect she gives them pretty good reasons for her whims."

"How do you know all this?" Ronald asked suspiciously.

"My Uncle got the sack, when he was an H.P., for kissing a Pro in the testing-room."

"But he's on the Staff now!"

"I know. He was so brilliant that they had to put him on it, after ten years. Thought everyone would have forgotten, I suppose. So they have, and she's a grand lady in Harley Street. But he'd have got on five years sooner if he'd not been so dam' silly."

"Well," said Ronald, "I'm jiggered."

"Thought you would be. Well, look here, old thing, just be sensible and chuck it. You've got a jolly good chance of getting on well—brains and prizes—and influence—and people like you. Don't go an' blow it all because of a girl's dimples. Besides—another thing. You know what nurses are. They're the devil, after the first few months. Half-educated, catty, scandalmongers, bossy—oh, I wouldn't marry a nurse for a thousand pounds."

"*She's* not like that," said Ronald.

"You don't know. You've only seen her on her best behaviour. You think about your work, old Doc, and don't be put off by the temptations of the flesh. Hang it all, it's not like you—"

Ronald said nothing at all.

2

An hour later, he was tumbling in a fury downstairs from Darwin Ward. His "firm" had a dozen beds there. Two were occupied by patients who had been operated on the day before, and Ronald had intended dressing their wounds—always the House-surgeon's duty on the day after operation. Afterwards, the job was left to the dressers or to Sister unless something unexpected happened to the patient's progress.

He walked round the ward with Sister.

"How's Daddy Four?"

The old man grinned. Sister said nothing.

Ronald glanced at his chart and went on.

"Has this boy been sick any more, Sister?"

"No, Mr. Dalloway."

It was the merest chance that made him study the chart closely and see marked on it that the child had vomited three times during the night. The night was, strictly, no concern of the day Sister. Ronald wrote a medicine on the board and went on.

"I think I'd better examine Mr. Sixteen."

Silently Sister turned back the clothes.

"Hullo, what's this?"

The man was under treatment for an abscess in a bone on his right leg. Today his left shin was swathed in bandages too.

"I 'ad a pain there all night. So nurse did put on a foment," the man explained.

Supposing I hadn't examined him! Ronald was thinking to himself. I shouldn't have done anything about it at all. Of course, Sister can do all there is to do without any telling from me. But then Terry would've come round this afternoon, and Sister would've pulled back the things as a matter of course, and I should've looked a fool.

He looked at the leg, felt it and covered it up again.

"Secondary abscess. That explains the temperature. Nuisance," he said. "Hot fomentations four-hourly, please Sister."

So the round went on.

"I'll do those two dressings now please, Ten and Thirteen."

Sister looked pained.

"They've both been done, Mr. Dalloway. You were later than usual, and I really couldn't keep the ward work waiting for you."

Dalloway walked over and looked at the two men. They both seemed pretty well. He supposed that he had better not worry them by having them undone again.

"I see. There's a man coming in today, a request of Sir Roland's, for investigation."

"Sir Roland hasn't an empty bed." Sister's stony calm underwent no change.

"Oh, bother. Borrow one of Mr. Terrington's."

"Mr. Terrington's are full too."

"Well, look here, Sister, he's coming in. You'll have to make a bed somehow. What about this one?"

"Both my couches are being mended, Mr. Dalloway, and that bed is going to be used. If you want a bed, you must transfer the little boy to the children's ward, where he ought to be."

Ronald snorted. The boy had been taken into Darwin specially at Sister's request, because his father was there. He was only six, and his rightful place certainly was the children's ward. Well, he wasn't going to lose his temper because Sister had gone in off the deep end over something or other.

"Right-o. I think that's all my jobs here then. Good morning, Sister."

He cursed as he ran downstairs.

Pedley was right. Sister Darwin was a great friend of Sister Theatre's. George must have sneaked about that silly business in the anaesthetic-room. What a green, lurid idiot he was not to have realised the beastliness of hospitals before.

3

During the lunch hour, he sat hunched in an armchair, its back to the crowd of noisy students who filled the Common Room.

Half-educated, John had said. Well, if she was, he could teach her things. That was one of the joys of her, she liked being taught.

She wasn't catty.

Wives very often were scandalmongers. A beastly nuisance in a doctor's wife. There was that case of Sir Francis Bolt, who had told a juicy story about a patient to his wife and she had published it at a tea-party with the result of a libel action and £1000 damages against Sir Francis.

Doctors' wives. If she got the sack because of him, he'd have to marry her. Then he wouldn't be able to go on doing unpaid hospital jobs for the experience they gave him. He wouldn't be able to take his Fellowship. He would have to go and be a G.P. in some mouldy town, and all his ambitions would be gone and his brains of no account.

His father would be terribly disappointed.

Dora hadn't liked her. Perhaps Dora had recognised some unpleasantness in her which he had missed. Women knew things about other women that a man would never realise.

For a long time he brooded, his thoughts racing from Anne to his work, his prospects, his brilliant past, his easy popularity, and back to Anne again. Presently he rose and went with lagging footsteps to the Theatre floor. He had to give Sister a message. Perhaps he would see her. It would be better if he didn't; if he did, she would give him that frank wide-eyed smile. If she did, he would be bowled over again. It would be pleasant to be bowled over again by that smile.

He looked in several rooms for Sister. In one of them a pale, fluffy-haired girl was cleaning Mr. Terrington's boots. He had never seen that girl on the Theatre floor before.

His heart thumped suddenly, then raced, and his face grew slowly hot and then cold. She had gone. She really had got the sack, because of him. He would have to marry her.

He didn't want to. Oh, he didn't want to. He wanted to stay on at St. Edmunds and become Senior Resident in his turn. He wanted to take his higher exams. He didn't want to settle down to be a dull, hard-working G.P., not yet. Not ever, if he could help it.

Perhaps he wouldn't be able to find her. She had never told him where she lived.

CHAPTER 6

1

ANNE had again completely changed her routine. She found the sudden difference dulling to the feelings. She did not miss the Theatre, or even Dalloway, half as much as she had feared. There was simply no time.

The Gynaecological Block had two wards, one for Midwifery, one for Diseases of Women, and the nurses took turns of duty in both. Sometimes Anne would be hurrying about with another nurse, double-lifting Jewesses of extraordinary bulk and power of lamentation. At others, she would be carrying a pair of minute, scarlet babies from the bathroom to their little red cradles at the foot of their mother's bed. She was always busy and generally tired. The lifting alone was trying, and there was no time except actual off-duty time for rest.

Most of the nursing there was dull. There were only about three diseases for all the patients to have. But she was immensely interested when she was allowed to go into the Labour Room and watch undisturbed the arrival of the babies. "You'll be doing your C.M.B. one day," the Staff-nurse said to her. "See as many labours as you can."

Sister was a little red-haired, short-tempered woman, a slave-driver to her nurses, inclined to be lazy herself. She nagged always and never praised. She had no great interest in her work, which she left as far as she could to the elderly Staff-nurse who had been in the ward for years; much more in the recently appointed Assistant

101

Gynaecologist, who was young and unattached. Anne avoided her and learned all she could from the Staff-nurse.

The "Gynæ Block" was separated from the rest of the hospital by a long passage. Those who worked there saw little of those outside. The Gynaecological students were very hard-worked elsewhere and only appeared in the wards when their chiefs were doing their rounds. The "Midder Boys," who attended the women on the District, were sometimes seen in the Theatre, sterilizing their instruments; but they were generally on the verge of being overcome by sleep. And the two Resident Accoucheurs only came when their help was required.

Anne did not see Dalloway at all for three days. She wondered vaguely what would happen next. They would have to meet somehow, of course. They were much too good friends to be cut off from each other by silly rules. Their minds fitted so well. She wondered if Ronald felt that too. He would probably be planning and arranging some way for them to meet. No one could possibly object if she were invited to his home at Hampstead, for instance. That was right away from hospital rule. Suppose they actually did ask her to go and ride. She would just have to say she hadn't her clothes in town with her. And if they insisted and lent her some of Dora's—well, she was sure she wouldn't fall off, anyway. She had often had dreams of herself on horseback, and she knew exactly what it felt like and how one got on and off. Ronald would be able to teach her to ride properly. He was probably just as good at that as he was at everything else.

On the fourth day, she spied him. She was at the top of the zig-zag flight of stairs, and she saw him through the banisters, just beginning to come up. They would meet half-way.

He did not see her until he was almost up to her. Then their eyes met for an instant; but the glances only touched the surface and flashed away, and he muttered "Good morning, Nurse," and hurried on.

Disappointment sat like a leaden weight on Anne's heart. She could feel it, physically. Yet, there had been nothing in that meeting noticeably different from any earlier one. They always called each other "Nurse" and "Mr. Dalloway" in hospital, always passed the stereotyped good day. But generally their eyes held each other, if only for an instant, probing deeply and parting reluctantly. Today, his had slid away from hers almost furtively.

"I suppose," she said to herself, "he's afraid of getting me into another row. Decent of him."

Then, "There was no one about. But there might have been at any minute. He won't take any risks for me. Besides, we mustn't be underhand or we shall spoil it."

Then, sensibly, "I was so looking forward to seeing him that I expected something more than usual. It was exactly the same as usual, really. Anyway, I've seen him, and I shall see him again."

She passed him in the garden, walking with another student and he took no notice of her at all. That was only sensible; even a good morning from a Resident to a mere probationer in the garden before everyone would have set people talking.

Sometimes the Gynaecological nurses had to go up to the main Theatre to take drums of dressings to be sterilised or to bring back sterilised things. Anne was never sent on these errands, and if, as once, she volunteered, the Staff-nurse was sent too, to help carry things. The second time she offered, she was sent summarily back to do some other task in the ward.

She realised that the porters eyed her with amused interest as she went out when she was off duty. Once waiting outside the hospital for a bus, she caught sight of a goffered cap inside Casualty window. Sister Casualty was watching her as she climbed up the stairs of the bus.

St. Edmunds' paternal eye was on her, unwinking. She felt surrounded by a wall of unfriendly faces; faces that were simply ordinary, sometimes even kindly, when she was just a Pro in uniform; but let her become a person, express an opinion, ask the reason for an order, even show an intelligent interest in her work, and they became inscrutable, enemies who would not fight and were too many to run away.

She came face to face with Dalloway once again, and instead of grinning with pleasure to see her, he flushed and looked uneasy.

Was he afraid that she had taken offence at his attempt to squeeze her hand? Perhaps she ought to have done so. The time and place had been most unsuitable, of course. But she had wanted sympathy so much at that minute, and it was an added proof that he liked her for him to show it. She was glad he had done it, glad. The only thing she was not glad about was that his aim had been so poor.

104

The next time they came together, she looked straight at him and smiled, the old tender smile. She had imagined the relief that would shoot into his eyes when he saw that she was not angry.

But the expression that met her was one of alarm, like that of an imprisoned animal. The two of them turned, blindly, and stumbled in opposite directions.

Anne felt all in a whirl. He was afraid of her. She had seen that. But why? Was it—could it be that he—he liked her so much that he couldn't trust himself to be discreet any longer, and so he ran away? She shook herself. People weren't really like that except in books. Certainly not educated, controlled people like Dalloway. Then—he must be afraid she was going to run after him. But he couldn't be. He couldn't think she was that kind of person, the kind of person who would pursue a man and exercise her wiles on him until he proposed to her in sheer desperation. "Their only chance of escape," his sister had said. But surely she had shown him that she was interested in her work and did not want to escape from it.

She forgot about the whole thing in the stress of the day's work; but whenever she had a minute's leisure, there would come back to her, with a catch of the breath, the realisation that some shadow was upon her, and her eyes would look round anxiously, and a little fear would gnaw at her heart.

She spoke of it, stumbling, to Belsize. Worldly wisdom and kindness of heart struggled in Belsize's eyes as she answered:

"No chance to meet now? No, not with everyone's eye

on you. He could write to you, of course—"

"I hadn't thought of that," Anne said. "I suppose he hasn't either."

"It's the only thing to do. If you do anything else, now, you'll both get the sack."

"Both?" Anne was startled.

"Oom." Then, after a pause: "Mr. Dalloway's awfully brainy."

"I know."

"He'll end in Harley Street, I expect. He's awfully ambitious."

Anne nodded absently. She was already walking away in the direction of the letter-rack.

She watched the letter-rack for days, and nothing came for her. The dull ache of disappointment was with her all the time; and at night, and between whiles in her work, she thought.

She had so enjoyed Dalloway. She wanted to hear him talk, to exchange ideas with him, to know he liked being with her. That was all. It wasn't much. But there was no one else whose ideas seemed to fit hers as his did. No one else nearly as interesting.

She was sure he had liked being with her. Why had he asked her to go out again with him, if not? Besides—there were lots of proofs—

If he hadn't liked her—liked her a lot—why was she such a fool as to have thought he had?

She wasn't a fool.

Perhaps things didn't mean the same to him as they did to her. Didn't mean so much. Her scale of values was quite different. It was all that business of education again. She might like him—love him, even—with her spirit and her body, but her mind would always be his inferior, because she had never learned to use it. They could never be equals, and that was intolerable. Perhaps it was just as well that he had gone away.

But had he gone away from her, for good? Couldn't she teach her mind to equal his, even now? She would make herself a fit companion for him, if only he would give her a chance.

Then her mood changed. He couldn't give her a chance, poor Ronald. She was hedged about by jealous women, he by jeering friends, and they must keep apart or be ruined. Both had their work to do. There was no time, no energy left over to fight the necessary battle to get together again.

Should she leave St. Edmunds, give up nursing and find some pretext for meeting him as a private person? But then, supposing he didn't really want her.

Should she write to him, since he hadn't thought of writing to her? But you couldn't write to a man just because he talked to you about your work and took you out once on a bus. Besides, there was nothing to say.

Once she saw him coming towards her along a corridor, and he looked up and turned aside hastily into the Casualty Department, where he could not possibly have wanted to go.

But that might have meant anything.

Then she didn't see him again for over a week. And then he came into the ward where she was, with the Junior Accoucheur and several students, and stayed there for half an hour quite oblivious of her presence. He wasn't pretending, she could see. He really did not know who the figure standing in the corner was. It was just a nurse, and nurses didn't concern him. She knew then that their friendship was over.

2

The beginnings of a philosophy of life came to her during the days which followed. She felt deserted, alone. There was only one person with whom she could be entirely herself, and he did not want her. She would always be alone, now.

Reaction, because she was a sturdy soul, came soon. She refused to be sorry for herself. People who were sorry for themselves were no good. It didn't matter what happened to one, it was the way one took the things that mattered. She found that mental suffering taught one many things. She understood the patients even better than she had done when she was happy. She tried to bury her discomfort in her work, and to a certain extent succeeded.

She wondered what most people did when they were hurt. Prayed, she supposed. Prayed that the things which hurt them might be taken away. She found that she could not do this. She could not, possibly, pray that Ronald should come back to her. It hurt her sense of logical cause and effect to think of doing so. If he was not the sort of person to want her more than anything else, as she wanted him, it was useless to pray that, by some fluke, he might be changed. She did not want him changed.

Besides, she did not think that God did change people just to please someone else. She had not thought much about God before. Now she saw Him, not as an all-powerful ruler who could, and would, suddenly perform a miracle to satisfy a whim; but as a great intelligence who knew everything because He had made it, whose creation followed a great network of laws which were dependent on each other and which could not possibly be broken. She felt that she could worship such an intelligence. But it offended her to think that its plans could be changed by the prayer of a mere human. Irreverently, she imagined a scene in the Headquarters of Olympus. "Everything going smoothly? Hullo, what's that? Anne Lee in difficulties? Can't get on without Ronald Dalloway? Well, well—" and some ethereal artisan would jam on a lever and a whole lot of cables would be thrown violently out of alignment, a whole lot of lives given a rude jolt; another lever would be moved and the cables would jerk, heavily, into a new pattern, and the almighty overseer would look at them a little doubtfully and say, "Well, I didn't mean to have it quite like that, but I suppose it'll work all right. If it doesn't we shall have to disconnect and try something else."

Oh no, that wouldn't do at all. You couldn't pray for other people's lives to be changed to suit your own. Definite actions led to definite conclusions. "Not a bus, not a bus, but a tram." Only Anne did not agree that the grooves in which the tram moved were predestinate. You could choose, when you came to the points, which way your tram should take; only, once you had chosen, you had to go on along that set of lines to a definite goal. You couldn't turn back. You might, perhaps, by a long and painful cross-country journey, get on to the other road which you wished, too late, that you had taken. So that all you could logically pray for was wisdom, that you might foresee a little where each of the roads led and take the one you really wanted. If she prayed at all at this time, it was that she should have the sense not to try to hold on to Ronald if she did come across him again. Anyway, it was no good praying that the laws of the universe should suddenly be suspended just because you found you had made a mistake. It wouldn't happen, and it was much better for you to learn from the experience and hope you did better next time. She felt that her little adventure was a very important experience, because it taught her, what her father had done his best that she should never learn, that men were weak and impulsive and silly and hated above all things to be made to look ridiculous. She did not hate them. She merely ceased to look upon them as gods. She embarked again upon her quest for knowledge with clear, widely opened eyes.

3

The three months Gynaecology dragged to its end. It made Anne wish more than ever that she had not been born a woman. They seemed to be burdened with so many useless organs. Then, having taught her that the things that happened to her did not matter, Fate tried to make her forget the lesson by treating her kindly for awhile.

She was sent to the Casualty Department, to learn what people look like when they are very ill indeed; to treat minor injuries and do no harm to serious ones; to diagnose infectious fevers at a glance and segregate them; to know who is telling the truth and who is not; and, as always, to clear up the most unpleasant messes and restore cleanliness.

It was a varied life, full of excitement. One never knew what would happen next. One turned from a child with running ears to a man with electric shock, without a blemish on him but as dead as a doornail; and thence to the unexpected birth of a baby. One looked down on a sea of anxious faces, bewildered by some sudden ill, dazed and resigned as so many cows at market; watched each one dealt with and sent shambling away by the young Casualty Officer to the Department most suitable for his case; heard snatches of their conversation—

"Moi Sam's in th' Infirmary, and Peg's abed, an' now this one's sick—"

"Missis 'Iggs is fell agin. Ten, that is, in nine year—last time was twins—"

"She's buried six o' consumption an' one wi' the inward convulsions—"

"Bill 'ere's got the inward convulsions I do think — threw 'imself back 'e did and rolled 'is eyes like a little dead thing—"

"Aw well. Reckon it's the will o' Gawd—"

Anne longed to fling herself on them and shout, "It isn't, it isn't, if only you'd try to prevent these things! If Mrs. Higgs wouldn't have quite so many babies and would keep her windows open and her floors clean—"

It wouldn't be any good, of course. Most of them would just, cow-like, not understand. A few would laugh tolerantly and say that nurses and doctors always had these fads. But perhaps one would take it in and act on it.

Anyway, she couldn't do it. It wasn't her job. Perhaps one day she would do Public Health work. It was all frightfully interesting, the more so because it was so practical and so human. The people liked her, because she was so interested in them, unlike the bright, hard type of nurse to whom they were all so many cases to be got through and sent away. She really minded when they were hurt, and somehow they knew it, though her pity came out in firm, quick action, not in tears.

"A jolly good nurse," the Casualty Officers voted her, and trusted her with dressings and taught her how to put in stitches.

She learned all she possibly could, and kept her real, personal self tucked tight inside her uniform, lest it should come peeping out and do harm and get hurt again.

She had one thorn in the flesh. Nurse Paley was in charge of the Casualty Observation ward. But Anne, being now a Senior Probationer, was not actually under her. The sour little woman was unpopular in spite of her undeniable efficiency. She preferred to watch a mistake made and then report it rather than to give the hint which might have prevented it. She lost her temper very easily and both nurses and Residents would now and then play jokes on her for the amusement of watching her flare.

One busy day a Casualty Officer rushed into her little

112

ward and told her to get a bed ready at once for a bad accident. Anne, not in the least taken in by the young man's bustling importance, reflected that it was usually the porter who came with news of a bad accident, and wondered what would follow. Nurse Paley reflected upon nothing but the extra work she would have to do and went grumbling off to do it. Hot bottles were prepared, dressing trays were dragged into position. The porters brought in the stretcher, all covered and solemn. A red stream dripped from it to Nurse Paley's spotless floor. Two Casualty Officers came running, and sent Nurse Paley off to fetch a blood-transfusion apparatus. Anne, still suspicious, watched at the door while she was away—and as soon as she was out of sight the stretcher was dumped without ceremony on the floor and the porters lifted out the gigantic coloured cardboard Charlie Chaplin who had been guarding the door of the cinema across the way. They had only just got him nicely tucked in when the Staff-nurse puffed into the ward again. She had half set up her apparatus on the table before she realised that everyone was laughing at her.

She scattered the men with her biting words. They stood outside, shrugging, inclined to be sulky. Why couldn't she take a joke properly with a laugh? They would have cleaned up her floor and brought all sorts of people to talk to her and see her distinguished patient, if she had behaved sensibly. Now she had spoilt it all. Anne, as they passed her, spread out her hands in a gesture of hopelessness. It wasn't any good trying to have fun with Paley. They grinned, wishing that Anne had been the subject of the joke.

No one would go into the little ward to take Charlie away. Paley had to heave him out herself and stagger with him to the door of Casualty and prop him there. He reappeared, later, back in his old place outside the cinema, and everyone was angry with Paley for making a frost of a good rag.

Paley vented her spite on Anne. "I suppose you think that was funny!"

"I think it would have been, if you'd let it," Anne said. She had never been able to take Belsize's advice and toady the senior nurse.

"Just as you think you'd have been Missis Ronald Dalloway if I'd let you!" Paley hissed, beside herself.

Anne's face lost its colour for an instant. "What d'you mean?"

"I saw your little game! Making eyes at him when everyone was at breakfast! Meeting him on buses and pretending it was an accident! I was inside that bus, let me tell you! I saw you go off to tea with the young man!"

"Oh, it was you, was it," Anne said coolly. "I thought it must be. Why did you sneak? It didn't matter to you what we did!"

"It wasn't the proper thing for a St. Edmunds nurse to do."

"I bet," Anne said, "you'd have simply loved to have done it yourself. Only you've never had a chance. And you never will have, if you go about looking like you do now."

Nurse Paley could do nothing but snort. In a minute

Anne saw her lip curl in a little triumphant sneer, and her head go up as she watched Anne out of the corner of her eye. Dalloway had come quietly into the Casualty Room, looked round and quickly departed. Anne hoped quite calmly and sincerely that Paley would go to hell and burn. She knew that she would, if a righteous lack of charity was a valid passport. She comforted herself by thinking that after all it was just as well the affair was over, for she had quite made up her mind that her only ambition now was to become a Sister—a really good, efficient and yet pleasant Sister, like Sister Southcliffe, only better still.

After Casualty she had a series of posts; the men's medical ward, which she took as evidence that her past had been forgiven; a women's medical; some strenuous months in the throat department, which she enjoyed, for it had a theatre of its own; more night-duty; and then, having passed her State examinations with credit, she had a whole year as Staff-nurse in Southcliffe Ward under Sister Southcliffe, who was more than half a saint and the rest a very wise and kindly sinner. She had learnt the art of nursing inside out by that time. From Sister Southcliffe she learned how to manage people, from the anxious relatives of patients to raw probationers and ward-maids. She learned to keep calm, not only to appear so, by the simple process of thinking of one thing at a time and putting behind her everything that worried and could not be remedied. If it could be remedied, she dealt with it. She stilled fear, saved lives so often that the process became a matter of no concern, and Residents' reputations again and again with a twinkle of enjoyment; and so grew from a callow girl into a quiet, disciplined woman. Under her uniform, however, much of the girl still lingered. Her brush with the pettiness and jealousy of hospital life had made her wary inside the hospital. Of life outside it she had no experience. She still thought it wonderful and its people brave and honest and just and all the other things she had been taught at school to think them. Her brown eyes often flashed a girl's mischief and sometimes a girl's quick hatred of injustice. She had kept, too, the child's happy courage and honesty and love of beauty. She had wallowed in the mud to find out all about it, and somehow had managed to come out of it clean.

4

"Sister Darwin's leaving to get married!"

So the rumour first went round.

"Who'll get her job?"

"Oh, Sister Tillyard, of course!"

That was obvious, Sister Tillyard having been Assistant Sister in Darwin ward for the last three years.

The burning question in the Nurses' Common Room was, who of the permanent Staff-nurses would be offered Sister Tillyard's position.

"Lee, for certain," general opinion said.

Anne even dared to think so herself. She had worked very hard, been given consistently good reports, and had several times unofficially acted as an Assistant Sister in emergencies. She got on well with everyone, and her aloofness, unpopular in a new probationer, gave her now an added dignity. She was quite the most outstanding of the Permanent Staff.

She wanted the post more than she had ever wanted anything. It was the ambition she had been aiming at for years. She had all sorts of plans. She simply must get it. Everyone expected her to. In a day or two she would be called to the Matron's office and given permission to wear the Sister's blue. In the meantime, she waited and planned.

It seemed to her that everyone was looking at her with envy during the next few days. Only Belsize, now on the Private Staff, surveyed her rather anxiously.

"Remember the last time you were sent for to the office?" she asked idly of Anne.

"Yes. I do. Isn't it ages ago?"

"Ages, it seems. 'Tisn't, really," Belsize said, and relapsed into silence.

It would be very different this time, Anne thought to herself. No nonsense about black caps now. She pulled herself up. She really must not say "this time" as though it was a foregone conclusion.

At lunchtime she sauntered through the groups of nurses to find her letters.

"Paley, of all people!" she heard someone say. "Well, she's waited long enough for it!"

"—Got into a mess with a Resident, didn't she?"

"—The mouldiest luck—have done much better!"

Paley, in a mess with a Resident? Never! Anne was out of earshot and level with Belsize.

"What's this about Paley?" she asked.

"She's got Sister Tillyard's job." Belsize's voice was toneless.

Anne felt the blood drain out of her cheeks. *"Paley?* Good lord, why?"

"She's not a bad nurse, you know!"

"But such a beastly person!"

"Sisters are always beastly people. I wouldn't be one for a thousand pounds. Besides, the Secretary's wife's her cousin."

Anne said nothing. Then, positively, "It was *me* they were talking about!"

"'Who?"

Anne nodded towards the group behind her.

"Those people. They said someone had got into a mess with one of the Residents, and that it was mouldy luck."

"So it was. The very mouldiest."

"Is that why I didn't get it?"

"Well—Paley's senior to you, of course—"

"She's never done emergency Sister."

"I know. Yes, I suppose it was that, really, old thing. I've been afraid about it all along."

"Have you? You knew they'd rake it up again?"

"They never forget things like that. They're afraid you'd be a rebel and go against tradition. It may be a bad tradition, all this narrowness and hatred of change, but there it is. They love it, the old ones, it excuses them for being single and dull and catty. Paley won't spoil it, she's branded with it already. She's safe. They're afraid of you. So you go, and the hospital suffers."

Anne glinted a smile at her.

"Thanks for that. But—it's fiendish."

"'Tisn't. There are other places then Edmunds. Better ones. You'll be glad one day."

Anne shook her head. Never.

"Never expect things," George said to her later, "and you'll never be disappointed. But you'll be a dull sort of a buddy all the same."

5

She lay awake most of the night. It was only a little trouble really, just as the other had been. But it seemed so big. It was such an enormous punishment, just for being green. Why couldn't they see she had grown out of it? She had worked so hard, for the hospital, and now they said she wasn't good enough for it. She felt that she could not stay there any longer, with no probability but of growing old as a mere Staff-nurse. She must go and fulfil her ambition somewhere else. She did not want to leave St. Edmunds, not a bit, but she felt that she would be even more of a failure if she did not.

She allowed a decent interval to elapse, then sent in her resignation to the Matron and looked out for another job.

PART II

ADOLESCENT

"Mad is the heart of love,
   And gold the gleam of his wing,
And all to the spell thereof
   Bend, when he makes his spring."

Hippolytus,
Gilbert Murray's translation.

CHAPTER 1

1

"SISTER LEE, Matron, please."

A shabby replica of the little Assistant Matron at St. Edmunds ushered Anne into the Presence.

The Matron of Princess Ida's Hospital for Children was in no way a replica of the stately lady at St. Edmunds. She was little and alert, with red frizzy hair and eyes that snapped. She looked like a rather bold rat, and she lolled in her chair like an insolent queen. Anne had disliked her at the preliminary interview. But she could not afford to refuse the first Sister's post to be offered her in London just because she did not like the looks of the Matron. Besides, the off-duty time was good, the work what she wanted, and the salary sixty pounds a year, which she considered very good too. Anyway, she had accepted the post and here she was.

The Matron glanced up at her. "Good evening, Sister. I'm just off to dinner with Doctor Finnemore, so I can't give you very long now. Sister Jonas will show you your room and your ward. You'll find the ward in a frightful muddle. Terrible woman, the last Sister we had there. I never interfere with my Sisters, I just gave her the sack when I found out what she was like. I hope you'll be more satisfactory. I'm sure you will. Good evening, Sister."

Then she was in a little square room with a bright fire. The wails of angry babies battered at her ears from the open window and door.

"This is your sitting-room," little Sister Jonas was saying.

"Thank goodness I don't have to sleep here!" Anne thought.

She tried to remember the landmarks of stair and corner as she was allowed to peep into the various wards and then taken upstairs to her bedroom. Then she was left alone, with the meagre information that supper was at eight-thirty in the Nurses' dining-room in the basement and that she would go on duty at eight in the morning and report to the Matron at nine.

2

"It's a nice ward!" That was her first impression as she came into it in the morning. It was tiled in white from the floor to halfway up the walls and finished with a dado of playing children. It had windows on both sides, and a balcony on one, over which a red and white sunblind flapped.

She passed down the ward, and noticed with sudden dismay a hillock of dust and crumbs under one of the cots. The ingrained tradition of St. Edmunds rose up within her in horror. "Good gracious, it's dirty!"

She went a little farther, and saw that two of the sheets were badly stained, that one of the red quilts was torn and another had never been hemmed. "And nobody's done any sewing for months!"

She came to her table, set at one end of the ward, and sat down at it to read the night-report and to think. No one had told her anything about her duties. She supposed she had to find them out for herself. It was a good thing Sister Southcliffe had taught her so thoroughly how to manage a children's ward. She looked up to see the Staff-nurse standing before her, and bade her good morning.

"Good morning, Sister."

The shade of anxiety on the girl's face stimulated her. She really was a Sister. This ward was her ward, her authority in it was absolute.

"I'll do a round now, Nurse."

The Nurse was disconcerted. She made faint protest.

"Sister never did a round till—"

"All the same, we'll do a round, Nurse."

She smiled down on the girl. She didn't want them to be afraid of her. Not unless it was necessary. They were so young, these nurses, some of them only eighteen, and it was such a terrifying job.

The Staff-nurse surveyed her with amazement, and capitulated. She had not met with firmness for a long time, and with a smile like that, never.

Long before the round was over, the smile had vanished, and with it the faint terror which had wrinkled Anne's brows since her arrival. She knew now exactly what she had to do. The whole place was dirty—floor, beds, utensils, everything. How anyone could send a surgical case into it she could not think. She must get it clean and make the nurses keep it so. Until that was done, nothing else need be thought of. She catechised the Staff-nurse as she went round, reading the names of the surgeons on the case-boards at the foot of each cot.

"Mr. Salter? What does he do?"

"He's Senior Surgeon, Sister."

"When does he come round?"

"Mondays and Thursdays at two."

"When does he operate?"

"Er—Thursdays, after the round."

And so on, through the list.

At the end of it, Staff-nurse ventured some information.

"Er—we don't have many operations, Sister."

"No?"

"Crossman ward gets them all. This isn't a very good ward."

"Oh."

So people did not put surgical cases into it. They just dumped children for whom there was no room anywhere else.

"Seen your ward?" Matron greeted her when she appeared in the office.

"Yes, Matron. It's filthy."

"Get it clean, then," Matron snapped.

"Yes, Matron. I intend to."

"Tell all the nurses to come here," she told the Staff-nurse after this brief interview.

They gathered round the table, as grubby and frowsy-looking as the ward itself, and she harangued them on tidiness and cleanliness until, at her word, they slunk away with underlips drawn in, and apprehensive brows. She forgot she was only just fledged. She was Sister Theatre, the Martinette; Sister Southcliffe, amazed that such things could be; all the St. Edmunds tyrants rolled into one incarnation of horror and wrath. And at the end of it, her own humorous, kindly self came out, and she laughed. The probationers had gone, and did not see; but the Staff-nurse had stayed behind for orders and met her twinkling eye.

"That'll do, Nurse. We *must* do something about it, mustn't we? Awful, I call it!"

The Staff-nurse was her woman from that instant.

Then a child was sick.

"Get a clean nightdress, Nurse! And a clean pillowcase too," Anne said when it was over.

"There aren't any, Sister."

Anne flashed an awful glance at her.

"Show me the linen-cupboard!"

Staff-nurse did so, silently. She was right. Except for a few sheets and a few rags which had been clothes, it was empty.

She thought she knew the worst then, but she did not. She saw children with bedsores, wounds that stank of infection, beds in an indescribable state of dirt, and she thought that nothing could be more horrible.

The House-surgeon lounged up, at nearly twelve o'clock, to do his round. She waited for him, starched and prim, with her back to the high wire fender.

He was greasy to look upon, his jacket had a waist, his shoes were pointed and his hair smelt of scent.

She disliked him intensely.

"Mornin' Sister. Nothin' to show me, have you?"

"There are several things I'd like you to see, Mr. Brown."

"*Are* there? Well, hurry up, then."

She led him round to the bedsores and the septic wounds, and he chewed his lip in silence. They were not nice to see.

"I just wanted you to realise what things were like when I came. I'm not responsible for them."

He said nothing. He had never seen those cases before, except their heads above the bedclothes. When his chiefs came round, he always assured them that they were "going on all right."

He led the way back to the fireguard and Anne followed.

"What do you want done with them? "Anne asked him.

"Oh, come, Sister, that's your province, isn't it? Pure nursing."

"You mean," she said stonily, "that I have a free hand?"

"Oh, yes. Do as you like. Immaterial. They'll clear up. I'm sure you'll do the best that can be done."

He grinned, and edged imperceptibly nearer to her. Before she had taken her mind off the various antiseptics that she might use, he had slid his arm round her trim, belted waist.

She whirled furiously away from him.

"Please don't behave like that in this ward"

He thrust his hands into his pockets and shrugged.

"Sorry. Thought you'd like it. Sister Jackson did."

She turned her back on him, then primly addressed him again.

"Is there anything else you want, Mr. Brown?"

"Er—no."

"Good morning. It's time I was seeing to the dinners."

She held open the door and he could do nothing but stroll out.

She was left alone, chattering to herself with rage.

"Little worm! How dared he! Filthy place, no nursing to do at all, no one with a penn'orth of sense in their heads. Give in my notice this evening."

Should she?

There *was* nursing to do. Not proper surgical nursing; but it was up to her to heal those sores and clean those foul wounds. And, presently, to teach those young nurses as she had been taught herself.

She looked through the ward dressing cupboard. It at least was well supplied. After dinner she would show those nurses how to do a proper dressing.

But when she climbed the stairs after the dinner-hour, she was met by a commotion in the kitchen, a stretcher borne by two porters, several weeping women and a grubby child.

"Case for your ward, Sister."

She swept past them to find the Staff-nurse.

"D'you know anything about this, Nurse?"

"What, Sister?"

"Don't they warn one, before they send up cases?"

"They're supposed to. It's on the regulations."

A porter handed her the child's admission slip. There was no diagnosis on it, nothing to direct her.

"I shall send for the House-surgeon," she decided, and took up the telephone.

"Be lucky if you get 'im," she heard the grinning porters agree.

"Mr. Brown?" came up the telephone. "He's out."

"Well, please send me whoever's doing his work. It's important."

She heard a murmuring. Then—

"Miss Thorn's coming," someone said.

"She's the Casualty Officer," the Staff-nurse whispered.

She had evidently roused the Resident by her urgency, for on the heels of her message came a little dark girl in the Resident's white coat.

"'What is it, Sister?"

"It's this case. I had no warning. I can't take cases straight in like this, I must be told when they're coming."

The girl's mouth twitched.

"I'm sorry. We never bother."

"Will you please bother in future?"

"We'll try. As a matter of fact, Sister Jackson always used to say there wasn't a bed. We knew there was, so we just sent 'em up without asking. She poked 'em in somewhere."

"I'm not Sister Jackson."

The girl's amused grey eye met Anne's.

"So I see. I'm glad."

"But I'm going to say the same thing. There isn't a bed."

"Oh, rot, Sister!"

"Perhaps you'd like to come and see."

She led Miss Thorn round the ward, showed her the grubby, tousled, slept-in beds which stood empty, the dirt, the squalor.

"D'you think that's a suitable place to nurse surgical cases in?"

"That kid I sent up," Miss Thorn said, "has a wound into his knee-joint."

"If you want him to get a stiff leg, or to lose it altogether, put him in here now. Next week I'll welcome him."

"Oom. All right, Sister."

"Take the case to Crossman and tell Sister he must go on a couch. No, I'll tell her myself. Stay here till I come back." Miss Thorn told the porters.

Their grins had subsided.

Later in the afternoon the House-surgeon appeared again.

"Ward been shirking work again, I hear," he said nastily.

Anne presented an unmoved front.

"I'm not taking in any more cases until I've got the ward clean."

He whistled. "We'll see."

"I suppose I'm taking a high hand. It's the only way. If I don't, I shall never make anything of it." So thought Anne to herself. "Is that how all Sisters get—like Sisters?"

She sought the Matron again the minute she was off duty, and explained herself.

"I'm not shirking, but I must get clean," she said.

Matron surveyed her with a faintly approving eye.

"All right, Sister."

3

There followed weeks of which Anne had no clear remembrance. She whisked about the ward with her sleeves up, scouring and polishing; she harried the nurses, made them do jobs three times over, pursued them with pieces of cottonwool (how she had hated Sister Theatre for that!), abused them until their faces were haggard and tears very near. At first they sulked and worked more badly than ever; then they realised that they would never be left alone until they had satisfied her, and worked frenziedly, cursing; then they realised that the ward really was beginning to look nice; that the sores were healing— one child had actually been sent home after a stay of two months—that they were learning the elements of nursing; and that there was truth in the Staff-nurse's reiteration, "She's a jolly fine person."

They began to breathe more freely. Anne's smile came sometimes and her whimsical phrases made them laugh.

"We're clean," she told the Matron, and the Matron came up to look and approved.

"Jack Horner ward's ready for patients," the message went down. The ward sat down to wait for them.

The nursing-staff was not idle. The ward had to be kept clean now, and kept clean it was. And in every spare moment Sister and nurses mended and hemmed and darned until it had nearly its full complement of bed linen again. Anne had written to all the relatives and philanthropic friends she had and soon there began to come parcels of children's cast-off clothes, bits to be made into bed jackets, and wool for operation socks.

She kept them busy. And the patients which they waited for did not come.

If Anne could have listened at the keyhole of the

Resident's Common Room she would have realised why.

"She's a tartar. I simply daren't show my face up there again! Don't for any sake send up a case that wants any treatment, or I shall have to go."

"She's all right. She was only shocked," Miss Thorn would object.

"She was jolly rude to J.B."

"I expect," stoutly from Miss Thorn, "J.B. was rude to her. He always is."

"It's only his little way. She'll have to get used to it."

"She won't, if I know her!"

"Then she won't get any cases. Not that she'll want 'em. Jack Horner's always been a dud ward. The nursing's simply vile."

"Oh, send 'em to Crossman. Sister Crossman's an old darling, do anything for you—"

So Anne sewed, attended to the minor ailments that came her way, did her best for the "chronics" for whom nothing could really be done at all, and ate her heart out for some work that should put her on her mettle.

"I shall go," she told her loyal Staff-nurse one day in a burst of despair.

"Don't, Sister. Look at those Pros."

"What about them?"

"They're turning into nurses. They're learning. You'll get them through their exams, anyway. That's something."

Perhaps it was.

Perhaps she would stay. But how she hated it!

CHAPTER 2

1

ON the heels of Anne's struggle came a letter from her youngest sister, Angela.

"I've sent you a parcel of clothes. Ours, when young. I had the greatest trouble to make Mother give them up . . . I'm coming up to London. I'm fed-up with home, so I've got transferred to the London office and I'm going to live in a hostel near Vincent Square. Can I come and see you some evening? I'll ring up."

Anne puzzled over it. Something drastic must have happened to make Angela desert her many friends in the north; and for her to ask humble leave to come to see her somewhat despised elder sister.

She came, one evening. Anne thought her quiet and pale, though she teased in her usual way at Anne's bright blue Sister's dress and at the little blue cape with red lining and red bands crossing over the chest.

"It suits you, though," she admitted. "You're jolly nice to look at, you know. Dignified. Never make a fool of yourself." She sighed.

"What do you want?" Anne laughed.

"Want? Pig. Nothing. Comfort, perhaps."

They tiptoed into the ward and looked at the sleeping babies, then drew up chairs in front of Anne's fire. Angela displayed her left hand, which looked queerly bare.

"I've broken with Jimmy," she said.

"Angela! Poor old infant! Why?"

Anne remembered her sister's radiant shyness six years ago, when the engagement had just been announced and she herself had left home. Angela had been so proudly secure then, so sure of the future. They had all wondered a little why the pair did not marry. But it was a risk, nowadays, to marry on a clerk's salary, and this explanation had satisfied the Lee family. Anne had seen very little of Angela since then.

"D'you want to tell me about it?" she asked.

"Yes. At least, there's nothing much to tell. He's married."

"Married? Oh, poor Angela! When?"

"He's got three kids."

"Oh, Angela! The wretch, the beast."

Angela stopped her.

"He's not. I knew, all along."

"You *knew?* And yet—you loved him? You were *engaged* to him?"

Angela nodded.

"Do still," she said briefly.

"You'd better tell me some more," Anne said.

"Tell you all of it. He got married to a French girl, during the War. He told me about it when I first met him, almost. We loved each other pretty soon. He couldn't hide it, nor could I. I thought he'd get himself divorced, of course. I was ready enough to help him. I was—pretty green, you know."

Anne said nothing.

"Shocked?"

"No. Lord, no. Puzzled, a bit."

"What at?"

"Why on earth you—let yourself love him."

"Couldn't help it. It just came. He loved me too, you see. It was—oh, pretty wonderful."

"And what now? "Anne asked.

"I couldn't get him to do anything about it. And then, at the New Year, he went over—she's in France—to see what he could do. And he's never come back. At least, not to me. He's in England."

"Hasn't he written?"

"Yes. He wanted me to go on as we are for a bit. Then he talked about the children. Said how nice they were and how well she'd brought them up. Three of them, Anne, two girls and a boy. I realised what an ass I'd been, then. I wrote and told him we'd better stop it. And he wrote back at once and agreed. I suppose that was what he wanted. Men have some queer idea that it's not honourable for them to be the ones who let go."

Then, after a silence: "But he still loves me. I know he does, It's some feeling of duty to the kids that's done it. Oh, Anne, we've had such heavenly times! I do want him back. He's so lovely to *play* with!"

She looked across with tragic eyes, then slid to the floor and burrowed into Anne's cool, starched lap. Anne felt her shuddering sobs and was suddenly frightened. Angela had never been one to let herself go. None of them did. Self-control was the most rigid of traditions, in all circumstances except perhaps of rage. She patted Angela and talked to her as if to one of the hurt babies in the ward. Presently the girl sat up and mopped her eyes.

"Haven't blubbed before," she announced. "Feel better now." She turned on Anne a watery smile. "Have you ever—done it?"

"Done—?"

Angela grinned. "Loved anyone."

Anne was comparing this abandonment of grief to her few angry, sleepless nights over Ronald Dalloway. She answered honestly, "No."

"Hope you never may. It's hell."

Anne, thinking with distaste of the various men she had known—her father, Dalloway, said, "I don't suppose I ever shall."

"I suppose it serves me right," Angela said. "I never thought of the kids, only of me and him. But, lord, it does make a vacuum inside one!" She went on: "I suppose, too, it's not only him that I want. It's the uprooting that hurts, as well. I've always thought of myself as—well, going to be married. I might've been, of course, if I hadn't been such a damn fool as to tie myself up to him. Sometimes I think it was worth it, but I don't know. I'm too old now to love anyone else. Besides, it makes me sick to think of it. I want him, and I want to get married. I—oh, I don't know what I do want!"

Anne smiled down on her. "You're only twenty-three, aren't you?"

"Years don't count. I'm ages older than you, for instance."

"What rubbish!"

"I am. I know all there is to know about people. And people are the only things that interest me."

"You're wise to come away. People are different, down here."

"Are they? I simply had to come. They were so scandalised, and so angry with him. A man at his office found out, and his wife told Edith. I simply didn't dare tell them I'd known all along."

Anne looked into the fire and asked the question which had been fighting to get out. "Angela—you're—all right?"

"All right? Oh, yes, thank goodness. I can't think why, though—" She looked up at Anne and said no more. They talked of other things until hospital rules sent Anne to bed and Angela back to her hostel.

Anne felt suddenly very old and very much of a spinster. Angela *was* older than she was. She had thought that she, too, knew all about people. But she had realised nothing of this passion which was deliberately stronger than tradition and common sense, which took youth in its arms and then tossed it away spent and sore.

Perhaps it was just because Angela was so young, and had lost none of her vividness, that it took her so hard.

2

The next day, Anne was free in the afternoon, and went to St. Edmunds to see Belsize, who was still on the Private Staff. She was "on call" and could not leave the hospital. So they walked together in the Nurses' Garden.

Belsize was monosyllabic—unusual in her.

"What's the matter with you?" Anne asked her at last.

Belsize poked a pebble out of its bed with her toe.

"Is it so horribly obvious?" she asked.

"You seem miserable. I thought you were extra tired, or you'd got a throat or something."

"I've done a silly thing," she said, all in a gabble. Sensible Belsize? Never.

"I've gone and fallen in love."

Ordinarily, Anne would have said, "that's not silly, carry on with it." Today, she exclaimed explosively, "Good heavens, you too?"

It was all round her!

Belsize laughed mournfully.

"Even me! I know I'm an ass. I thought perhaps—*you'd* think I wasn't such a bad person."

Anne pulled herself together.

"You're a jolly nice person," she said warmly.

"Only?"

"Only—so sensible."

"That's what everyone says." She scraped an impatient foot along the ground. "Anyway, I've done it."

"Well—why worry?"

"Why worry!" she almost shouted. "She says, why worry! Anyone can see *you've* never done it, my good girl! I thought you had!"

"I haven't," Anne said meekly. "I thought I had, too."

Belsize glared at her.

"I s'pose I'd better stop talking to you about it," she said.

"Do talk. Unless you don't want to."

"I do want to. It's the only thing I do want to talk about."

Anne linked arms with her.

"Come on. Talk."

139

"I nursed his sister for six weeks. They live at Wimbledon. He's a month older than I am. He's—rather ugly, I think. But simply charming. That's the only word. I know I'm an ass. I expect every woman he meets does the same thing."

"Does he—?" Anne hesitated.

"That's just what I don't know. They were all most awfully nice to me. Didn't treat me like a nurse a bit. He used to take me out in his car almost every evening after the first week. We talked a lot."

This was more understandable. More like her and Ronald.

"He's taken me out several times since I've left them, too. They're awfully grateful—it was pneumonia, and their Doctor said the nursing saved her life. I suppose it did, it always is the nursing in pneumonia. But, anyway, I always go as his sister's guest. I go to meals sometimes, too, and I've met lots of other girls there at different times. Oh, there's no doubt he likes me. He's—kissed me. And we went to a dance, and he—said things. Only, nothing definite."

They paced round the garden and moodily looked at the vegetable beds.

"Sometimes I think he doesn't—ask me—because he thinks he's too poor. He is, compared with his family. And I want to rush and tell him I wouldn't care if he hadn't a bean, I'm used to it. And then, I'm not sure. He's the sort of person who's always had everything he's wanted, never been disciplined much. I wonder sometimes if he can feel deeply, if the niceness isn't mostly on the surface, like—"

"Like a lettuce which has never been tied up and hasn't got a heart," Anne suggested.

Belsize gave the ghost of a gurgle. "Yes. Exactly like that. What'll I do, Lee?"

"Wait, I suppose."

"I *can't* wait! I can hardly sleep a wink, and I'm so tired I can scarcely crawl. I keep on wondering and wondering." She blew her nose explosively. "You don't think," she asked, "I can tell him I don't mind being poor?"

"You can convey delicately that you prefer simplicity to wealth."

And so the conversation went on, straying, but always coming back to the original subject. Poor Belsize had got it very badly indeed.

"And she's older than I am," Anne told herself. "And so sensible. It isn't only because Angela's young, then."

She thought about the two of them for the rest of the day. "Angela, loving a man who's married and has children and never minding that she's upset their whole lives. And Belsize, going silly about someone who's been kind to his sister's nurse just because he's been brought up to be polite and never really given her any encouragement. I don't see how they can," she told herself.

But, as she went to bed, she honestly confessed to a great curiosity about this emotion which was so much stronger and more lawless than she had supposed. Sensible Belsize! And well-brought-up, self-controlled little Angela!

CHAPTER 3

1

ANNE ploughed through her round of peevish children, hardly ill at all yet not well enough to go back to their squalid homes and foolish mothers. She looked up sometimes, satisfied with the bright, clean ward with flowers in every corner. Sister Jackson had never had flowers, could not be bothered with them. A young probationer passed her with a little smile, very clean and trim. Anne remembered her on that first day, with her grubby apron, grimy nails and hair standing out in wisps round her cap. They had reacted very well, these girls, to her ferocity. That particular one was giving medicines, punctual to the minute. She had dinned into them the importance of punctuality and tidiness. Trivialities? Yes, but trivialities were important, as long as one didn't let them dominate. How ridiculously things did recur, and how solemnly one preached doctrines that years ago one had hated like sin.

The ward door opened slowly, and Miss Thorn, the Casualty Officer with the black hair and the honest grey eyes, looked round it.

"May I come in, Sister? I know it's after the proper time and that you're very stern with us—"

Anne laughed. She liked the girl.

"Yes, come in. I'm only stern with some people."

"I came to say I'm sending you up a case. Boy of eight with an acute appendix. He's pretty ill. I expect he'll be

142

done soon."

"Done? Theatre, you mean?"

Anne could hardly believe that a real emergency case was coming to her.

Miss Thorn nodded, a glint of mischief in her eye.

"Yes. Why, don't you want it?"

"Want it! Rather. I've been so bored—"

"That's all right. I only thought I'd break the news to you."

"What will Mr. Brown say?"

"Oh, he's gone. Didn't you know? His time was up yesterday, and the new man's not coming till tomorrow, so we're managing. I thought you'd like to make a start as soon as possible."

"I suppose *he* thought I couldn't nurse a bad case." Anne said tentatively.

"What? On no, not that, Sister. He was just frightened of you. You were rather fierce to him, weren't you?"

"Fierce! He didn't know how to treat me," Anne told her shortly.

Miss Thorn laughed. "Poor J.B. He—" She appeared to remember her loyalites suddenly. "He was quite good at his job, you know. Lots of exams. Right-o, Sister, I'll send the boy up. Put him in one of Mr. Salter's beds, will you?"

She went away, and Jack Horner ward became a scene of great activity. Now, Anne thought, I really shall be able to teach these Pros something. They were ready for emergencies now, they had their groundwork all solid waiting for them.

She set them to get the bed ready and to put into

practice the treatment of shock which she had unceasingly taught them. Then the boy arrived, curly-haired, blue-eyed, terrified by the pain and the bad taste in his mouth and all these strange people. He broke into a wail, and she spoke to him and he was quiet. A good thing, she thought, that children always took to her face. They all wanted to stroke the peach-red, velvety cheek.

She spoke to the mother and the friends who supported her. "Wait in the corridor. I must see to him first." She looked at him, set the Staff-nurse to undress him and went back to the mother.

"He's my only one. Lost 'is father, in the War. But 'e talks to me like a little man and takes care o' me. Is 'e bad, Sister?"

"Yes. They'll operate almost at once."

The woman's face was white and set.

"'Is father died after an operation," was all she said. "Try not to worry, Mother. We shall all do our best for him."

She left the woman there, and went into the ward again. What would they like done to the child? It was awkward, with no House-surgeon to direct her. Still, she knew well enough what used to be done at St. Edmunds and that ought to be good enough for any hospital.

"The new case is ready," she rang down to Miss Thorn after some minutes of gentle rapid action.

"Thank you, Sister. Mr. Salter will be here in about half an hour."

"He looks awfully bad," Anne ventured. "Shall I give him a rectal saline?"

Silence. Was the suggestion not approved?

Then: "Yes. Good idea. Er—very gently, Sister."

Anne chuckled. At St. Edmunds, even a Staff-nurse would have been blown up if she had been told—actually told over the telephone by a Resident—to deal gently with an acute appendix. One learned things like that in one's first year. But these people didn't know her. She had to prove herself.

"Yes, Miss Thorn," she meekly said. "I'll go and do it right away."

Presently the Senior Surgeon came, looked at the child's tongue and laid a hand on his abdomen.

"Yes. Theatre, as soon as you like."

Then they were all in action in the Theatre. Anne had not been present at an emergency operation for months, but the routine came back to her without effort. Then it was over, and she was taking the unconscious boy down in the lift; and then, in the ward, the struggle began.

He was sick, again and again. He was restless, calling for his mother and moaning with pain.

Miss Thorn looked in, ordered some morphia, and went away, and Anne resumed her watch by the bedside. The ward Sister was not required to hang over a case like this. She knew that. But—he was her first emergency, and he was bad. Worse than they had thought, Mr. Salter had said when the incision was made.

He lay quiet after the morphia; but his cheeks seemed to grow greyer and his eyes more sunken, and to Anne's watchful fingers his pulse seemed weaker. She rang down to Miss Thorn again.

She'll think I'm in an awful nuisance. Can't help it, he is so bad. "Hullo? Miss Thorn, may I give another saline? He's been vomiting awfully."

"I'll come up."

They bent over the cot together.

"Give it under the skin, I think. The quicker he gets it inside him the better," said Miss Thorn.

So it had been the right thing to suggest.

Miss Thorn stood by and watched. Anne found that terrifying. She must do it very well, under this scrutiny.

"Do you like it given here?" She stood ready with the needle poised.

Miss Thorn laughed.

"Go ahead, Sister. I'm learning."

That was all right. They realised that she knew her job.

The child seemed to rally after the fluid had been absorbed. When Anne went off duty at half-past eight he had not been sick for over an hour and was sleeping quietly. She was so pleased with him that she sent the mother home for a night's rest.

In the morning she went straight to see him. He was still there, propped up in the tilted cot, but looking terribly ill and sunken-eyed.

"Still vomiting," the Night-nurse reported.

"Aren't we going to save him? We must, he's her only kid—and my first emergency," she added to herself.

She waited feverishly for someone to do a round. Presently Miss Thorn came in, followed by a man. The only thing Anne noticed about him was that he had a big head and very big feet, and that he was very young.

"This is Mr. Ashe, your new H.S., Sister. How's the

boy?"

That was the question Anne had been waiting for. Mr. Ashe did not interest her in the least. She led the way to the cot.

"Bad," she said.

They all stood looking at him. Miss Thorn passed the new H.S. his notes and chart.

"Appendix, done last night. He'd been ill two days. Perforated, of course, and general peritonitis."

"Not much of a chance, has he?"

The young man's voice was pleasant, cultured and respectful. But Anne felt she hated him. Not much of a chance!

"He's pretty mouldy," Miss Thorn was admitting.

The H.S. made a suggestion and Miss Thorn agreed.

"Write it on there," she told him. "See, Sister?"

Anne nodded silently. They must save him, they must.

The three of them went on round the ward.

"He's the only acute case? "Mr. Ashe said.

"Yes. Sister's just been spring-cleaning," Miss Thorn told him shortly.

He nodded, perfectly satisfied with the explanation.

2

They did not save the little boy. He seemed a little better, then grew rapidly worse in spite of all their efforts, and died during the afternoon, when his mother had gone home. Anne and Mr. Ashe watched the end of his little flickering life.

"Poor little beggar. I say, Sister, what about that poor

147

woman? Shall I tell her?"

She liked him for that. He had been very helpful and sensible, too. She felt as if they had worked together for a long time.

"Oh no. That's my job. I'll do it."

He sighed with relief.

"Sure? You'll do it a lot better than I should, of course. I've never done such a thing in my life."

Anne nearly said, "Nor have I and I'm terrified!" She smiled sadly instead.

The woman just looked at her, wide-eyed.

"Oh—I wanted him so, I wanted him so!" she cried out.

There was nothing to say. Anne murmured what she could, and presently the sad little figure plodded away downstairs.

Anne went and sat on the edge of her bed, gripping the ironwork underneath it.

She had wanted him so—wanted him so. Poor woman. What an idiot she, Anne was, to mind like this. Ward-sisters didn't mind deaths. They were just part of things, and the Sister's job was to get rid of the relatives as quickly and quietly as might be. *She* wasn't a proper ward-sister, not a bit of it. She mustn't have feelings, she must squash them. Ridiculous idiot. Well, she'd better take him to the mortuary.

3

In the morning the ward was all quiet and clean again —and dull. No more interesting work for a while, Anne feared, after that failure. She had done her best, but it wasn't a very experienced best, and probably the medical officers had seen that. She did not know enough to realise that the child had already been beyond help when he came in, that he had only been operated upon as a last, almost hopeless chance.

Then, a minute after nine-thirty, the earliest hour at which the Residents were allowed in the wards, in walked Mr. Ashe. "Morning, Sister. I want to get the hang of these kids. Can I do a round, please?"

Anne, clipping on her cuffs in a hurry, reacted to the briskness. This was more like proper hospital routine. The weeks of sewing, cleaning and bullying began to look like a preparation instead of the nightmare they had seemed.

It did not take them long to look at the few children Anne had left. They stopped at a cot where a fat two year-old sat bolt upright, his chin tucked into his chest, his eyes rolled up to see without being seen. "What on earth's he doing?" Ashe asked when Anne had explained his illness and the treatment he had been having.

Anne laughed. "Being ashamed of himself."

"Why? What have you been doing, bad lad?"

The child's lip trembled and Anne said, "Better not ask. He always lets us know when it's all over, but never before. Nurse! Teddy wants you!"

A Pro hurried along with a wry smile and put up a screen, and they went on to the next bed.

"Rickets? What are you doing to him? Osteotomy?"

"Presently," Anne said. "Mr. Salter wanted him dieted and exercised first, to get his muscles stronger."

"Bit of a job," Ashe commented, "to exercise a thing that size."

"Look, I'll show you—"Anne lifted the baby out of his cot and sat him on the floor. "Now then, Smiffkins, show off!"

The little thing looked at them solemnly for a second, then settled himself with his bandy legs in front of him, his bandy arms at his sides and set off at a great rate with his tail as a pivot and his heels and hands as propellers.

"That's how he goes. He's never walked. He didn't even do that till a day or two ago. Just sat still and wailed."

"Priceless sight! Here—what's your name—Smiffkins—come back!" Ashe raced after the child.

"Now for a howl!" Anne thought.

But no howl came. Ashe swung the baby up, talked to it and brought it solemnly back, its face buried in his white-coated shoulder, one eye looking out unwinking and contented. It let him feel its legs and arms and prod it without a murmur.

"Thank goodness for someone who doesn't make them yell," Anne said to herself. They had shrieked at the very sight of J.B.

Smiffkins, whose real name was Horace Smith, pulled the young man's nose and said "Da."

"Not guilty," Ashe told him at once. "I'm afraid my rounds will take an awful time, Sister, unless you sternly refuse to let me play with them."

"I'll harry you, when we're rushed," she promised. He looked such a baby himself that she felt like telling him to wash his hands for dinner or tying a bib round his neck, rather than taking orders from him. "We're slack now, of course."

"Quite. Oh, that reminds me. There are two cases coming up. I ought to have told you at once. There's an appendix and a grubby little kid with a burnt leg. I said you'd ring down and say if you'd got beds."

She went to do so, gladly. He wasn't going to hold up her failure against her, then.

"What d'you like on burns?" she asked when she came back.

He rubbed his chin. "Picric? Why ask me? Students don't have much to do with burns, you know, Sister."

"Students?"

"Well, I've only just stopped being one. I only qualified a fortnight ago."

She stared at him, amused. "You're honest, anyway. Most Residents pretend they know everything."

"No good pretending. Sisters *do* know everything, don't they?"

She smiled, her tongue trembling to say that this was her first job, too. But—it was such fun to be a Sister who really did know everything!

"No," he went on, "it's no good pretending, to experienced people like you. You only see through us. Besides, it's not the way to learn. I do know a certain amount, of course. What do *you* like on burns?"

This was delicious. She went over in her mind the burns whose treatment she had watched. "What about that new tannic acid treatment?"

They discussed burns, probing each other's mind.

151

He made a movement towards the washbowl, and she automatically poured out water for him and held the towel ready. He threw her a glance of surprise, unused to being waited on. They went primly to the door together, and he held it open for her to pass out first. It was her turn to be surprised and his to be unconscious, then. She had been brought up to treat doctors as tin gods, with respect. He had discovered that Sisters are among the terrible ones of the earth, goddesses who can make the life of a House-surgeon easy or burdensome, to be placated and treated handsomely. So that each was astonished and a little flattered by the respectful friendliness of the other.

Outside the door he stopped. "Sister, I'm proposing to fill up your beds. No objection?"

She stiffened. She was longing for work, but she must not overdo it. She knew these young men. They would stuff in case after case, until the nurses were run off their legs and even the couches were occupied, if they were allowed to.

"I like two beds left for emergencies," she said firmly.

"Yes, of course. You don't mind emergencies?"

She nearly said, "I love them," but that wouldn't do. "I always do my best to make room for a serious case, Mr. Ashe."

The boy's eyes twinkled ever so slightly. "Right-o. Good morning, Sister."

He ran downstairs, and Anne scuttled into the ward to make ready cots for the two new cases. It was splendid to be busy again.

CHAPTER 4

1

THE OTHER Sisters, hitherto inclined to be watchful and remote, began to make overtures to Anne at about this time.

"Jack Horner getting to work again!" little vivacious Sister Theatre said across the table at dinnertime. "We haven't had an operation-list from it for about a year, but there's a good long one for tomorrow."

"Jackson was a slacker. She's gone and got married now, to a poor man, too, so if she slacks any more there'll be trouble!"

"Did you have an awful job, Sister Lee?"

"Pretty fierce."

"What's the new H.S. like?"

"Nice infant. Knows his job."

"Didn't get on with J.B., did you?"

"I was glad when he went," Anne said soberly.

"Taking a few o' my emergencies, I hear," said Sister Crossman.

"Yes. D'you mind?"

"Mind! I'll be thankful to be rid of them. I'm getting too old for the Theatre. I'm sixty-five, you know. Oh, I used to be a dab at it in my day. Used to assist Sir Frederick Reeves—Mr. Reeves, 'e was then—and 'e said 'e never had a better. Nurses can't assist now. Too nervous. Not like the nurses in my young days. Don't know what work is. Nor espree de corpse neither. Plaster Samuels, they are—"

One of the other interrupted her rudely. "Did J.B. sauce you, Sister Lee?"

"Only once," Anne said grimly, and they all laughed sheepishly.

"Jackson loved him. She was that sort. I think she had hopes. But J.B.'d got his head screwed on the right way—"

"Heavens," Anne thought, "do they always run a body down like this when she's left?"

Old Sister Grossman leaned across to her again.

"You come an' 'ave some coffee with me after dinner. I'll tell you a tale or two."

"Thank you very much, Sister."

2

She followed the old lady in her elastic-side boots, and picked her way between knickknacks and whatnots and occasional tables in the crowded sitting-room. The walls were plastered with photographs and the chairs with chenille and cross-stitch cushions.

"Sit down. Sit down."

Anne did so, gingerly. Surprisingly, Sister Crossman produced excellent coffee and cigarettes, which she smoked herself with enjoyment.

"Those wimmen won't let me talk," she confided. "Like the sound of their own voices best, the silly 'addocks. I know I'm old an' out o' fashion, an' I don't spend all my time nosin' out romances that aren't there an' backbitin' an' they don't like that. Lot o' balmy 'addocks, gossipin' an' talking'. A hospital's a terrible catty place. I expect you know that, Sister."

Anne nodded.

"You come from Edmunds, don't you?" the old woman went on. "I was trained there myself—"

"*You* were?"

"Yes. But that was thirty years ago an' more. It was very different then."

They plunged into tales of the old hospital, and the time flew.

When Anne at last got up to go, the older woman followed her to the door.

"You be careful o' these wimmen."

"Which women?"

"Sister Theatre and her lot. You can either go in with them, which you won't because you aren't their sort; you can be their enemy, which isn't wise, because they'll give you 'ell if you are. They're strong and they're mean, so they can do anything, even get you the sack. Or you can keep yerself to yerself an' be perlite to them. That's the best plan. They keep thinkin' they'll get you, then."

"I expect I'll do that," Anne said. "I'm rather good at keeping myself to myself."

Then, thinking the other might be hurt, "Will you come and see *me* sometimes, Sister?"

"I'll see, I'll see. I'll come if you want somebody. Good night, Sister Lee."

3

The ward took up most of her thought now. The beds were full, mostly of children who were really ill. Dressings alone took all the morning to do, and there

155

were operations four afternoons a week. And all the cases were doing well. The nurses liked being in the ward, and thirsted for the knowledge which Anne was always ready to give.

Some of the children were charming. She loved their funny little ways, and she had grown so used to their wailing that it hardly troubled her.

There was Douglas, who for the first few days had shrieked and hidden himself when anyone had approached his cot. He had been brought to hospital because of his temper and his fits of ungovernable crying. Someone had discovered that he had a disease of his ear, and so, that crying and rage were due to headaches, not wickedness. He was to be operated on, but first to be accustomed to the ward and tamed a little. He was quieting down now, and even smiling.

There was Harry, a coster boy with an abscess in the bone of his leg. He called Anne and Ashe the most appalling names all the time his dressing was being done, and directly afterwards would beckon Anne to him and say:

"Sister—did I say anyfink? I'm sorry, Sister. I didn't mean it. No, you didn' *really* hurt, not a bit. Sister—tell the Doctor I didn' mean it!"

Smiffkins was still there, sitting solemnly in bed now, his straightened legs on splints. He crooned little songs to himself as he sat.

Then there was Henry. He was only two months old, very thin and very lively. He had great blue eyes and a long upper lip which he stuck out like a hood as he

156

earnestly applied himself to the examination of his fingers or his toes. He had something wrong with his stomach and had to have it washed out twice a day. But he didn't seem to mind, he loved everyone and pulled their fingers just the same. Anne loved Henry best of all, he was so little and anxious.

Mr. Ashe came round punctiliously every morning at half-past nine, did himself any of the dressings that were particularly unpleasant, tickled the children and talked to them; but Anne wouldn't allow that for very long, there was too much work to do. He discussed treatments with her as with a colleague—which indeed she was, only very few House-surgeons realise it. His profession is as dependent on hers as hers on his.

"We'll do that, Sister, don't you think?"

Sometimes she would say yes and the thing would be done. Sometimes she would suggest something else, and they would wrangle for a few minutes and sometimes his view and sometimes hers would carry the day. Generally hers, for she did not put forward ideas unless she had proved them.

Sometimes she would question—

"Why? You didn't do that with the other one."

"No—but that was quite different. That one was caused by one thing and this by another, when you think it out—wasn't it, Sister?"

She would say yes, then. He never seemed to realise that her knowledge did not go anything like as deep as his did, that it was only her greater experience which made her so much wiser. She did not tell him how little she really knew. It was such fun to be looked up to. And in return, she was utterly loyal, carried out his orders to the letter, and never spoke to a soul of the gaps in his learning, only of his good diagnoses and his careful thought.

She grew to understand that he could be depended upon, that he never minded being sent for if she was in doubt, that in a crisis he would always lend a hand and do his sensible best and never think himself too hard-worked. It was good to know that she had someone behind her, that she had not to shoulder the whole responsibility of her thirty children. So often, a House-surgeon was nothing but a careless youngster to be carefully watched for mistakes rather than followed.

She did teach Ashe many things, but only those she honestly knew, such as bandaging, which doctors never learn. She loved doing that. It was stimulating, to show off her hard-earned knowledge. She was afraid he would stop respecting her if he knew what surface knowledge it was.

Sometimes the outer world obtruded itself, in the shape of Angela and Belsize. She worried about them a little, they both looked so miserable and moody. But there was no help but her sympathy that she could give.

4

One afternoon when she had nothing immediate to do, Anne was standing in her favourite position against the fire-guard, watching the babies. She turned, at a sound, and saw Miss Thorn and Ashe in the doorway.

"Sister, we're bored!"

She smiled at them. "Well, what then?"

"We're *bored*, Sister!"

"What do you want?"

"Henry!" they said, both together.

She laughed outright then. Babes, they were, ridiculous, learned babes.

"Come in. You can have him. He's been squealing all the morning."

"You see," Ashe explained as they went to Henry's cot, "we're on Casualty, and it's such a horrible wet day that nobody's come. There was one Hebrew lady who forgot to bring the child and wouldn't tell me what was wrong with it, only that she wanted 've red medsin, like *blood*, Doctor!' I gave her Parrish's Food, it was the only red medicine I could think of. So now we're bored. Are you ever bored, Sister?"

Anne heaved up Henry, kicking and grabbing. Miss Thorn took him absently and balanced him over her shoulder.

"Bored? Yes, often. At least, I was before you came."

They both bowed, absurdly, and Henry wabbled.

"Be careful! I mean, before you snowed me under with work."

"Oh, how dull. What do you do when you're off duty?"

"Bus ride. Read. That's all."

"Don't you go and see people?"

"Don't know many. My home's up north."

"Oh," they said. "That's mouldy for you. Don't you go to theatres?"

159

"Sometimes. I can't afford it often, and besides, it's no fun alone. I'm afraid I'm a dull person."

"Oh no, you're not," they said positively.

"Look," Miss Thorn said. "I'm going to put Henry down here and watch him kick. He's trying to catch his toes I Isn't he a lamb?"

"I want one, too!" Ashe demanded. "I'll have Douglas."

So Douglas, his head all bandaged now, was brought and set on a rug. Ashe built towers for him and he obligingly batted them down.

"And Ruth."

Ruth, a fat three-year-old, joined the group.

"And that gross baby—John, isn't he?"

John provided a diversion by crawling over to Henry and smacking him. He was a large, bloated child and did not approve of Henry's slim liveliness.

The Residents sat on the floor beside the children and Anne stood over them all.

"Why don't you sit down, Sister?"

"Not allowed to, while you're here."

They stared at her.

"Oh, rot!"

They rushed at her and forced her into a chair.

"Matron would have a fit!"

"She's out," Ashe said. "I saw her go. She had a feather in her hat and stockings like fish-scales. She said she was going to Piccadilly."

They all shouted with laughter.

"Why shouldn't she?"

"Why, indeed? Very suitable, poor lady."

"Come on, Henry. Have a brick. You've sucked that toe long enough."

They stayed there for an hour, talking nonsense and playing with the children. Then someone rang up for "a doctor for Casualty," and they haggled as to whose turn it was to go.

"Thank you, Sister, for letting us come."

"I'll put John away, if you'll put Henry."

Ashe dumped fat John in his cot, where he set up a howl of disgust, swept Douglas up and carried him off on his shoulder to his, and threw the bricks after him.

"All tidy? Come along, Doctor."

They went, smiling and waving from the corner of the stairs.

"Nice things! Hope they'll get bored again."

Apparently they did. They often came, after that, in the afternoon, or in the evenings, after the babies were washed. Once Ashe insisted on bathing Henry himself, and nearly drowned him—or so Anne and Miss Thorn said. They always came together and always talked the whole time. Sometimes they would talk of Cambridge, where they had both been; Anne loved listening to them, and wished more and more that she had been there herself. Sometimes they talked of books, and she joined in, sometimes argued about "shop" and turned to her for a casting vote. Sometimes she could give it and sometimes she could not. They were so frank that she forgot to pretend that she knew everything. They didn't seem to think it a disgrace not to know things, they took it for granted that no one could be omniscient. She

161

remembered, smiling, the Dalloways' faint disdain if they surprised a gap in one's education. These people realised that education was going on all the time.

She enjoyed life very much.

5

One night, "those wimmen" invited her to coffee. She went, curious to see more of them. She found Sister Theatre, Sister Outpatients, Sister X-rays, and Night Sister, gathered like witches over a fire in Sister Theatre's room, amid black satin tumpties and small china dolls in various stages of undress.

A dead silence greeted her knock; then someone pushed forward a chair for her and poured out coffee, and talk buzzed on again.

"Sister Crossman's dyed her hair again! She's overdone it this time. Looks like brass!"

"Silly old thing. Why on earth can't she retire?"

"D'you hear the story of her prayers this morning —her Staff-nurse told me. 'Our Father 'chart in 'Eaven—Now 'oo's supposed to 'ave swept under that bed, it's full o' flick—you go an' get the broom, Nurse Smith, as soon as ever we've done 'ere— 'Allowed be thy name—'; she could see under the bed when she knelt down, she never looks at any other time!"

"D'you know, that new H.P., Miss Johnson, had the cheek to tell me when to let Jimmy Goddard get up! As if I didn't know when to let a heart case up! Think they know everything, these brats of Residents! I kept the kid in bed another day, just to show her!"

"That's right, Sister, you teach 'em their place!"

"There'll be wedding in the Residents' Common Room before long, I'm thinking!"

Anne had not contributed to the conversation. But now they all turned and looked at her.

"Don't you think so, Sister Lee?"

"Think—what? I've never been in the Residents' Common Room!"

They cackled at her.

"You don't need to go into it! What about Miss Thorn and your new H.S.? They're always together. Oh, *we've* seen them slinking into your ward of an evening, to canoodle without the others seeing them!"

Anne laughed. The thought of the two "canoodling" was too absurd.

"They're just a pair of infants," she said. "They scrap most of the time or play with the babies."

"Oh!" they said all together. "You needn't be afraid of giving them away! *We* know!"

"I saw Miss Edmunds and Mr. Bligh kissing each other again last night," one of them said, blowing out clouds of cigarette smoke.

"*Did* you? How?"

"My room looks right down into the Common Room. I can see everything that goes on, if I lean out, and they never pull their curtains."

Mr. Bligh was one of the younger visiting surgeons. Sister Theatre's eye rolled often and enviously in his direction. Miss Edmunds was a House Physician.

"How did Missis Squee treat you this morning,

Theatre?"

"Oh, snappy. She's got an awful down on me. Lee's her pet darling just now."

They all turned to Anne again, expectant.

"*What?* Missis Squee? I don't know what you mean!"

"Aren't you an innocent! Missis Squee's the Matron, love, and she's so pleased with the way you've pulled that ward of yours up that she holds you up as a little white angel to all of us gross mortals."

"*Does* she?"

Anne was pleased, in spite of the sarcastic tone.

"Oh, it won't last long, don't you worry. She changes her favourite about once a month, and the deposed one has a filthy time. She's had you for some time now, you're about due for a fall. Haven't you noticed how nice she's been?"

"She's been quite amiable. I thought she was always like that."

"Ohl You wait."

"You don't half use your eyes, Sister Lee. You miss half the excitement of a place like this if you go about with your eyes shut."

"Missis Squee's gone to dinner with Mr. Salter tonight. She told me so. She isn't half proud of it!"

The room was filled with their shrill voices and cackling laughter. They had nothing to talk of, except this petty gossip, half of it surmise, half of it definitely untrue. Anne sickened of it suddenly and longed for the bracing severity of St. Edmunds, where the Sisters were martinettes indeed, but not chattermags like these, and the Matron a real queen, severe and narrow, but—respectable. These "wimmin" were not respectable even to the outward eye. But, of course, she reminded herself, she did not know what the St. Edmunds authorities were like when they were gathered together off duty, in their rooms. Just as bad, perhaps, in a more majestic way.

As soon as she could, without offending them, she excused herself and slipped downstairs to her own sparsely furnished room. It smelt very fresh after the mixed odours of coffee, cigarettes, and scented soap which she had left behind her.

6

She sat there for some time, stretched out, doing nothing, yet fully awake, as those only can do who tire themselves right out, physically and mentally, by the end of the day.

Presently she got up and strolled across to the ward kitchen on the other side of the corridor. Night-nurse would be bringing her some cocoa in a little while. She did not want it, after all that coffee. She would tell nurse not to make it.

She turned round as she came to the door, at the sound of voices in the ward. Ashe and Miss Thorn came out quickly, almost on top of her.

She smiled and held out her hands to them, spontaneously. She was so pleased to see them. They looked so frank and cheerful, and she had before her only the vision of Sister Theatre's slanting eyes and Sister Outpatients' leering, pouting mouth.

They took her hands, one each, swinging them to and fro, and stood there laughing.

"Hullo, Sister! I bet you've been asleep!"

"I haven't—I haven't!"

"What are you doing here at this time of night, anyway?"

"Sitting in my room, just. I came over to see about some—some cocoa."

"Cocoa!" they said, smacking their lips.

"This," said Ashe to the air, "is the first hospital I've ever been at—"

"We know that," Miss Thorn said rudely, "to our cost!"

He glared at her.

"The only hospital I've ever heard of—shut up—which doesn't give its Residents a Midnight Feast. Sardines or dog's body or even only biscuits, and drink."

"They generally do," Miss Thorn allowed.

"We need it," he went on. "We work hard from 9 a.m.—yes, I do, we're not all sluggards like you!"

"I'm not a sluggard!—I do—"

"Dumb-bells every morning on the roof! Yes, I've seen you!"

"I do half an hour's M.B. swot while you're wallowing in your bath!"

"—From 9 a.m. to 12 midnight and sometimes later, with about five minutes for meals, and we get *jolly hungry!* An' we have to buy vittals out of our pocket-money and go without fluid. No wonder we get const—"

"Shut up!"

"Get hospital throats!"

"What are you laughing at, Sister? We're *grousing!*"

"Come and have some cocoa with me," Anne gasped.

"Oo-oh! I've got some mixed biscuits! Miss Thorn announced, and sped away to get them. Ashe lounged against the kitchen door and watched the cocoa made.

It had in days gone by been a strict rule that no Residents were allowed to set foot in a Sister's sitting-room. But since the advent of women Medical Officers the rule had been relaxed and tea-parties were relatively frequent.

They arranged themselves in front of Anne's fire, Ashe spread out in a chair, Miss Thorn squatting on the rug.

"I'll pour out!" she said firmly, and pushed Anne into the other chair. "Mayn't I, Sister?"

"Of course, if you want to!"

Ashe took out cigarettes and offered them. Anne was surprised at the easy communal spirit which had invaded the room. To the others it was perfectly natural, just a continuation of the atmosphere of University and hostel, where nightly gatherings were common enough and it was immaterial who provided room and food.

Miss Thorn voiced that view.

"Nice. Just like Girton," she said, and then Anne understood. She wanted to hug them for bringing the atmosphere within her reach.

"It's boiling, Sister. These cups? Tony, move your great feet."

Ashe glanced down at them placidly.

"They are large, aren't they? Make me look like a beastly puppy!"

He was like a puppy, awkward and yet graceful, fumbling and yet surefooted, and his wide grey eyes looked out with trusting interest above a wide mouth that was always on the verge of a grin. His hair was generally untidy and so were his eyebrows. He just missed being good looking, but he was strong, and queerly sensitive for a young man at an age when most of his kind are enveloped in a stout hide, thinking of nothing but themselves.

"Come on, Fido, then—have a drink."

He took a cup hastily from Miss Thorn and balanced it on his knee. Anne pushed a table towards him.

"Thank you, Sister. We've just shot what we thought was an emergency into your ward. Now we're not quite sure it isn't a measles."

"Oh no—not really?"

Anne was really anxious. A measles would mean quarantine for goodness knows how long—more weeks of boredom.

"It isn't a measles—it's a mastoid. Bet you tuppence, Tony."

"Haven't got it. Pay day soon."

"Rabbit! No, it is a mastoid, Sister."

"That's all right."

"There was a man in the bus today I wanted to kill," Ashe rattled on with a story of a fat man who had annoyed him just by being fat and how he had induced him to get out before he meant to.

"Little warrior!" Miss Thorn said lazily, and he kicked her.

They went on to talk of railway journeys, rhapsodised over holidays they had spent on the Yorkshire moors, and talked of sheep and dogs. Anne had seen the trials often in her childhood, and shyly told about them, and they listened eagerly. Then the conversation turned to peat fires, coal and the latest coal crisis.

"Did you see Raine's article in the *Race* last week?" Ashe asked Anne.

She shook her head.

"I never see the *Race*."

"It's a good paper. I get it every week. I say, would you like it when I've done? Don't say yes if it 'ud bore you—"

"I'd love it!" Ever since she had first come to hospital, Anne had missed her family's arguments on current events. It would be splendid to renew them with these two.

"I read the *Current*," Miss Thorn announced. "It's run by women. No, Tony, it's not about clothes. If you ram your *Race* down Sister's throat, I shall ram that. May I, Sister?"

"Rather."

"Oh, won't there be some fur to fly when we start talking," Ashe prophesied.

"May we come again, Sister?"

"Whenever you like," Anne invited fervently.

"You'll tell us if you're too tired, or anything?"

She laughed. "I'll tell you."

"We'll have to go and open that wretched child's ear now, I suppose. Good night, Sister."

Anne sat and smiled in front of her fire. She felt very

middle-aged—but it was lovely to have these infants seeking her company. She wondered why they did. The great gulf between nurses and doctors, cleft by years of education and training, seemed not to exist when they were with her. They were all just people, active minds sharpening against each other, players playing pitch-and-toss with hardly a miss between them.

She liked them so much. They were just the sort of people she had always wanted to know.

They would make the jolliest pair, if there should be a wedding. Love would not throw them away disappointed. They were too well-balanced for that. That was what she was herself, of course, sane and well-balanced. Angela and Belsize weren't.

CHAPTER 5

1

THE contented weeks passed in a smooth stream. Children came and went; hours of strenuous excitement punctuated the routine of hard work; at meals Sister Crossman rambled on, the other Sisters giggled and gossiped, sometimes snapped and spat insults at each other when they were extra tired; off-duty times were filled with bus-rides, walks and books, observation more eager than ever because it was to lead to discussion afterwards; and almost every day ended with a gathering in the little room by Jack Horner ward. Sometimes Miss Thorn and Ashe came; sometimes other Residents knocked sheepishly as well; and sometimes one or other of the pair came alone. They were becoming such friends, the three of them. It was sheer joy to work with one's friends. One did one's best, simply to please them, it was a duty no longer, and they were always there to back one up. Anne's eyes were brighter and her cheeks redder than ever, the dimples showed more often and the smile came and went. Her nurses were happy, though she was still stern with them when it was necessary, and the children loved her.

The Matron troubled her a little, now and then. Her manner was less sugary now and she would come and prowl round Jack Horner ward as if she was longing to find a speck of dirt to pounce on. Anne took good care that there should never be any, and the thwarted lady would gibe or revile her for some sin that had never been

171

committed or some omission that existed only in her imagination. She always let off her querulous steam so on her Sisters, once she was sure that they would not turn and leave her. She loved to rail at them as at a set of schoolgirls, knowing that they dared not answer back for fear of losing post or testimonial. It did not trouble Anne much—she recognised it for what it was and did not think it personal spite directed against her. Besides, she was too happy to bother about it. She knew her work was good. People whose opinion she valued more than the Matron's told her so quite frequently. She pitied those who had no outside interests and were dependent on the goodwill of the hospital for their content.

Her outlook was broadening every day. She was no longer a half-educated nurse, with no thought but for medical honours and the smiles of young doctors. She was no great talker, but she could listen and comment intelligently on all the topics which interested the outer world, she was not afraid of asking questions, she was self-sufficient.

And then a cloud descended, menacing her happiness.

Miss Thorn's six months as Casualty Officer were over and she was going. Would the evening gatherings come to an end? Miss Thorn was so cheerful and so popular, she seemed to hold the others together. Anne felt as if she could not live without the stimulating company of the young Residents now. Sister Crossman was senile, the others were cats, the nurses were just adoring girls; and there was no one else.

All the Residents and most of the Sisters saw Miss

Thorn off in her taxi. Another girl came in her place, and hospital routine went on.

In the evening Ashe came up as usual and sprawled in the armchair.

"Dull without Betty," he said. "The new woman's a hag. Talks too much. So I've left her down there alone."

"What's Miss Thorn going to do?" Anne asked.

"Holiday, then M.B., then I don't think she knows. She's a good person. They all are. I was at school and Trinity with her brothers. I've stayed with them a good bit, too. My father's in India, and Mother died when I was eight. The Thorns used to take pity on me in the holidays."

"It's bad luck to have no people of one's own," said Anne tritely. Then: "Or is it? I'm not sure."

"Depends on the people. Her's are ripping."

"They would be. I mean, you can tell they are, from her."

"It's funny," he went on inconsequently. "How one remembers school, and school holidays. That time's more real to me now than Cambridge, or even Hospital. Isn't it to you?"

"Mine," Anne said with a smile, "is so long ago." He looked at her, appraising.

"Is it?"

"I'm twenty-eight."

"I'm only twenty-three," he said ruefully.

"An infant."

He humped his shoulders.

"Rot. I don't think one changes much, once one's grown

173

up, do you?"

"I don't know. What's being grown-up, anyway?"

"Ceasing to trust people, I think. Knowing that one's alone. Medical education grows one up, that way. People never tell the truth to their doctor. I don't believe a single person now, ever. I weigh and add and subtract, whatever they tell me, and never expect anything until it's there. I don't believe in justice any more, either. There's no such thing. I don't know why they teach us that there is, it only makes it hurt more when we find out it's a myth."

"Does it hurt still?" Anne asked.

"Still hurt?"

"That there isn't any justice, and no one to trust?"

He considered.

"Why—yes. Sometimes. Why?"

"Then," she smiled, "You're not grown-up. When you are, you'll take it all quite calmly. It won't matter. Nothing'll matter. You'll just look out tolerantly on everything, like a sphinx."

"Nothing that *happens* matters now," he said sharply.

She jumped.

"Only—the way one takes it," she finished.

"How did you know I was going to say that?"

"I didn't. It's what I've said to myself, for ages."

"That matters, still to you?"

"Rather. Of course."

"Then," triumphantly, "you're not grown-up, either."

"No," she said a little sadly, "I don't think I am. It must be very comfortable, to be grown-up."

"Comfortable! Who wants to be comfortable? *That's*

being *dead!*"

"I want to be," she said obstinately. "So would you, if you'd mugged at home all your life and then *nursed!*"

"Poor Sister! Tell me," he wheedled, "about—school."

She flushed.

"I didn't have any, to speak of. Father didn't approve of it for girls."

"That's why you're so eager, and—and young, now. People who've been stuffed get blasé."

"Do you like it?" she said, surprised. "I've always been so ashamed. And then, you didn't seem to mind. You didn't despise me for it, you and Miss Thorn. That's why I liked you. I didn't have to pretend, with you. I've always had to, before."

"Sister, how funny I We liked you because you were so honest, just *because* you didn't pretend. Nearly everyone does."

"I was honest with you because you were honest with me."

He laughed. "I remember. You said so."

"Yes. I was so surprised."

"Education," he said, "is all bosh. It gives people a common language, that's all. It's what you're like underneath it that matters."

"Most people don't think that."

"Most people have nothing underneath it. They've shelled themselves over with education and prejudice and convention and died inside of suffocation."

"But unconventional people—cranks—are horrid," she objected. "They're always unbalanced."

175

"Cranks aren't unconventional. They've made new conventions of their own and stick to them instead of to the old ones, that's all. They're just antisocial. We're unconventional, and so are you. We don't let customs hamper us. We're ruled by our own ideas of what's right and wrong, and apart from that we do as we like."

She pondered. "I suppose that's true."

They were silent then. Their conversation had never before become personal. They had always talked of things and theories. Somehow the loss of Miss Thorn had made them more intimate. Anne was glad. She had sometimes wondered, before, if they had just used her room because it was convenient, and talked to her just because she had let them use it. But they hadn't. They liked her, had talked and thought about her. They were really friends. She never had any real friends before.

So she settled down again. Her room was not invaded every evening now, but very often Ashe would wander up alone and sometimes bring others with him. He brought his books sometimes, and sat in a corner, reading for his higher examinations and sucking his pipe. Anne kept very quiet then. He said he came there to work because the new "Aggie" talked too much. She wouldn't disturb him for anything.

2

She still went often to see Sister Crossman and listen to her quaint wisdom, but the other Sisters had quite stopped asking her to their rooms. She was not sorry. They were polite to her at meals, and that was all she wanted.

She thought sometimes that Sister Theatre's slanting eyes looked at her malignantly, but then, their normal expression was not exactly pleasant. Night-sister sneered, too, at some of her comments to supper-table conversation; but then, she didn't comment very often.

She did not always go down to supper, but had it occasionally in her room. There was such a lot to do in Jack Horner ward to keep it up to St. Edmunds' standard. As soon as she had made one batch of probationers efficient, they were reft from her, and another lot, greener than ever, sent instead. Matron had discovered early that she was a good teacher.

One evening she was even more tired than usual. She had been on the run all day long and felt she could not face that crowd of magpies.

She called the Ward-maid.

"Minnie! Tell Sister Jonas I shan't be able to get down to supper until nine and ask her to send it up, will you?"

Presently the maid brought the tray and set it in her room. She sat down, sniffing appreciatively, for she was hungry.

She lifted the covers of the dishes one by one, full of curiosity. Soup, toad-in-the-hole and a big apple gob. Not a bad dinner, for hospital.

She took a spoonful of the soup and immediately blew it forcibly out of her mouth on to the floor. It tasted almost like pure vinegar, and left her raw and sore as if it had been a mustard poultice. She stirred it with her spoon. That sediment *did* look like mustard. Well, made-up mulligatawny soups could be pretty vile, but she had never met with one as bad as this.

She turned to the "toad." It was a nice colour scheme of brown and yellow. She nibbled a bit of the latter. It was quite cold and there was a prickly taste about it. She examined the meat. Meat? There was none, only crusts of bread thrust into the holes were the meat should be.

She realised then that someone had either blundered or played a joke on her, and turned over the apple-dumpling to see what had happened to it. The top fell off the bottom, and revealed a knob of coal inside.

She sat still for a minute or two, wondering who could have done it. If it was just a joke, it was an ugly one, to deprive a hard-worked person of her largest meal. For she knew that she was unlikely to get anything more. She did not think she had any enemies, certainly among the kitchen staff.

Perhaps—she really had been pretty fierce to her last new Pro, but Pros did not have a chance to tamper with one's dinner. Perhaps the Pro was a cousin of the kitchen-maid.

Or—perhaps Sister Theatre's eyes were really malignant; Sisters were treated as school-children by the Matron, it was not a far step to imagine them behaving so.

She carried the tray into the ward-kitchen, emptied the soup down the sink, and was drying the edge of the soup-plate when the Night-Pro came in. The Night-Pro had been trained in Jack Horner ward from her arrival, and held Anne in respect but not in awe.

"Sister! Whatever are you doing?"

"Somebody," said Anne, unsmiling, "has been playing

jokes with my dinner."

The Night-Pro prodded it.

"Pig-dogs! Haven't you had any?"

Anne, thinking of the horrified spit when she had tried the soup, laughed with real amusement.

"Not a drop," she said.

"Wretches! Whoever did it, Sister?"

"I don't know. Never mind—unless you've got a spare egg."

"Of course I have. I'll bring you in something in a tick. You go back and sit in your armchair."

Anne went, and presently heard little squeals of horror in the passage outside. The Night-Pro was spreading the news. That was a pity.

Then a knock came on the door. She looked round, expecting the egg. The Ward-maid sidled in, sheepish and anxious.

"Sister, please, I couldn't get any more toad. But here's another dumpling!"

"Minnie! How did you get it? I shall have a lovely dinner now. I believe Nurse is boiling me an egg. Thank you very much."

The maid beamed.

"I'm glad you'll have something, Sister. It was a silly joke! I'll keep this hot in the kitchen till you've finished the egg."

She vanished, and in a minute came another knock. On the tail of it, the cook flounced in, a big tray slung at the end of her stout arms.

"There you are, Sister!"

She humped it down.

"There wasn't any more toad, but there's a lovely kipper for you! And another apple gob. And some coffee, to make up for it being late!"

"However did you know?"

Cook clasped her hands over her stomach.

"*That* Sister Jonas! Came an' giggled about it! I told 'er off. Then Sister Crossman came an' tipped me the wink you wouldn't get any more. So up I came. Dirty trick! Be'avin' like a set o' schoolboys!"

"Cook—who was it?"

"That Sister Theatre an' 'er lot! I 'ate 'em! Treat me like a flea!"

Cook stood still, breathing hard. It was impossible to imagine her imprisoned between a finger and thumb or flattened upon a cake of soap.

"But how did they do it?" Anne persisted.

Cook snorted.

"The Matron's out an' they can do what they like with Sister Jonas. They made the soup out of everything out of the cruet. They turned the syphon on to the toad an' took out all the meat, an' put coal in the apple gob instead of the apple. That's all."

"It was the soup, and the prickly taste of the toad that I couldn't fathom," Anne said. "Thanks most awfully, Cook."

She ate the kipper. The Nurse brought in a scrambled egg and she ate that. Two of the apple dumplings she demolished, but when the Night-Pro came with two more which she had filched, Anne presented them to the Night-nurses with her compliments. She drank the coffee, and settled down very contentedly with a cigarette. Practical jokes betrayed one's enemies, but they made one realise unsuspected well-wishers too.

Another knock revealed Sister Jonas, calling quite unnecessarily as she went round to collect reports from the wards.

She looked at Anne with a half-frightened snigger.

"Dinner come up all right, Sister Lee?"

Anne despised her. Silly old owl, why couldn't she wait till the morning to find out what had happened, instead of butting in? Probably the other Sisters had sent her.

"Yes, thank you," she said affably. "Very good dinner too. First decent soup I've had since I came."

Sister Jonas blinked.

"Apple dumplings all right?"

"The apple was burnt. But Minnie got me another one, and Cook sent up an extra one for luck. So I did well."

Sister Jonas could quite evidently not understand it at all. Anne continued to beam upon her.

"E—that's all right, then. Good night, Sister Lee."

Anne cocked a snook at her back and when she was well out of the way, strolled along to Sister Crossman.

"What did they do it for, Sister?"

"Umph. Balmy 'addocks."

"I know. But why did they do it?"

"Jealous, o' course. Anyone could see that."

"But what on earth of?"

"We 'ad a bad lot o' Residents before this lot," the old lady said. "They—those wimmin—useder have them to

181

tea and play cards. Mr. J. Brown, 'e was the last o' them. They don't go down wi' this lot, those wimmin don't. An' you do. So they're jealous."

"Oh," said Anne, relieved, "is that all?"

"Isn't that enough? I *told* you to keep on their right side—an' then you go an' do a thing like that!"

"Like what? I didn't ask the Residents to come and make friends. It just happened."

"They won't believe that, don't you worry, even if it's true."

"Of course it's true!"

"Oh, well, I believe you. You won't 'ave any difficulty in getting' off with a doctor if you want to, with that smile on you. *They* do want to. Only thing they think about. An' they're not as young as they useder be. Like me!" She laughed shrilly.

Anne snorted.

"What rubbish! Why, these Residents are just babies!" she said. "Anyway, it doesn't worry me now I know what it's all about."

"You be careful, or it will worry you," was old Sister Crossman's last word. "It'll worry you a lot. I know I'm old an' out o' fashion, but you just take my advice an' don't annoy those wimmin if you want peace and quiet."

CHAPTER 6

1

ANNE tore open a letter from Angela, and almost at once let out a long, horrified whistle.

"We couldn't bear it any longer," Angela wrote. "He came to see me last night, and we talked for ages. He's told her about me, and she's been simply awful about it. By the time you get this we shall have gone to Italy together. He's got to go, on business, which makes it easier. I don't know what'll happen then. I've written to the family. Stick up for me to them, if you get a chance. But don't worry about me, I'm so relieved that I don't know what to do, and I *know* that it's all going to turn out well."

Anne was standing by the window in her room, reading the letter by the light of the spring evening. She read it again, wrinkling her forehead in anxiety. Angela was so very young.

"Am I in the way, Sister? You look worried." Ashe's pleasant voice came to her from the doorway.

She turned, glad to see him.

"I am worried. But you're not in the way."

It was noticeable how, since Miss Thorn had gone, their conversation had dropped from its high impersonal plane. They still greedily read the papers and wrangled about the views they found there, still laid down the law sometimes on morals and manners; but often they wandered in the fields of reminiscence, learning eagerly about each other's past. Tony Ashe had been to a Country Grammar School

183

and had gone on to Cambridge and thence to the Central Hospital on scholarships. He had come to Princess Ida's merely to fill up time while he waited for a House Appointment in his own Medical School. He was going to take up Surgery if he could, for he shared Anne's enthusiasm for that art. Anne found him very simple and straightforward and, above all things, very kind. She never knew him to lose his temper, except at gratuitous unkindness. At the sight of it he became very cold and grim, and if it persisted he seemed to burst, and let loose floods of trenchant language upon the offender. She had seen that happen in Outpatients' one day, to a mother who was nagging her ill, sniffling little girl.

He came in, balancing a surgery book on his hand, and sat down.

"Can I do anything about it?" he inquired.

"No, I don't think so. I don't think anyone can."

He looked across at her gravely and then settled himself in his chair.

She wondered what he would say to Angela's story.

"It's my young sister," she said. "She's only twenty-three. Such a pretty kid."

"Kid?" he snorted.

She laughed.

"She's the youngest. Perhaps we babied her."

He grinned, placated, but asked no question.

"She's gone and run away to Italy with a man," Anne went on.

He looked up, startled.

"Is that so very shocking?"

"It is, rather," she told him. "He's married. Very married—three children."

"Oh, lor! What's he like?

"She says he's all right. She would, of course. I've not met him. I knew there was an affair, some time ago, but she said it was all over."

He sucked his pipe.

"D'you want to go out an' fetch her back?" he asked.

"Can't. She just says Italy. I don't think I would, either, even if I could. People must be allowed to live their own lives, even if they do make a mess of them."

He nodded agreement.

She told him the rest of the story.

"It's hard on the other woman and the kids, however you look at it," he said.

"Unless—she's got someone else too."

"Yes. You've no word of that, though, have you?"

"No."

"It's cruel." That was utter condemnation. "Think of the job she'll have to keep those kids. They ought to have thought of that."

"Angela's such a child," she pleaded.

"Yes. He's the most to blame. But she ought to have thought, too. She oughtn't to be such a child. It's not fair to other people."

"You mean, it's our own fault, for bringing her up like that?"

"Partly, I expect. Isn't it?"

"I don't think," she answered his unspoken thought, "that the rest of us are like it. Not nearly so much. She's

185

spoilt."

He looked across at her.

"People oughtn't to be too—innocent, nowadays," he said.

"I'm afraid she's going to suffer for it," Anne said presently.

"How? Why?"

"She thinks it's going on forever, the love part of it."

"Don't you think it will?"

"I don't think his will. I supposed he loved the other woman once. And I doubt if anybody's does, ever. It's just a phase, loving people, isn't it?"

He sat up straight then.

"D'you think so, really?"

"Yes," she said stoutly, "I do. I think one can love anyone, if one knows them well. If one understands them. Love them just quietly and happily, I mean. The other sort, the sort that carries you away, isn't love at all. It's physical attraction, and it dies. That's what they've got, I expect."

"Neither of those is love," he said positively.

She laughed, a little bit scornfully.

"D'you think I don't know?"

He got up.

"I think you're talking through your hat!" he said crossly and walked out.

She sat still, disconcerted. Now she'd annoyed him. How—how simply horrible!

He imagined himself in love, she supposed, with Miss Thorn. They weren't lovers, just dear comrades. You could be that with anyone, if you understood them. Most people didn't give one a chance. But she did wish he would come back. She felt, like the Hebrew women in Casualty, very veek in the stomach. Loneliness was much worse when you'd had companionship.

Then he came.

He stood in the doorway, grinning at her, and she did not know whether to look at him or not.

"I'm sorry, Sister. It was rude of me."

She did look at him then, and her smile was very shamefaced and glad and amused.

"I'm sorry too. I was aggravating. And I didn't know what I was talking about, really."

He met her eyes, pleased.

"D'you mean that?"

She shook her head rather wearily.

"Oh, yes. I only know it's a mistake to expect joys to be permanent."

He just nodded at her.

"You wait. You just wait," he said.

She was very glad to have her dear comrade back again. How *had* she lived when she was all alone?

Angela was lucky. Yes, lucky. She would never be alone any more.

2

The next week was filled with visits from the Lee family. They stormed at Anne for not preventing the catastrophe, at Angela for disgracing them, at the man for luring her away, and ended by weeping hurt, noiseless tears that Anne could not help herself but join. She was so sorry for her mother and the aunts. It was so difficult for them at their age, to have all their levels torn up, their standards flung overboard. But she annoyed them by refusing to condemn Angela.

She saw them off, sadly, at Victoria, for Croydon, where they were staying with another aunt, and went back to the hospital. It was a pity they took it so hard, felt so responsible for Angela. Of course, they *were* responsible for her. They had made her. But so many other influences had moulded her that they had inevitably lost control. That was what they could not realise.

She was tired when she climbed up to her room. These upsets wearied her much more than work.

There was an envelope on her mantelpiece. She turned it over idly. It hadn't come by post. She opened it, and read the typewritten slip.

"The attention of the Residents and Nursing Staff is drawn to the following extract from the Hospital rules:

'No Sister or Nurse is to go at any time into the Residents' rooms or Common Rooms. Sisters and Nurses are also forbidden to allow Residents in their sitting-rooms or in the Nurses' Home. Residents are not expected to be in the wards except between 9.30 a.m. and 12.30 p.m., and after 8.30 p.m. except when accompanying the Honorary Staff or when specially summoned to attend an urgent case.'"

She turned quite white as the meaning penetrated her mind.

Why had the Matron suddenly resurrected that old rule?

Was it just because of her and Ashe? They hadn't done anyone any harm. They were both sensible people. Matron was nothing but an interfering old cat.

She heard a small commotion on the stairs, and looked out of her door to see what it was. Ashe was running up, two stairs at a time. When he reached the top and turned the corner towards Jack Horner ward he saw her and made a jerking motion downwards with his forefinger. She leaned quickly over the banisters and looked over into the well below. Sister Outpatients' sitting-room was down there, and from the door of it "those wimmin" craned their necks upwards to see where Ashe was going.

She met him in the passage and he called loudly to her.

"Hullo, Sister! Had a good evening?"

She answered him primly, at the top of her voice.

"Very, thank you, Mr. Ashe. My people are in town—"

"I've just put a child into your ward," he shouted and disappeared through the ward door.

She went into her room and shut the door, and waited until she heard the door below her closed, too. Then she crept out again, and into the ward kitchen. From there, she could see him come out.

He came soon.

"This is the devil, Sister," he said with comical dismay.

"Shall we have to keep their beastly rule?"

She nodded.

"I'm afraid so. I shall get the sack if we don't."

"Damnable! I say, have we got you into hot water?"

"I don't think so. This is the first I've heard of it. I expect it's just a fad of Matron's."

"It's a nuisance of a fad," he grumbled. "I shan't be able to do a stroke of work. Can't I tell her I'm working in your room because it's quiet?"

She smiled as she shook her head.

"She'd never let you."

"Wouldn't she? Well, I'm angry. And must I really keep out of the ward?"

"Unless I summon you," she told him.

He grinned.

"Well, summon me very often, won't you?"

"I will. Very, very often."

She felt quite cheerful again at that. It was a pity their evenings were spoilt. But—he wanted to be summoned. And the whole thing would soon blow over.

She went to her bedroom and undressed, and waited outside the closed bathroom door.

Out of it, in a minute, came Sister Theatre. She looked at Anne with her malignant, slanting eyes.

"Yah, baby-snatcher!" she said, then drew herself up. "We felt it our duty to go to the Matron."

3

Anne was furious, simply furious. She jabbered with fury as she sat in her bath. How dared they? How dared they judge her with their nasty, dirty, grown-up minds? They didn't know what friendship was. Horrible, sniffing, prying *bitches!*

She turned on herself then. She had been green again. She might have known what they were like. All Sisters were like that, after their first job. She would be like it too herself soon. How could she help it, after all these disillusionments?

She stalked about proudly during the following days, never lowering her eyes to look at one of them. It was an impossible position. The Sisters did not speak to her, except Sister Crossman, of whom she saw very little, because they were seldom off duty together. The nurses and the maids all knew what had happened—they had seen the notices and heard the giggles of the triumphant conspirators. Those who had worked in Jack Horner were angry, and did not scruple to say so; the others were suspicious and scornful; so that the hospital was filled with friction; none of the usual borrowing and exchanging went on, difficulties were frequent and tempers short.

Anne found her ward forever invaded by the Assistant Matron and her crony, the Sister Housekeeper. They always had good reasons for their visits. They would prowl round the bathrooms and kitchen as if searching for an intruder hidden there, and come out baffled. They would officiously bring Anne's letters up to her room when she was off duty, and come to her there in the evenings with questions about the day report.

One afternoon she did call Ashe up to the ward to see a child who had been operated on in the morning. He had hardly joined her when Sister Jonas pattered through the door.

Anne summoned the Staff-nurse with a nod.

"Tell Sister Jonas," she said loudly, "that I'm sorry, but I am engaged with the House-surgeon at present."

Sister Jonas withdrew, gobbling. The Residents had precedence, even over the Matron, and no one but the ward Sister and her nurses was permitted in the ward when one of them was there. She had made a mistake.

But after that incident, she and Sister Housekeeper were not content with prying into the bathrooms. They buzzed round the ward itself, talking to the children and looking at their case-notes. They soon knew as well as Anne did when a very ill child was in Jack Horner and what was the matter with it. They were not going to countenance Ashe's presence there out of the proper hours. They were not particularly concerned with the younger Sisters' jealousies; but they were jealous themselves for the authority of the Matron's office, and would not allow its rules to be set at naught.

As soon as Anne realised how thoroughly she was being watched, a demon entered into her. She was not going to disobey the rule, and be dismissed, that would have pleased them too well, besides making life very difficult for her. But she would give them a run for their money.

One evening when Night-sister looked in on her, ostensibly to ask some official question, she found the door locked, and heard a scuffle behind it, and in a minute Anne came out, very red-faced and tousled, and withstood stoutly all efforts to penetrate into the room. When she had gone, Anne chuckled, and poured a jug of steaming water, over which she had been leaning since Night-sister had first begun her round, down the sink, and curled herself up again in her solitary chair. She was eyed with great solemnity by all her enemies the next morning.

Another evening, she threw her window wide open and sat herself just inside it with a book. From Sister Outpatients' room below came the sound of voices joined in after-dinner gossip. Anne found her book amusing. Indeed, it was the amusement of it which had given her the idea. She read bits of it aloud to herself from time to time, and burst out at intervals into gusty laughter. The bits she read were generally conversations.

She had been so diverting herself for nearly half an hour before she heard the door below her open, and almost at once her own handle rattled and Night-sister came in with a rush.

"Er—we thought you'd like some chocolates!" she said, holding out a box.

Anne took one.

"Thank you. This is *such* a funny book," she went on affably. "Have you read it?" Night-sister barely glanced at the title.

"No."

Her eyes were roving round the room. She dropped a chocolate on the floor with a little squeak, and pursued it under the sofa, and rose again visibly put out. There wasn't even a kitten hidden there.

"I'm afraid," said Anne politely, "that I've been laughing rather loudly at this book. I hope I haven't disturbed you."

"Oh, no," Night-sister said. "Oh, no, not at all. Er—good night, Sister Lee."

Anne found unholy delight in these pranks. One cannot come into daily contact with pettiness and not become a little petty oneself, and she had been enveloped in it for over six years now.

She sometimes, when in mufti, wore a signet ring on the fourth finger of her right hand. She put it on the left hand one day instead and turned it back to front so that only the plain gold band showed. She hid the hand shyly under the table at dinner, and only flashed it out occasionally for an instant. She counted certainly on some lynx eye catching sight of it, and she was not disappointed. Conversation languished at that meal. All the evening she was left alone. But at breakfast next morning Sister Jonas sidled amiably up to her.

"What's this rumour I hear about your engagement, Sister Lee? You've been so quiet about it that some people are going further and making it a wedding ring! Do let me see it and congratulate you!"

Anne surveyed her stonily.

"I don't know anything of such a rumour," she said.

"Oh, Sister. At dinner last night!"

Anne spread out her bare, workmanlike paws.

"I don't wear rings on duty," she said.

That evening she wore the ring as usual on her right hand. She saw Sister Jonas dig Sister Theatre in the ribs.

"Eeee! Mistook the hand! Silly ass!" she was squeaking, Sister Theatre looked malignant daggers across the table and shook her head.

4

But her enjoyment of her enemies' discomfiture was only episodic. On most days, Ashe did his round in Jack Horner in the mornings, with the ward nurses hurrying about him on their tasks; dressed a few of the children's wounds, with Anne and a nurse to help him; talked shop and departed. Sometimes they had a few minutes' conversation over the washbowl, but it was of the scrappiest. Often the Assistant Matron would look in, and they never knew when she might not be upon them. When they met in the passages they would exchange a word or two, but that was all. The evenings were barren and lonely.

"Look here, can't we go out to tea together?" Ashe grumbled one day.

She shook her head, remembering her experience at St. Edmunds.

"I think it 'ud be foolish, just now."

"We could meet somewhere—oh, damn, how silly and furtive it sounds! It's their fault."

"I *hate* it!"

"Well, let's just go out together, in front of them all."

But she would not have it, and he stumped away, sulky.

And then she began to live in the most terrible panic which had ever assailed her.

At St. Edmunds, authority, goaded by jealousy, had quietly nipped a friendship in the bud. Was the same thing going to happen here? If it did, she couldn't bear it.

She turned over in her mind Ashe's suggestion of going to the Matron and asking permission for him to work in her room. She would assure her that there was nothing in it but that, the Matron couldn't disbelieve her. Then she realised that she did not know which side the Matron had taken, or whether her dignity had kept her outside the quarrel; and her courage failed her.

The next day, even their brief intervals of conversation were forced and awkward. There was so much she wanted to say to him, that she could not marshal it at short notice; and he was still sulky.

Authority and jealousy were winning.

She climbed wearily up to the Theatre with the first operation case. Generally she loved Theatre days, as she had loved them during her training. The Theatre at Princess Ida's, too, was very pleasant. It had three walls entirely of glass, and a frosted glass roof. It seemed, on bright days like this, to be a bubble suspended in the blue sky, with birds hurrying and clouds floating by it, all above the smoke and grime of London; and inside the bubble, the rapid, unhurrying precision of the surgical team.

The anaesthetist was taking a long time to anaesthetise the first case. Everyone in the Theatre was ready. Anne was standing, her gloved hands resting on each other in front of her, so that they should touch nothing else, staring out at the sky. She felt her eyes travelling, following a cloud, then coming back with a jerk to the confined space of the room. They lighted on Ashe, sitting waiting on a stool, gowned and masked in white. He was looking at her. Slowly, she realised his expression. It was like nothing she had ever seen before, inquiring, longing, devouring, loving.

His eyes held hers for a long brooding minute. Then she heard the door of the anaesthetic-room open and tore her glance away.

Her pulse was racing, her cheeks flaming under her mask.

Authority was not going to win. He didn't want it to, either. The two of them could flout authority, and jealousy too.

The afternoon passed in a dream of swift action. Nothing escaped Anne. She was everywhere exactly when she was wanted. She always worked better when she was happy.

She was still happy when she went to bed, though vaguely disappointed. She had expected that something would happen, although she had no idea what the something was, and although her reason told her that nothing was even remotely likely.

5

The following day was a busy one. One of the children who had been operated on was a little girl with a most puzzling condition. She was very ill, and nobody quite knew what was wrong. The X-rays showed a shadow in the region of one of her kidneys, and the Surgeon had gone boldly in, expecting to discover and remove a stone, only to find none. So the severe operation had been undergone without the child being one penny the better. Anne was alarmed about her, fearing that she might not get over the shock of so large an incision; Ashe was perturbed at his own and his chief's misdiagnosis, very anxious to arrive at a decision as to the real cause of her condition.

They pored over her for a long time in the course of the morning round. Ashe's last words on leaving the ward were "Keep her going, Sister. Don't let her die!"

Anne had cheerfully smiled and given instructions for the closest watch to be kept on the child. There was something stimulating about a really difficult case. The child had all her thought and care then, everything else was subordinate.

During the afternoon, the little girl seemed to collapse. Anne rang down hastily for the House-surgeon.

" 'E's out," came the laconic answer. "Miss Fox is on."

"All right. Ask him to come up when he comes in," Anne directed. She wasn't going to have the new "Aggie," who talked too much and didn't know a thing. She could do better than that by herself.

She set to work to revive the child with hot bottles and subcutaneous salines. The child was tossing restlessly, making herself worse with every movement.

Ashe would have ordered morphia. She knew that. Miss Fox would have refused it, she knew that, too. Miss Fox didn't approve of morphia for children. She said their pain didn't matter, because they didn't remember it.

Anne sent the Staff-nurse off on an errand, and quickly dissolved the appropriate dose of the drug and injected it. She must do this, if her professional conscience told her to; but she must not set an example of independence to the nurses. When the Staff-nurse came back, she was standing watching as before. In a quarter of an hour, the child was sleeping quietly, her pulse getting stronger with every minute of rest.

When Ashe came up, the danger seemed over.

"Elsie worse?" he asked at once.

"She was. She got horribly restless."

"Did you have to get Miss Fox up? Oh lor—with her views too! I wish I'd been in!"

He went over to the cot.

"She's better now. I didn't have Miss Fox. I—I gave her a sixth myself."

He looked at her quickly.

"You're a brick, Sister. Morphia was the only thing."

"I thought you'd say so. I didn't know what to do. She'd have died without it, and Miss Fox would never have allowed it."

"It was the only thing possible. Thanks awfully. I simply had to go out."

"If it got about that I gave the morphia without permission," Anne said, fingering the cot rail, "there would be a shindy. It would be the last straw."

"It won't get about. *I* know when I can trust a person. Don't you?"

"Yes," she said, "or I wouldn't have dared to do it."

"It was the only thing," he repeated. Then, half laughing—"Sister, there's nobody like you! You're such fun, and one can trust you so!"

Anne flushed and smiled and looked him bravely in the face.

"That's all right. I'm glad you didn't mind."

She turned away, expecting him to go, now.

But he didn't. He stayed there, bending over the cot, and she had to go back and face him.

"Sister," he said, so low that he might have been speaking to the child, "I do—love you."

He was looking up at her then, his eyes strained and anxious.

"But you know that," he said.

"I—didn't," Anne whispered.

"I—can't help it. I tried not to. I tried not to tell you, too. But—I can't go on like this."

"Like—what?"

"Never seeing you."

They were both holding the cot rails, leaning backwards with stretched arms.

"It's—beastly," said Anne.

They stared at each other across the sleeping child.

"Do you—mind?" he asked, very quietly.

"Mind—what?"

"Me—loving you so?"

Anne took her hands off the rail and stretched them out to him, her eyes dancing and her head thrown back.

"Mind? I love you! Oh, so much!"

He took her hands and they stood so for a second then separated, laughing at each other.

"What *would* Sister Jonas say?"

They strolled towards the door together. The Staff-nurse scuttled across their path, throwing them a hurried, excited look.

"She saw!" they breathed.

Anne laughed.

"Doesn't matter. *She* won't say anything."

At the door they stopped. There was no sign of a spy. Ashe's face took on an air of great resolve.

Look here," he said. "We must do something about this. We shall burst if we stay here. Besides—there are such billions of things to talk about."

"It's my weekend off," she told him.

"I can get off, too. Could we—would you—go away?"

"Rather. Where?"

"The Downs. It's open. We can talk secrets at the tops of our voices. I know the very place. Saturday afternoon till Monday morning?"

She nodded, her eyes shining at the wonderful prospect.

"I'll arrange it all," he said. Then—"Good afternoon, Sister."

Her dimples came.

"Good afternoon—what?"

"Good afternoon, Sister. We must, while we're here."

A goffered cap appeared above the banisters.

"Good day, Mr. Ashe," she said solemnly. "I'll let you know if there is any change."

It was not until Anne was off duty and alone in her room that she realised fully what she had done. Then it came to her so suddenly that her heart felt like a lump of stone.

She was twenty-eight and a hospital Sister. One of the most unpleasant body of women on this earth, in embryo. And she had told this boy of twenty-three that she loved him, and had promised to go away with him.

It was wicked of her. She had been carried away. "Those wimmin" had forced her hand. She would grow old and cross and narrow when he was at the height of his strength and wisdom. She must write to him and say that it was all rubbish, and tell him to marry Miss Thorn.

If only Miss Thorn hadn't gone away it wouldn't have happened. It must not go any further. He and Miss Thorn would marry, and she would go and stay with them and be their friend.

She took out block and pen, then pushed them away.

She couldn't do it. She couldn't give him up now; she couldn't.

She would go away with him and let him see how dull and old she was, and it would all fizzle out quite quietly and naturally, and she would come back and be a hospital Sister again with a wonderful memory behind her.

She thought she knew what Angela had felt like, now, and what had come over sensible Belsize.

INTERLUDE

TONY ASHE and Betty Thorn were having tea together at the Plane Tree.

"And so," Betty smiled at him, "it's all settled?"

He looked across the teacups at her, his eyes bright with excitement from which amazement had not yet faded.

"The weekend is. We're going to Glynde, to the forge, where I used to go with Martin. Mrs. Hewitt'll put us up without any fuss."

Betty nodded. "Tell me about it."

"Nothing to tell!" he mumbled, and she chuckled.

"I just blew off in the ward, over a half-dead kid," he went on. "I couldn't help it! It was simply awful, never seeing her except when we were doing rounds. I didn't mean to be in such a hurry. She seemed most frightfully surprised. I can't think how she didn't spot it ages ago!"

Betty took another scone. "She's not on the lookout for things like that, thank goodness. It was funny, wasn't it, how you were smitten that very first day? When she wasn't thinking about you at all, only about the small boy."

Tony grunted. "Oom. I thought I was just being silly. And then, the more I saw of her, the more it grew. And when I didn't see her, it simply *shot* up "

"You're sure about it, Tony? That it doesn't matter her being older, and a Sister?"

"She isn't a Sister except when she's in uniform," Tony objected, "and hardly, even then. She's just herself. So

203

much herself that it wouldn't matter what shell she put on, Sister or charlady or duchess or—or lady-help. She'd show through every time. And I don't see why I should worry about the age question if she doesn't."

"You're a lucky devil," Betty said. "She really is a rare person. I felt that the first time I saw her, too. She had me up and ticked me off about something—"

"I know I'm lucky. I can't think why, either. I say, Bet—I do want to thank you. It would never have gone through its first stages without you. I should never have got to know her."

"A chaperone," Betty remarked, "is a very useful bit of furniture. Without one, the headstrong young go on too fast. The affair outgrows its strength and finds itself gasping in air too rarified for it. Then it collapses and shrivels up and no one can think why. That's true, Tony. I've seen it happen again and again in people who are left quite to themselves. Our grandmothers weren't such goats as we like to think them."

"I believe you're right," he agreed. "I've seen it, too."

"I suppose," Betty said, turning serious all of a sudden, that if they're left to themselves they do nothing but kiss and paw each other and think that's all there is to it. Probably it *is* all there is to it. Those things ought to be just signs that the people are fond of each other. And then, when they get tired of kissing, or something prevents it, they find there's nothing else behind and the whole thing goes up in smoke. If you can't have the pawing and stuff, the friendly part grows instead, and when the time for pawing comes it really *is* mostly a sign and that's why it's so—precious. Isn't that right, Tony? You ought to know."

"S'pose so," Tony agreed unwillingly. He began to hum—"Oi'm an honest lad though Oi be poor, And Oi've never bin in love avore—' That's the truth, you know. It's odd, isn't it, when you think of what most chaps are like by the time they're qualified."

"Most. Not all," Betty said. "I know several who are quite chaste, and they're the nicest."

"Betty, you ass. There's a difference between being chaste and not having any inclination to be anything else."

"I know it," Betty said solemnly. "It's having one's nose kept down to one's work. If you're really keen to get on there's no time for your emotions to get a look in."

"You don't think it's feeble—to have had no experience by my age?"

"No, I'm damned if I do. I think it's a jolly good thing. Twenty-three's not Methuselah. I hate these masculine young men, myself. They're—oh, not civilised."

Tony grinned. "There are better things than being civilised. Honestly I think I'm funking a bit. I've never talked about these things like most people have. Martin's too old and Hugh's too young, and the rest of one's crowd are too smutty." He hesitated and glanced directly at Betty. "It strikes me as odd that I can talk to you. You don't mind? I want to know how women think about it— because of Anne."

"Mind? Goodness, no. If two medicals can't talk sense about it, who can? Specially when we've known each other since we were born!" She went on presently: "I shouldn't think there's anything to funk, with Anne. She's awfully understanding. And I should think—I don't know, but I should think—she's as ignorant as you are, in that particular way. She's got that young look—"

Tony moved uneasily. "I think she is, too. But I'm just a bit afraid of letting us both down."

Betty spoke lightly. "I shouldn't worry about it. It's silly to let one's reason butt in on a matter that's purely instinctive. You're much less likely to let yourself down if you keep calm than if you flap."

He laughed. The unconcern was so like Betty. She excelled in common sense. "You're a lamb, Betty."

"You're lucky, you know," she said, "to have had to be restrained. You've got the friendship part of it well going first. That's the part that lasts. Reproduction's only incidental, although everyone makes such a fuss about it. That's why old people love better than young and friends better than lovers. Young people are too full of life—too lusty. They get the two things muddled, and think the least important one is the whole thing. You're lucky because you'll have them both."

Tony grunted. That was the worst of Betty; she let her mind run away with her. She embarrassed one. And she was never embarrassed herself. That was why she was so good at her job.

She led him back to talk of Anne, and he did so, fervently, until the end of the meal.

CHAPTER 7

1

ANNE and Tony met at Victoria, five minutes before their train was due to start. That much risk of being seen together they felt they could not be bothered to avoid.

Tony was in flannels and an old tweed coat, Anne in grey wool. They both carried walking sticks and looked very much the tramp. They surveyed each other with broad grins and walked up the platform smiling. People turned to look at them because they were so evidently happy.

2

They left grey, old-world Lewes behind them and climbed up a steep path behind some limekilns, and then they were on the downs. The sky was misty blue above, the earth below blue-carpeted with violets. The clear lines of hilltop rising and falling divided earth softly from sky all round them.

"Oh—look!" Anne pointed to a valley, sunk in the shadow of late afternoon, where men with wagons and fat white horses were taking straw from a stack. They watched the picture, clear, tiny and far away. Then they settled their rucksacks more comfortably and stepped out along the path of turf, while the wind made waves in the silvery grasses at their sides.

They did not talk much, just called each other's attention to the lovely things they passed, and now and then stole sidelong looks at each other and laughed for joy.

They came to a dewpond and watched a grey wood pigeon drinking, dipping and lifting its round head in the air. They scrambled, panting, up the steep sides of the Roman camp. Tony was first at the top, and bent and stretched a hand to Anne. They stood together, looking down on the flat plain intersected with little rivers and dotted with cattle. The sun was setting in a pale pink and primrose sky and everything was still and sweet.

Anne felt that she could not bear the minute to end. She wanted to stand there forever. She felt Tony move towards her, turned to him quickly, and they kissed each other and sprang apart.

"T—Tony! We must have been visible for miles!"

"Who cares? I've been wanting to do that for five months!"

"Let's do it again," said Anne.

They did, and took longer over it. Then, hand in hand like children, they dropped down sheer over fields into Glynde, where goats with tasselled beards wagged horns fiercely at them.

They walked through the sleepy village, peering into gardens of golden daffodils over banks of primroses. They came to a house whose door was an upturned horseshoe of warm brown wood. Tony, who had been dawdling along the road, stopped there and said, "Here we are!"

A brown-haired, rosy woman met them, with two

sleepy children clinging to her. They made friends silently with Anne while Tony talked to their mother.

Then Anne and Tony were in a tiny room, crammed with chairs and tables, draped with antimacassars and dotted with mats, the window blocked with plants in pots. Anne clasped her hands and gasped as she looked round it. She was quite unused to cottages in the country. Tony was amused. "You wait till you see the bedroom—" He looked quickly at her and away, but she was quite calmly prowling among the china ornaments.

Mrs. Hewitt bustled her upstairs for a wash. The bedroom was all that Tony had hinted. The deep-set, tiny window was bordered with starched lace curtains, dragged at their waists into wide sashes of pink silk. There were pink bows on the bedposts and on the elbows of the looking glass. The bed had pink silk petticoats veiled with lace. It was all spotless, incredibly stuffy, and smelt of lavender. The ceiling was so low that the clumpings of the children in the attic above seemed to rebound from Anne's head as she stood.

She washed in rainwater and puzzled why it gave such a polish to her nose. Tony hated powdered women. He said so very often. She dusted the shine carefully and rubbed the powder off again. Perhaps he wouldn't notice such a very little powder. She felt that she would squint if she did not subdue the glare a little.

She could see the appreciation in his eyes when she came down.

"You are jolly to look at!" he said shyly, and she smiled at him and stroked the bristles on the back of his neck as she passed him.

They sat down to a great meal of ham and milky eggs and homemade bread and butter. Anne found the little room very cosy and intimate. She felt as though she must be giving out a glow of happiness, and indeed her wide brown eyes did seem to shine with it. Once she put out a hand and brushed Tony's, and they grinned at each other, with their mouths full, in great content. They talked spasmodically and Anne was not embarrassed by their silences. Outside, through the square of window, the sky was deep, luminous blue, with the downs humped up into it and the lamp's reflection swung in it like a moon.

"Let's go out," Tony said when the meal was finished. He was restless in the little room. He linked his arm in Anne's as they passed between the daffodils. Anne breathed deeply. She could not tell which she loved best, the moments when they were quiet, happy friends, like this, or those when they were lovers. She thought suddenly, curiously, of the night which was before them, and as suddenly some inhibition turned her thoughts off like a tap.

They paced past the church. Glow-worms twinkled in the hedges and bats flew over their heads. Tony laughed at Anne's little squeaks of amazement. She was so unused to country things, so full of curiosity about them, like a child. They climbed a stile and a grassy hill, and looked over the crest of it. The moon sailed there, pink like a great ripe peach. It seemed to Anne that all the beautiful things she had dreamed of during her girlhood had become realities during these last few months. She smiled at herself. How idiotic, to have wanted to stand and look at a pink moon with some loved person. And how jolly it was to do.

They strolled back, presently, and talked of bed, for they were tired. In the little parlour, Tony fumbled with his rucksack and coat and put them on a chair by the door. He came to Anne and hugged her suddenly. "Good night, darling Anne. Sleep well."

Anne, drawing back from his close embrace, looked at him, questioning, not understanding what he meant. He flushed, "I'm going—next door."

"I thought—"Anne began. Tony mumbled, "I don't want to rush you."

Anne was on the point of saying, "Rush me as much as you like, my darling!" She got as far as looking him frankly in the eye, and something she saw there stopped her. She said gently instead, "That's dear of you, Tony," and saw relief flood his face. They kissed each other again, very tenderly, and Anne climbed up the rickety stair and waved from the top.

She really did think it was dear of him. After all, she was not going to give up her job just yet, and it would be an awful complication if anything happened. It was just like Tony, to think of her before himself. As she arranged herself in the great feather bed, she chid herself for being disappointed.

3

In the morning, blue sky above, mist below and a tang in the air, they were on the road again. The lower slopes of the downs were studded with chalk flowers, tiny gems which Tony picked out of the dew for Anne to see—cowslips, squinanceywort's pink crosses, lady's slippers with fiery toes, pink orchises with spotted leaves and the queer fly and bee orchids which she had never seen before. The slope was steep on this north side of the great ridge, and the grasses quickly grew silky and the flowers fewer. Anne and Tony scrambled and panted, rested and scrambled again. When they were nearly at the top, Tony rushed ahead, stumbling in his eagerness.

"Wait, Anne! I must see if this is the place! Wait till I tell you!"

So Anne waited, leaning on her stick.

"It is!" he shouted, presently. "It's the place I wanted us to hit! It's simply heavenly. Come on, quick!"

She floundered up the last few yards and joined him on the top, just west of Firle Beacon. In front, far below, the sea stretched, delicate blue edged with silver lace. Behind, the weald lay, patterned with trees, dotted with pointed spires, and beyond it the blue haze that was the North Downs.

"Worth it?" Tony asked, proudly, as though it was his.

"It's perfect," said Anne.

4

They tramped slowly along the ridge's backbone until they came to the Beacon, and there Tony flung himself down.

"Lunch? I think so. Don't you?"

Anne turned out the contents of his rucksack.

"And," he said as he munched, "I think we'd better talk—about things."

"What things?" Anne's heart sank suddenly.

Tony settled himself on his back, gazing into the faraway sky.

"Well," he began, "I'd like to get married at once, of course. Wouldn't you?"

Anne gasped. "No. Yes. I don't know. We can't, anyway."

"I know. At least, it would be silly to."

Anne had pulled herself together. "It would be wicked," she said firmly.

"Oh, not as bad as that," Tony objected lazily. "The question is, can you bear to stay on at that hole for eighteen months or so? Wouldn't you rather go home? Or—anything else? It's just while I'm doing House-jobs. I'll get a practice after that. I could get one now, of course, if you'd rather. Only I do want to be competent. If I can do a few special jobs to get experience, and get my Fellowship, we'll do far better in the end. D'you see?"

She was silent, and he sensed her to be unresponsive and rolled over doubtfully. "You do understand, don't you?"

"Of *course* I do!" Anne saw that he had misunderstood her silence. "I wouldn't spoil your work for a moment. You know that."

"What is it, then?"

She answered in a little voice, her face turned away.

"Tony, dear, I can't marry you, ever."

"What d'you mean? Why?"

213

"I can't. It would be wrong of me."

"Why? Aren't you enjoying—this?"

"I've never enjoyed anything so much in all my life."

"Well? Is it me? Don't you love me any more?"

"I love you awfully. That's why."

"I think you're being silly."

"I'm not. I'm so much older. And I'm a hospital Sister. You know the sort of petty women we turn into. I'm beginning already. I can feel it coining on. I snap, and I mind about little things that don't matter."

"You'd better take it in time," he said solemnly, "and marry me before it gets any worse." He chuckled. "Anne, I do love you! You, a petty woman!"

"Tony, you *must* be serious! It's important!"

"I know," he said, suddenly quiet again. "It's frightfully important. Go on."

"I'm dull and uneducated and I don't know how to call or go to tea-parties."

"You talk," Tony said with heavy scorn, "as though you were a barmaid!"

"I might almost as well be. You don't know how people outside despise nurses!" She thought of Dora Dalloway. "They say, 'Oh, a nurse!' as people who've lived in China say, 'Oh, a black-and-tan'. Pity and distaste all mixed up with scorn. I don't want people to talk like that about your—your wife, Tony. You'd hear, and it would spoil things and anyway it would spoil your practice."

"It wouldn't have the slightest effect on either the practice or me," Tony said placidly. "I should think what idiots they were. Besides, they'd jolly soon change their

214

tone when they saw you. I say, Anne, do you know how lovely you are? Do you know what your smile's like? Have you ever listened to your own voice?"

"Tony," Anne said faintly, "you're mad!"

Tony crooned to himself: "I like to be mad. It's jolly being mad. Darling Anne, stop being a donkey. Honestly, I want to know if you can wait. If you can't bear the idea, we'll do the thing right away and I'll go as someone's assistant. I bet I'm as good as lots of G.P.'s already."

Anne wanted to hug him. She was almost crying with eagerness to make him understand.

"Tony, you *must* see I'm dull! I've got nothing to talk about! I've got nothing behind me, like you and Betty have! You'll be tired of me in a year!"

"Well," Tony said practically, "we shan't be married in a year. That is, unless you decide to do it now, which you've said you won't. So if I'm tired of you—you idiot, Anne—we can quietly drift apart. What more do you want?"

"It's all most unsuitable," said Anne.

Tony edged closer to her. "What d'you feel like," he asked softly, "when we're together, just the two of us? When we're together, anywhere, in any circumstances?"

Anne drew in a long breath. "Just content. When you look at me, or touch me, sort of shining with happiness. But generally, completely, absolutely content. And whenever you surprise me—you do, sometimes—it's a happy surprise, never a nasty one."

"I feel like that, too," he said. "No hurts or jars. No possibility of any. Don't you think that to live together, like that, would be the most wonderful thing?"

Anne looked at him. He was smiling a little, his untidy, boyish hair ruffled, but his eyes serious, so happy and so sure of himself and her. She dropped her cheek on his hand on the grass. "All right, Tony."

"Only," she went on, after a minute, "you must promise, *promise* that if you get tired of me before the eighteen months or whatever it is are up, you'll say so. None of your silly 'honour bound' business! Promise?"

"All right, Anne," he mimicked. "Promise!"

5

When they went on again Anne walked in a dream. He wouldn't let her go. He wanted her, even after a whole day alone with her. He felt the same happiness as she did.

She skipped, and Tony chaffed her.

"I can't help it," she said, "I'm so happy!"

"I feel," he said, "as though I should never be able to stop grinning. Even at the Matron and Those Wimmin."

Anne's mood changed. "Don't talk of them. I wish I was never going back. I wish we could build a magic hut in one of those fairy-rings and live there. You'd go out and gather mushrooms and dew and I'd keep it tidy with a broom of—what does one make fairy brooms of, Tony? The sort that you can use as a motorcar when you're not wanting it to sweep with—"

Tony could contain his pocket no longer. "I've got a fairy-ring!" he announced. He brought it out, silver, with a single big sapphire. "It's to remember our blue weekend by—blue sea, blue sky, blue violets, bluebird—

216

everything."

"Tony, you darling! Put it on, please!"

Tony did.

Presently they awoke to the world again, and, since there is no tea in fairyland, set out for Alfriston. They found a cottage with a sloping garden full of flowers, and there an old, apple-cheeked woman brought them tea and homemade cakes and honey. Small fluffy chickens cheeped round their feet, picking up cake-crumbs. A chaffinch hopped on the table and ate from their plates. A puppy and a kitten rolled together in the grass. It was as nearly Fairyland as might be.

CHAPTER 8

1

ANNE did go back, late that night. She went straight to her room and slept the sleep induced by open air and exercise, until five. Then the thousand questions hammering at her consciousness had their way and she woke, and could not sleep again.

What should she do? That was the theme which recurred, again and again. For although Tony had lulled her misgivings, he had not destroyed them. While she was with him, she saw him as a man; young, certainly, but sure of her and of himself, able to hold his own. But when they were apart she thought of him again as the absurd, learned infant, teasing, playing with Betty Thorn, as capable of quick happiness and deep hurt as one of the babies in her ward. She could not play with this boy Tony. When he and Betty Thorn had played together, she had never joined in, only listened and laughed. She could no more play pitch-and-toss with words as they did than play the fiddle. She felt old and ponderous beside them. And yet—Tony loved her, although she was old and ponderous.

When the Night-staff brought her tea, at seven, she was tired out with this whirligig chasing of past and future. She drank the tea and dozed off again, a thing she never did. When she woke again, in a flurry, it was ten minutes later than her usual time for getting up. She tumbled out, still half asleep, and raced along to the bathroom.

218

Everything went wrong, of course. The bathroom was a swamp, left by some careless person in a hurry. She dropped her towel into it before she saw what it was like. At breakfast, the porridge was burnt and the kipper cold. It was quite a frequent state of affairs, but today it seemed to be so to spite her. Sister Crossman champed and smacked her lips as she ate. Sister Theatre, whose gentility was no more than camisole-deep, helped herself to jam with her buttery knife and put back into the rack a broken half-slice of toast which had been on her jammy plate.

A filthy life. Anything to get out of it. Their only chance—Dora Dalloway's words came mockingly into Anne's head.

"Have a good weekend, Sister Lee?" Sister Outpatients had sensed and resented her aloofness, her lingering preoccupation with the real world. Anne felt her weekend smirched by the other woman's interest in it.

She nodded, coldly. "Yes, thank you, Sister." Some demon prompted her to add: "I've been away, staying with my fiancé."

Squeaks of surprise went round the table. "Then it *was* an engagement ring!"

"Show it to us, Sister!"

"Who is he? Do we know him?"

Panic took her. "I don't wear rings with uniform. No, he's no one you know."

Now it would be all over the hospital, and Tony would hear of it and think she could not hold her tongue. She must see Tony. Supposing they put two and two together.

Everyone knew that Tony had been away for the weekend too.

She rose and excused herself. "I've a lot of things to see to before the rounds." Matron nodded benevolently and she left the table.

Until nine o'clock she lurked by the ward doors at the top of the stairs. It was a blessing that the Residents used the staircase which passed close to Jack Horner ward. When Tony went down to breakfast, she was discreetly carrying some flower-vases from the ward to the kitchen. She smiled at him over her shoulder.

He twinkled at her. "Morning, Sister. Had a good weekend?"

"Very nice, thank you, Mr. Ashe. Did you?"

"L-uv-ley!"

They had approached each other, and she spoke to him rapidly. There was no one in sight, to see or hear them.

"Tony—they saw my ring—I've said I spent the weekend with my fiancé and that he's someone they don't know!"

He grinned. "O-ho! Ashamed of me, are you?"

"Tony!"

"I know. I should have done exactly the same myself. Always tell whackers to noseys."

"I'd so much rather they didn't know more than that yet. Besides, I should get the sack, if Matron knew."

He nodded agreement. "We don't want to broadcast it. If anyone asks what I've been doing, I've been camping with the Boy Scouts."

He left her, laughing. She hated herself as she watched

220

him downstairs. Why had she told them even that much? Perhaps in self-defence, because she knew that she could not keep the news of it out of her eyes. Or was it in triumph, because she knew they would be mad with envy?

The next minute, she was assailed by a probationer from the Theatre floor, a black-eyed, insolent girl who had been trained by Sister Theatre and imitated her.

"Sister says, would you be so good as to return the tongue-forceps and the kidney-dish and the two towels which you took down with the patient on Friday."

Anne brought her thoughts back with difficulty to the trivialities of the present. Some things had been brought down on Friday. The rule in her ward was that such things were washed, and taken back to the Theatre by the Senior Probationer as soon as they were finished with and the return noted in the report. The Senior Probationer *might* have forgotten them, although one did not forget matters of habit like that. And Anne herself *might* have not noticed the omission of the note in the report, though she was observant enough as a rule. She could not remember with accuracy anything which had happened just before the weekend. However, one had to keep one's end up in questions like this, and she retorted at once:

"The things were sent up on Friday evening just as usual."

The Theatre-Pro eyed her. "I'll tell Sister she must have made a mistake."

"Please do," Anne said coldly, and went into the ward. There she was overtaken by a number of dressings which

221

needed doing at once, and forgot the incident.

But it was not long before the Pro was down again. "Sister says the things were not returned and she wants them for her inventory."

Anne wondered why on earth Sister Theatre should be doing an inventory in the middle of the month. She probably was not doing one at all, had mislaid the articles and wanted an excuse for venting her envy on Anne.

"I shouldn't have told you they'd been returned if they hadn't," she snapped, and turned back to her dressings.

"Sister Theatre said I was to wait for them," the Pro said, propping herself against a cot as though she meant to stay there all day. Anne wondered what Sister Theatre had been saying about her. Probationers as a rule treated her with respect. She took not the slightest notice of the girl. She could wait as long as she pleased.

She waited until that dressing was done. When Anne passed on to the next, she began to fidget. Presently she said quite meekly, "Have you forgotten—I was waiting, Sister?"

"No," Anne said. "You know, Sister won't like you to be away so long. You'd better believe what I've told you and go back."

The girl stared. On the Theatre floor, Pros were either petted or treated as dirt. There was nothing between. She said, "Thank you, Sister," mechanically and went. Anne called the Staff-nurse and sent her for the day-report. Under Friday's date was duly entered: "Returned to the Theatre one tongue-forceps, one kidney-dish, two towels."

"And I remember taking them," the Senior Probationer added, when she was asked about the matter.

Anne placed the report open on her table and went on with her work.

Then the Pro intrepidly returned. "Sister says she knows you had other things to think about on Friday, but that she really must have those instruments," she said. She was biting her lips to hide her smiles. She knew quite well what Sister Lee was supposed to have been thinking about.

Anne lost her temper. She could not imagine what Sister Theatre was getting at, or why she took the trouble to send her insolent messages which meant nothing at all. She said, "You can tell Sister that my report book's open on the table here if she cares to come and read it."

"She said I wasn't to come back without them."

"And I say I won't have you waiting about in my ward. If you want to stay on this floor you can stay in the passage." She flung the Pro such a look that she wisely withdrew. Anne saw her balancing herself against the wall outside, and presently heard her go upstairs. She was sorry for the Pro, being batted like a shuttlecock between her two wrathful superiors; but reflected that if she had behaved with more tact she would have been better treated. She would never get on in the world, that Pro.

In a few minutes there was a flurry of starched skirts, and Sister Theatre's little slanting eyes flashing fury.

"Sister, will you *kindly* return my property when I ask for it? And please treat my nurses properly in future when they're sent down with a message!"

223

Anne for reply produced her report book. But Sister Theatre's only retort was a sniff. "Anyone can cook a report book. Burnt your own towels and lost your tongue-forceps down the sink, I suppose, and think you can make up your deficiencies out of mine! Well, you can't."

Anne simply gasped. The rigid tradition of honesty at St. Edmunds, of owning up the very minute you had a loss or a breakage, or made any sort of a mistake, had left her unprepared for this. She said forcibly, "My towel-drawer and my instrument cupboard are both intact, thank you. And if they weren't I shouldn't choose things out of yours to fill up the gaps with. I wouldn't touch them, not with rubber gloves on!"

"How dare you be insolent to me! Everyone knows you don't care two pins about your work! All you think about is *men* and currying favour with the Residents!"

The utter untruth and injustice of these insults left Anne gaping again. She was not enough of a psychologist to recognise the very common trait of getting one's fist in first by fastening one's own faults on one's enemy. She only knew that Sister Theatre was a toad.

"My work's a good deal better than yours and you know it! What about those taps I heard Mr. Salter grumbling about? *My* ward's *clean!*"

"Taps! Ho! I'm not an electro-plater, am I? You're forgetting I was on duty in your ward while you were away with your young man! I never saw such a filthy place, never in *my* life! Top-tidy, that's what your ward is! I told the Matron so!"

Anne, having worked like a galley-slave to make her

224

ward the cleanest place in the whole hospital, felt like nothing so much as punching Sister Theatre's head. There was nothing else one could do against such barefaced lying. That, to a St. Edmunds nurse, from someone who had been trained at God-knew-what little provincial dustheap of a hospital. She gripped the top of the banister tightly to keep her fists under control, and said what she thought, with embroidery.

After that, they went at it like a couple of fishwives. They stamped side by side up and down the corridor hissing insults. The scene only came to an end because Anne felt tears of rage in her eyes and whirled into her sitting-room and banged the door. She sat in her armchair, literally sobbing with anger. How dared that woman say things like that about her, how dared she! And the whole thing entirely uncalled for and without foundation. It was just like hospital life, everything topsy-turvy. Things which really mattered, like death and saving life and courage and pain, passed unnoticed, and these little petty jealousies and irritations ruled the roost. You were much more likely to lose your job because another Sister hated you than because you were dishonest, dirty and untrustworthy. How could anyone expect to remain an ordinary, normal person in such an atmosphere? How could one hope ever to be normal again after living in it?

She regained control of herself and walked quietly into the corridor. It was empty. The vixen had gone back to her den. Anne went on with her work, with tight lips, knowing that by midday the story would be all over the hospital; that there would be two versions of it, one from the Theatre floor and one from her own nurses, and two factions, one following her and one Sister Theatre, which would not be on speaking terms for some days.

Tony came to do his round, and she tried to tell him about it. He grinned over the dressing he was replacing and said: "Dreadful woman! How they do flap over nothing at all, don't they? Damn her eyes, for making you cross!"

He didn't seem to see that it mattered being told your ward was dirty as long as you knew it wasn't. When the round was over, he went up to the Theatre with a message, and Anne sulked. If *he* had been spoken to as she had, she would never have gone near the person who had insulted him again, officially or otherwise.

The midday post brought her a letter from Belsize, a hurried scribble which seemed literally to drip happiness. She was to be married in two months' time. No more nursing as long as she lived. They had found the dearest little house at Clapham Common, and Jack would go up to town every day. They were frightfully busy, buying furniture.

Anne was so envious that she nearly wept again. If only Tony hadn't got to do House-jobs. If only they could get married in two months' time, even if it did mean pigging it in two rooms. She would ask him if it couldn't, possibly, be managed.

He came along the corridor, very spruce and clean, his eyes full of dreams as he smiled at her. And she knew that she could never ask him to live uncomfortably, without all the pleasant things he was used to, or to forego his ambitions, and see the dreams fade and his eyes grow anxious and tired. It would not be fair. She would wait for that year and a half. And if she did wait, she would grow stern and gimlet-eyed, and hard, a cool, efficient machine. She would forget, even, to encourage Tony to play. She had already forgotten how to play, herself, and all the charity would ooze out of her and leave her dried up and old inside her shell of print dress and apron.

For the rest of the day she went about as upright and unbending as a poker, an image of the Martinette, her lips pressed together and misery in her eyes. She knew now something of the history of those Sisters at St. Edmunds; why their minds were so much older than their bodies, why dear Sister Southcliffe looked so wistful, why the Martinette had become so grim and sharp.

2

Late in the afternoon, Anne had to take the next day's operation list from her ward to the Theatre. She thought of sending it by a nurse; but reflected that, if she did so, Sister Theatre was quite capable of swearing that she had never had it and not getting ready. Anne pinned the notice on the board and called the attention of the Theatre Staff and Theatre-pro to it. Sister was nowhere to be seen.

As she returned along the little passage which led only to and from the Theatre, the door of Sister Theatre's sitting-room was opened and Sister popped out her head. She drew back at once when she saw Anne, and shut the door. But she was a little clumsy in her movements, and Anne caught sight of a man standing just inside the room; a tall man who could be no one but the Staff Anaesthetist. She smiled grimly to herself. There was no actual rule that the Honorary Staff should not go into the Sisters' rooms. But they were expected to be above any such conduct, and a flirtation between one of them and a Sister would be looked upon with the greatest disfavour. Even Anne could think of no reason for such a visit except a flirtation, specially with Sister Theatre and the anaesthetist as the parties concerned. Anyway, if it was anything else, why had she looked so guilty and bobbed back in such a hurry?

3

When she came off duty, Anne was sent for to the Matron's office. She could not think why. She wondered for a second if Sister Theatre had had the idiocy to report her for the morning's episode. Well, if that was so she had a weapon to hand which she would not hesitate to use.

The little ferret-faced Matron looked up at her from behind the desk and began without preamble. "You really must try and get on better with your colleagues, Sister Lee. I've had a complaint from Sister Theatre—not the first, though I've ignored the others—"

Anne felt wearily that she simply could not cope with these people. She supposed that Sister Theatre had picked the silly squabble just so that she would get the sack, because they were all envious of her and hated her. Well, she would see to it that Sister Theatre got the sack too.

She heard the Matron out.

"The things had been returned, Matron. It was entered in the book and I made Nurse go through the cupboards to make quite sure as well."

"It wasn't so much the property as the rudeness with which you treated Sister and her nurse that was the trouble," the Matron said.

"Rudeness!" Anne burst out. "What about Sister Theatre's rudeness? It was every bit as bad as mine, and none of it true!"

The Matron looked vaguely about her. "That may be. I don't like this constant dissension." Anne, her tongue trembling to treat perfidy with perfidy, and suggest that the Matron should keep a strict watch on Sister Theatre's room, was visited unbidden by a vision of St. Edmunds; St. Edmunds, where the discipline was stern, the Sisters dragons; but where there was a sort of rough justice, none of this pettiness, this suspicion, this small vulgarity. At St. Edmunds one was loyal, at least, to one's kind. One didn't bring in counterclaims to rebut an accusation, one took it standing. She heard Sister Southcliffe's voice—"You mustn't *do* it, Nurse! It isn't *Ed*-munds!" Well, St. Edmund might have turned her away, but she still belonged to him. She couldn't go sneaking to the Matron about Sister Theatre's private affairs, whatever might be said. And, she acknowledged to herself with a grin, if it came to private affairs she hadn't much of a leg to stand on herself.

She allowed gravely, "I'm afraid I am a bit difficult to get on with, Matron. If only they'd leave me alone everything would be all right."

She saw that the Matron's little sharp eyes were fixed on her. There was not much, of hospital affairs, that those eyes missed. Surprisingly, Anne noted in them a glint of amusement, almost of kindness.

"There are some people, Sister, who are incapable of leaving anything alone."

The Matron had arrived at supreme power in her small world before all her charity had quite dried up, and now something, Heaven knew what, had drawn it to the surface. Perhaps it was merely that she was pleased with herself for having seen through Sister Theatre's silly little plot to get rid of a hated rival. Perhaps just that she had an eye for a good Sister and did not want to lose her. Anne never knew for certain what had prompted her to act as she did. She would not have been surprised if she had been told that the Matron knew all about herself and Tony down to the smallest detail.

She drummed on the table. "You've been having a trying time since you came to us, Sister Lee."

Anne jumped. She had not expected sympathy. "Er—not more than one looks for, in a new post, Matron."

The little woman smiled as though at an inward joke. "You're looking tired and worried. I think it would be a good plan if you took your holiday now instead of in September."

She looked up under her eyebrows and Anne simply opened her mouth and shut it again.

The Matron went on, conversationally. "Mr. Salter's going away next week, so there won't be very much going on in your ward, anyway. I've heard of quite a good

Holiday Sister I can have—from your training-school, by the way—"

Anne actually smiled. To leave Jack Horner to someone from St. Edmunds would be bearable, and to get away just now—to have time to think—was what she longed for.

"—so will you arrange to be off for a month from the day after tomorrow?"

"I—I—it's awfully kind of you, Matron. I could go home, of course. It's quite true, I am tired."

The ferret face relaxed ever so slightly. "I can see you are. I know you had a fight with that ward. It's a good ward now. We'll see it doesn't go down while you're away. The Holiday Sister will be there on Tuesday night. You can show her round on Wednesday morning and be off by midday. Good night, Sister."

4

At supper, Sister Theatre watched Anne at first with the greatest anxiety. Then she became almost ludicrously friendly. She cut bread for her, carried her plate away, helped her to pudding, made amends in every ostentatious way she could. Anne wondered whether she was placating a dangerous enemy or speeding a possibly departing one. She did not give her any help at all; thanked her politely for her services and looked down on her with a kindly, tolerant smile. What if she need not after all be drawn down to these people's level? What if she could rise above them and prove herself a proper companion for Tony after all?

It was not until, feeling quite light-hearted, she had sat down in her own room, that she realised that Tony's six months as House-surgeon would be over in three weeks. When she came back from her holiday he would no longer be there.

PART III

ADULT

He that bends to himself a joy
Doth the wingéd life destroy.
But he that kisses the joy as it flies
Lives in eternity's sunrise.

BLAKE

CHAPTER 1

1

ANNE spent a troubled night. She wanted to go away and yet she didn't. In the morning she was engulfed by her work, and had no time to think.

At teatime, Betty Thorn walked into her room. Anne sprang up in pleasure and surprise. Betty shut the door behind her. "I'm not a Resident any more, so I can come into Sister's room, can't I?"

"Rather." Anne was fumbling in the cupboard for an extra cup and plate. "There are only biscuits," she said regretfully.

Betty laughed. "Didn't come for food. Came to see you. I say, Sister, I'm so awfully pleased—about you and Tony!" She sat down on the arm of Anne's chair and hugged her impulsively; and Anne, who had no women friends with whom she was really intimate, and who had missed her sisters' demonstrations all these years, hugged her in return and wondered whether it was possible for her to be any happier.

They talked in the old comradely way as they had done before Betty had left the little hospital.

"I came really to get a testimonial out of Doctor Hooper. I've just finished M.B. and I'm putting in for a job at the North London," Betty said.

"You're looking tired. You want a holiday."

"I am tired. M.B.'s nothing but a trial of endurance, nowadays. If you can hold on to the end without your

235

brain going to a jelly, you get through. Otherwise you don't."

"I'm going for my holiday tomorrow—" Anne launched into the story of her interview with the Matron. "She simply pushed me off. I'm certain she knows about Tony. If she does, it's jolly decent of her not to push me off for good."

"She knows a good thing when she sees it," Betty said lightly, and Anne was inordinately pleased. She minded a lot what Betty thought of her, partly because the girl was so sensible, partly perhaps because of the trust Tony had in her opinion.

"Oh, but it will be good to get away from this place. Not that I haven't enjoyed it. One lives—" Anne stretched her arms.

Betty glanced out of the window to the crowded grubby street, alive with raucous children. "Oh, yes. One lives."

She watched the people in silence for some minutes, then whisked round to face Anne. "Sister! Where are you going for your holiday?"

"Home, I suppose. There wasn't any time to make proper plans."

"Will that be fun?" Betty asked.

"Not very. Mother and one sister run a sort of boarding-house, since my father died. They're kept pretty busy. And the others are away."

Betty came across and took her hands eagerly, squatting on the floor by her side. "Would you—could you come home with me for a week first? It's quite—quite amusing, at home; there are such a lot of us. They'll be longing to know you. And Tony could come for the weekend, if you liked. He generally does, when he's free. Do come."

"I'd simply love to," said Anne.

2

The next day found her with Betty in the dusty little train which plies between Liverpool Street and the Essex suburbs. They were met at Wroughton by a weather-beaten Morris and two youngsters whom Anne took, at first sight, to be both boys. Both had sleek black heads, their faces were almost identical, and both wore Fair Isle jumpers. When they greeted Betty, however, she heard with surprise that the voice of one was high and musical and the other deep and burry.

"Evadne and Hugh," Betty said. "This is Anne—Tony's Anne."

They were laughing up at her and pulling at her suitcase. She and Betty packed themselves into the back of the car. Betty looked round and asked, "Who's driving?"

"We are. At least, Hugh was and I'm going to. Don't you remember even *now* that we've had a birthday?" Evadne scolded.

"Goodness, so you have. They have driven before, Anne, don't be nervous. Only they couldn't have licences, so they couldn't drive in the village, because everyone there knows how old they are. See?"

Evadne took them very efficiently along the road which skirted Epping Forest. Presently they turned into a lane, and almost at once into the garden of a low, white house.

Anne found the family much like Betty; unassuming, yet sure of themselves; friendly and pleasant-mannered, yet shy. They received her immediately as one of themselves. She was "Tony's Anne," a person; not that queer phenomenon from whom anything might be expected, a trained nurse. She reacted to the atmosphere at once; became herself friendly and pleasant-mannered and only becomingly shy, instead of prickly and defensive as she often was with strangers who might have patronised her if she had given them a chance. She saw herself behaving really as a rather attractive person, instead of the gauche, dried-up spinster she had feared to turn into. It was funny, she thought, how she did not know at all, now, what she was like as a person, only as a hospital Sister.

She tried to sort out the Thorn family. There was Marian, the eldest, who lectured at the School of Economics. She was easily distinguished, a quiet, observant woman with kind eyes and a clever turn of phrase. She was older than Anne, her hair already grey. Martin, the farmer, who came next, was away on his farm. Nancy, twenty-seven or so, was married. She was staying there with her baby boy, because her husband was in the Navy. She was brighter and more talkative than Marian, but she had none of that hard, unkind wittiness which had made Anne long to do battle with Dora Dalloway. Betty, several years younger than Nancy, was separated by a gap of seven years from the twins, who played together like puppies and reminded Anne more than any of them of Tony. Dr. Thorn was a big, quiet man and his wife a

238

charming small slip of a woman, apparently his exact opposite. Anne saw that both were watching her almost critically at first, and then, after they had talked to her for a while, that they softened all at once and treated her as a friend.

"We're awfully fond of Tony," Mrs. Thorn said presently; and Anne knew that she was passed and approved.

She looked back on that evening as one of the happiest she had ever spent. She felt so at home with the Thorns. They might have been her own family, if she had had brothers and if her father had not been so set against educating his daughters. It was just as homely, just as full of life and laughter, with an added breadth and culture which actually, although Anne did not know it, extended back for generations. After the next day, spent lazily in the garden playing with the dogs and rambling with Betty and the twins in the forest, she felt as though she had known them for twenty years. When, in the evening, Betty announced that she had a headache and was going to bed early, Anne was not at all shy of staying in the garden with the rest of them. Indeed, she was enjoying herself so much that she would have been most disappointed had anyone suggested that she should go to bed too.

Mrs. Thorn lingered with Betty in the hall. Anne heard Betty say, "No, it's nothing really. I think I've got a cold. Aspirin and a hot bath'll settle it. I'll be all right in the morning."

But in the morning Betty was definitely not all right. Mrs. Thorn, bustling anxiously about the house, replied to Anne's questions. "Pain in her chest. She had pneumonia, five years ago. Her father's having a look at her."

Dr. Thorn came down, his stethoscope still hanging round his neck.

" 'Fraid so. It *may* just be flu, of course, but I'm afraid not."

There was a chorus. "Oh, *rotten* luck!"

"Poor old Betty, just when she might have had a holiday!"

And Anne, her hands clasped together in her eagerness, burst into the family condolences—"I can nurse her! Do let me stay and nurse her! May I, please?"

They all turned and stared at her, as though they had forgotten she was there.

"But—it's your holiday, too!" Evadne exclaimed.

"Doesn't matter. Do, please let me." She turned to the Doctor. "You know how nursing counts in pneumonia. I really am quite a good nurse, and I won't be in the way!"

Dr. Thorn looked her over and smiled. "It's most awfully good of you. And we should have to have someone, Marian's too busy and Mother's not very fit—"

Mrs. Thorn protested feebly. "But—you're tired, yourself. You *ought* to have your holiday."

"Betty's been so terribly decent to me," Anne said. "It would please me so much to pay it back a bit."

That settled it. Anne and Betty's mother went up together to the bedroom on the nursery floor. Betty had rolled up her one pillow and was leaning against it, breathing painfully. She smiled and held out a hand to Anne.

"I'm sorry—to be such a loon—when I meant to give you a good time. I must've got—flu. I got up—and then I fell over and had to—get back again."

"I should think you did!" Anne said. "Now you'll just stay there and do as you're told!"

Their eyes met, amused at the position in which they found themselves.

"I only want—to be left alone—" Betty said, and shut her eyes.

Anne and Mrs. Thorn scoured the linen-cupboard for pillows. A maid brought up coal, and Anne lit the fire herself because, she said, she knew how to do it without making a noise. She fetched hot water and bore down on the bed with a basin. Betty protested that she did not want to be moved.

"I won't hurt you. And you'll feel heaps better for it." Anne subjected her to the kindly firmness which St. Edmunds had inculcated, and Betty resigned herself. When she had been washed and, with Mrs. Thorn's help, propped up on her hillock of pillows, she achieved a smile.

"Goodness," she said. "What a difference it makes—to be done—by a proper nurse! I hardly knew—you were doing it. Last time, Marian nursed me—and it was hell!"

"You be quiet!" Anne admonished her.

"I'm glad you're here!" she insisted on adding.

Anne left her and went downstairs to make the patent

concoction of lemon and glucose with which the pneumonias at St. Edmunds were always fed.

"She's an awfully trying person to nurse. Won't let you do anything for her!" Marian confided gloomily. But Anne found her perfectly docile.

"It is pneumonia, isn't it?" she asked her father, later in the day.

"It is. But don't worry your head, you're strong enough for it."

"I know. And I shall be all right with Sister—with Anne."

There was little to do for Betty, really, except to ease her pain with poultices and see that she was comfortable and give her the frequent drinks she longed for. It was the need for incessant watchfulness which would become wearying. At any hour her heart might fail or her breathing become difficult. Anne insisted on staying up with her. The night was always the worst time.

She was restless. Anne arranged her pillows again and again, and once, because she was so hot, took matters into her own hands and sponged her all over with tepid water. After that, she settled down and slept.

The next day she was worse and the pain gave her no rest at all. So they gave her morphia and Anne's watchfulness could not be relaxed for an instant. Tony rushed down from town, but she could only smile at him and pant out, "Can you—spare Anne—for me?" and smile again when Anne said it didn't matter a toot whether he could or not.

In the afternoon, Mrs. Thorn took charge while Anne

slept. At six, Anne came back, because she could not bear to leave her patient during the critical hours of evening.

After that, the days and nights were one long vigil, for Betty grew steadily worse and weaker. Mrs. Thorn, Marian, and sometimes Evadne and Hugh, watched during the day while Anne stole some sleep. Martin, the farmer, came up from his farm. It seemed that Betty was a particular pet of his. He was the helper Anne liked best for her; he was solid and sure like the Doctor, yet quick at the uptake like Betty herself. Remembering Betty's hint— "it was hell"— he was the only one of them whom Anne would allow to help with the lifting. He could do that even better than she could herself. All the actual nursing she insisted on doing herself. Sometimes it was cold sponging that was needed, sometimes sedative and sometimes stimulant. She slipped down in the bed and had to be propped up again because she could only breathe sitting up. There was always something to be thought of.

Anne was happy. She was quiet and bright-eyed and gentle in the sickroom and she hummed about the house. She knew that, according to hospital law, she ought to have put on uniform, asked for another nurse, and definitely taken on either night or day duty, not done everything that was wanted in both night and day. But she wasn't a hospital nurse, here, she was Anne Lee, Betty's friend, who happened to have a thorough knowledge of nursing, and she could do as she liked. And what she liked was to nurse Betty herself.

One night, when Anne was alone with her, Betty just

243

lay and babbled. At first Anne could not hear what her interminable conversations were about or who they were supposed to be with. She did not try, seriously, to hear. People who were very ill always babbled. But towards morning the babble resolved itself into one phrase—"Tony—must have what he wants. Tony—must have—what he wants. Tony! Tony!" Even then Anne was too tired and too much occupied to pay much attention to it.

On the sixth day Betty was so bad that they were sure she would die. Anne, or one of them, was constantly holding the tube from the oxygen cylinder to her nostril, because that made her a little more comfortable. She lay there panting, a little blue, hardly conscious.

Tony had brought down the Senior Physician from the Central to see her. But he could do nothing which had not already been done. She had had vaccines, everything. The issue, if in anyone's hands, was in Anne's.

Tony was almost beside himself with sorrow. "She'll go, if the crisis doesn't come today," he said, when he had tiptoed for the second time from her room. "She's such a *useful* person! Why should we lose a person like that—and keep so many perfect old horrors?"

"It will come," Anne said.

Tony smiled. "You know much more about it than I do," he confessed, and Anne smiled too.

The crisis did come, at four in the morning. Anne was with her, as she lay panting, her pulse racing, moaning to herself. Martin was crouching by the fire. Anne had told him that she might want help that night, and he had stayed up. Suddenly, beads of sweat began to stand out on the girl's forehead. They could mean only one or two things—she was dying, or the crisis was taking place. Her breathing became almost imperceptible, but, it seemed to Anne, easier.

"You mustn't think she's better just because you want her to be," Anne gabbled to herself. "You must be sure." She prepared her hypodermic of strychnine and digitalin which the Doctor had left, in case it should be needed. Then her finger on Betty's wrist felt that the pulse had slowed down and was steady without being weaker, and she saw that the perspiration was bathing her all over. It was time for action.

She called to Martin—"Martin, give me that warm jacket!"

Martin jerked up swiftly and brought it, and Anne took off the soaked coat and put on the dry one and wrapped a blanket round.

Betty opened her eyes. "Drink o' water, please!" she said faintly.

Anne went to get some milk and brandy. The crisis was over, the only danger now was collapse. The brandy would guard against that.

Her pleasant reflections were disturbed rudely by Martin's cry from the bedside. "Anne! Do come!" She rushed back to the room.

"She moved, and then I couldn't feel her pulse," Martin was whispering, agonised.

The collapse had come all too soon. Betty lay cold and still. Anne whisked her pillow away and deftly laid her flat. "She'll be all right!" she said, from the depths of her experience. "She's sweated. They're always all right, once they've sweated." She injected the stimulant from the hypodermic.

"She's dead!" Martin whispered, unbelieving.

"She isn't. And she won't be, if we do the right thing. Get me some water-bottles and don't stand there like a boiled owl!"

Martin was galvanised into action by the abuse. He rushed away, and Anne stood waiting, hardly breathing in her anxiety. Betty must come back, she must. She was— they were all—so terribly fond of Betty.

Betty drew a shallow, shuddering breath. Her pulse tapped at Anne's fingertip and gradually grew in volume. Martin came hurrying back with the hot-water bottles.

"She'll do," said Anne.

The colour came back as they watched.

"She's sleeping now. There's nothing more to worry about."

Anne went away, then, to her own bed. She felt so weary that she could not do another thing. Martin tried feebly to keep her. "What shall I do if it happens again?" he pleaded.

"It won't," Anne said hard-heartedly. Then, relenting, "I shall wake if you call, I sleep awfully lightly, and I'm only next door."

She slept for eight hours. When she woke and stumbled into the next room, Betty was awake and smiling at her.

Tony came in, threw one look at Betty, and then had eyes for no one but Anne. "Jove, old thing, you do know how to nurse! I never thought you'd save her!"

Anne was conscious of a great relief that it was all over. That was all she thought of. It was something like the relief she had felt when she knew that her Father was not going to live on, paralysed, but die without having known what was taking place.

There was still nursing to be done, of course, and Anne did it and enjoyed it. She seemed quite simply to have become one of the Thorn family. After ten days she and Betty went down to Martin's farm in Kent. None of them would hear of her going home.

CHAPTER 2

ON her first morning at the farm, Anne was awakened by a puzzling combination of soft scents and sounds. She had never in her life stayed at a farm before. She had lived in the great towns and spent her summer holidays in apartments at the sea.

First, the birds awoke. One tentative pipe, then silence. Then a little trickle of notes. Then a series of couplets, as if someone was practising so as to be quite sure of his song presently. Then a chatter of sparrows—she recognised that—and then a shrill squeaking which drew rapidly nearer and was gone as a shower of black meteors fled past the window. Anne caught sight of forked tails. "Swallows," she whispered to her drowsy self. "Swallows!"

The cuckoo called softly, far away. Then, close at hand, another new sound began: "Quack-*quack!* Quack-*quack!*"

Anne kneeled on the bed and put her head out of the window. Below her was a square of grass, and on it a black hut out of which came a single file of white ducks, solemnly waddling, yellow feet splayed, yellow beaks turning this way and that, intent on their journey to the pond which gleamed away to the left. Anne laughed at them.

To the right, a line of red-tiled buildings stood. From them came a subdued clatter of pails, a gentle lowing and the busy "tork-tork!" of hens.

Shifting her gaze to the front, she drew a breath of delight. Before her stretched a sea of white foam, stirring in the morning breeze. She caught a glimpse of whitened stems beneath it, of grass between the stems. It was May, and the cherries were in blossom. The sun rose beyond them and stained them faintly pink.

A group of oast-houses caught her eye and fascinated her; queer red pyramids, capped by grotesque cowls. The fragrance of the cherry blossom floated up, mixed with the smell of wood-smoke and of the cowyard, warm, earthy, friendly. Drawing back, she caught the room's scent—lavender from the sheets, and the faint tang of the oil from the lamp which had lit her to bed. The whole made up the indescribable scent of a farmhouse, which forever afterwards made Anne feel happy and at home.

A man came round the corner from the cow-houses, two shining pails swinging from his brown hands. His shirt was open at the neck, his hair, wind-blown, stood up sturdily from his brow. A pair of grey eyes looked up frankly at Anne and he smiled. Martin Thorn was at work again. She waved to him. They were such a dear, friendly family, she could hardly believe that three weeks ago she had only known by hearsay of their existence; and here she was pitchforked into the very heart of their life.

Someone knocked at her door. Mrs. Batty, Martin's housekeeper, came in with a big can of hot water. She was a little rosy countrywoman. Anne had liked her at first sight. She could not imagine the Thorns with unpleasant domestics.

They entered into conversation about Betty's breakfast and whether Anne would like a bath.

Anne breakfasted alone. Martin had had his, hours ago,

and Betty's was taken up to her on a tray. Sitting in the cool dining-room, looking out on the leafy garden, Anne felt that she had never known such peace. The bustle, the noise, the bickering of hospital life, here seemed impossible. Yet this place had a bustle of its own. She was sure that Martin and Mrs. Batty had no more leisure than she was used to herself.

Martin came in when she had nearly finished, and drank a cup of coffee with her. Another smell came with him, and she sniffed, inquiring. He laughed, and said, "Cows. I've been milking."

Anne said, "I like it."

She took stock of Martin Thorn. She had noticed him before only as a solid person who might be depended upon to help with Betty. Now she became interested in him as an individual. He was broad and strong, she knew that already; fairer than the rest of the Thorns, with more blue in his grey eyes than they had, but with Betty's own steady look in them and just the sober twinkle of amusement which came and went in Betty's. He showed to advantage in his rough country clothes. Anne had never met a farmer before. She decided that she liked them. Martin's quiet, natural way of talking and then falling into silence was a pleasant contrast to the bedside manner which a doctor seems never able quite to shake off. She did not, of course, think of Tony as a doctor. The bedside manner had not got hold of him yet.

Martin answered her. "Would you like to see where it comes from? I can show you round, and then you'll know your way if you want to explore."

She rose. "I'd love it. I'll just see Betty's got all she wants."

"I'll wait here for you," he said, and began to fill his pipe.

Anne came down with a coat and they went along the stone hall and out at the back door together, collecting a spaniel and a terrier on the way, and across the square of grass where the ducks had been, into one of the tiled barns. There was a sound of chewing, and Anne found herself looking across a manger into a pair of enormous, liquid eyes.

She drew back. "I'm—rather afraid of cows!" she confessed. "They're so big and horny!"

Martin's sunburned face became a mass of little wrinkles. He said nothing, but stretched up to the rack where the hay was and brought down a little wriggling handful of fur.

"D'you like this better?"

Anne made a cup of her hands and he laid the furry bundle in them. It mewed and moved its head about aimlessly and clawed her. She hugged it and laughed.

"It's very young! Yes, I like this. It isn't that I don't like the cows, exactly; I'm just not used to them and I don't know what they're likely to do next."

"They're very gentle, once they know you," Martin said. "Sometimes one will take a dislike to you and give you a kick or bat you over the head with her tail. It's generally a new one, and I always think it means she's been ill-treated. But it's no good trying to milk a cow that does that. She'll hold on to it and you won't get any. You have to turn her over to someone else. As a rule they're placid enough. They're lovely to look at, don't you think? See her broad brow—and Daisy's coat here, like satin."

Anne contrived, led by his enthusiasm, to see some beauty in the great sleek creatures. One little Alderney she really did like, with its pretty colouring and its dainty, slender ankles. Martin seemed pleased with her for picking it out as one to be admired.

He took her into another shed. "There's a new calf in here, if you like young things—"

It was a sturdy little chestnut bull calf with a curly forelock and blue eyes with long lashes. Martin offered it his fist and it staggered to him and curled its long tongue round his hand.

"Rough, like a cat's—see? They use them as combs!"

Anne touched the tongue and laughed at her own boldness.

They came out into the farmyard. Two small piebald pigs scuttled away from them, squeaking.

"There are such a lot of *funny* things on a farm," Anne said. "One couldn't get dried-up and grim, like town people do."

"Yes, there's plenty to laugh at, if you're the sort of person who finds animals amusing. I do, of course," Martin said. "It's seeing them as people, as if they were human, I think. I dare say that little pig wasn't thinking about me at all when he bolted that apple under my nose and looked up out of one eye—but he looked as guilty as a naughty schoolboy!"

"He did—goodness, what's that?"

"That? Why, the little pig's mother!"

An enormous pink sow, with a turned-up nose and the most evil expression, wobbled across in front of them, grunting. Anne shuddered and Martin scratched the sow's back with a stick. "I bet she's no worse than some of your slum mothers—"

"She's very like some of them," Anne said.

They entered the cherry orchard, cool and damp under its canopy of white tassels. An urchin scampered away from them and clambered into a tree.

"He's one of Mrs. Batty's boys. She's got a whole tribe of them. Batty's the cowman. They have the cottage across the meadow," Martin said.

Anne silently contrasted the lot of the Batty boy with that of the London children to whom she was used; then put the London children deliberately out of her mind.

Beyond the orchard was a great meadow of short turf. On one side it fell away into a dell, full of uncurling bracken and scoured with rabbit-burrows. Hundreds of rabbits skipped away at their approach, and Anne must stand and watch them bob up one by one and come back with watchful ears. On the other side it was open, except for scattered oak trees. Martin took her to the top of a rise and she looked out over the Medway, a gleaming streak with hop-fields and blue hills beyond it.

"I keep this bit for the sheep," Martin was telling her. "I've still got some lambs—see?"

They watched the antics of a group of them, ridiculous creatures with furry leggings. Anne turned a glowing face to Martin: "Oh, look at them—look at them." She was entirely unselfconscious. She had simply never seen such things before. She watched the lambs and Martin watched her, with a little sober smile on his face. He felt just like that about the lambs himself.

"I could watch them all day!" she said.

"You may," he told her. "I'll have to get back now, but there's no reason why you should come. Go anywhere you like, as long as you shut all the gates—"

Anne smiled at him. "I think I'd be always good if I lived in a place like this. Heaps to do, and all these lovely places, and no one to backbite and hate one. You've no idea of the difference. You can't have."

"Animals are pleasanter than humans. More Christian," he allowed. "Of course, it's a hard life in a way. One works hard, and sometimes a bad season comes and makes all the hard work seem wasted. It keeps one from getting a swelled head—one's so helpless if nature takes the bit in her teeth. Keeps one's brain active, too. If you do have a bad year, you've got to find a way to make it up to yourself—or starve. The bad farmer will bet, or borrow, and come a cropper as often as he makes a bit to tide him over. That's not a good plan. I spent last winter inventing a tractor wheel, and the one before I tried out a pig-food on the lines of those native foods which are germinated before they're used."

"Did they—make a bit to tide you over?" she asked.

"Oh yes. The food's patented and most of the up-to-date people are using it. And the wheel got the gold medal at the Agricultural Show. I'm just beginning to get Royalties on it."

"But it's not everyone who can do things like that," Anne said.

"No. But if more of them would use their brains on their work and not on fantastic plans to get something for nothing, there'd be less talk about 'the plight of the farmers.' They've got no sense, most of them. Of course, making something for nothing's an awfully tempting thing to think of, and we're not an educated body on the whole, worse luck." He looked across the fields and then down at her. "I don't know why I'm holding forth like this. You're a good listener."

"I'm interested," Anne said at once. She really was. She so seldom heard anyone talk any shop outside her own. She did like to hear people talk of things they really knew about. It was speculation which was not backed by knowledge which bored her. She said so, and Martin nodded and agreed.

"Nonsense, like the twins', or horse sense. That's what I like to hear. None of your vapourings. You should hear some of the vapourings of the students Marian brings home! Aged about eighteen and discussing world politics as though they'd the experience of sixty. And spiritualism, that's the sort of thing that gets them, where you can have any opinions you like because none of it's capable of proof. I'm not educated. I went into the Army when I ought to have been at Cambridge. But I do at any rate know I'm not."

"That's what I feel like myself—"

Anne had thrown a last look at the lambs and they were walking back together. "I must get Betty's breakfast tray.

255

She'll be wanting to get up," she said in excuse as Martin hesitated. As they went, she shot questions at him, and he answered them, carefully, taking her intelligence for granted as she took his knowledge. She could not think of what situation she was reminded. Then she remembered the old night-rounds with Ronald Dalloway. Only Martin had none of Ronald's pompous conceit. He was older, of course, and simpler, than Ronald. A nice, honest, trustable person. All the Thorns were trustable.

He pointed out an old, gnarled tree in the cherry orchard. "That's the one we call the step-tree," he said. "You can get right to the top of it by the time you're about ten. We all started on it at the age of six—or younger, it may have been. It's too old to bear much fruit, but I haven't the heart to grub it."

"Six? Were you here then?" she asked.

"We used to spend all our school holidays here. It belonged to Mother's father. It's her's now, I rent it from her."

Anne was quiet, imagining the Thorns running wild. She spoke her thoughts. "It's the dearest old place. No wonder you're all so nice."

He smiled again, at that. "I'm glad you like it. It isn't everyone who takes to a farm. We simply love it, of course."

She was thinking, "There ought to be children here. Not only the cowman's boys." She did not speak that thought aloud. That was Martin's business. And after all, the twins were hardly more than children.

When she reached the house, she found a letter from

Tony; a letter full of excitement that she should be on the farm which he knew so well, urging her to be sure to make Betty show her this place and that; full of the horribleness of Princess Ida's without her, although, he said, the holiday Sister seemed to know her job; he was glad he had only a few more days there. The letter was almost like Tony himself chattering. Anne held it, half-ashamed, against her cheek for a second, then tucked it into the pocket of her jumper.

She made Betty's bath ready and tidied her room for her, and then they sat in the garden in the sun; and presently strolled about, for Betty must show Anne the barn where they used to have a castle in the hay, the cave-like insides of the oast-houses, and the dairy. There they found Martin again, and he showed them the intricacies of the cooler and the separator.

"Why, it's just like a Theatre! Just as clean!" Anne said, and Martin bowed absurdly and told her about the rigorous inspections to which they were subject and pointed out the "clean milk" ritual which the milkers had to go through. The cowman and the boy, rough and sunburnt, moved about with a gentle caution which, to look at them, one would have thought impossible.

After lunch they sat in the sun again and Betty slept and Anne read drowsily. After tea—a real country tea of Mrs. Batty's homemade bread and country butter—they ambled into the village. It was the most restful existence imaginable.

That day was typical of the days which followed. The fine warm weather held and Betty regained strength rapidly. She was able to take Anne for the rambles which she and her brothers had inherited from their mother and her brothers, by river and hop-garden, up to the blue chalk hills and into the green water-meadows. There was one very special expedition, through a village so old and lovely that Anne could hardly believe it was true, into a green valley shut off by pinewoods, where a little river runs; it sings by a field-path, rushes down a miniature waterfall, then broadens into a wide, slow mere with monkey-flowers nodding all around and the velvety leaves of mint giving off their heavy scent; then feeds a white mill with a water-wheel, and finally disappears underground to come out again no one knows where.

Martin's eyes met Betty's, twinkling, when they came home from that walk, still subdued and glowing after the sight of so much beauty.

"There aren't more than half a dozen people in the world we've taken there," he told Anne. "We're so afraid of it being invaded. It's so lovely and so peaceful, now. We only take our very chosen there."

"Anne was a chosen ages ago," Betty said.

"I guessed she was," Martin said, his eyes contentedly upon her. And again Anne could not think of what she was reminded.

She had never had such a holiday. She deliberately put out of her head all thoughts of Princess Ida's. When she thought of Tony, it was in terms of the weekend at Glynde. She refused to let anything worry her. The present was too wonderful for anything to interfere with her enjoyment of it.

CHAPTER 3

1

ONE night when Anne had begun to undress, Betty knocked on her door and came in, laughing, with hardly a pause.

"Martin's got two new baby pigs down in the kitchen. The mother overlaid them and he's reviving them. They're collapsed. He thought you might like to come and help."

"Pigs? How priceless!" Anne caught up her dressing-gown. "Was the mother that old horrible we saw in the yard? She looked wicked enough for anything!" She thought of herself, "What nonsense I'm talking! And they don't mind a bit how silly one is, the darlings!"

Martin had the two pink, snub-nosed creatures in blankets in a basket by the kitchen fire. They lay quite quietly. Anne could only tell that they were breathing by the quivering of their little stout sides. Martin made room for her beside them.

"Why—they're exactly like babies!" She stroked one of them gently with her finger and found that its bristles were like silk. She bent lower, and smelt a fragrance much more like that of a very young baby than of a pigsty. She looked up and laughed. "Those Pigs! I always thought pigs were filthy creatures! These are simply sweet!"

One of them had a great bruise on its head. The other, as Martin turned it over, seemed unmarked.

"They're getting better," he said. "They're warm now

and they've stopped shivering. We'll give them a drink."

He produced a medicine bottle of warm milk and brandy and began to fit a teat on to it. He was clumsy, and Anne mechanically stretched out and took it from him. He lifted one of the little pigs out of the basket and offered it to her. It hung, unresisting, his hands under its armpits, blinking.

"You do it. I'm sure you're better at bottling babies than I am."

She sat down and took the little thing in the crook of her arm. It looked up at her out of its pink, ugly little eyes, and in a minute had the teat in its mouth and was sucking greedily with great swilling noises. Anne chuckled. "Ridiculous thing! I'd no idea you did this with them! D'you often have to?"

Martin and Betty stood watching her, amused at her preoccupation with her task. To Martin she seemed just a charming woman, still with much of the child in her, as he had in himself. To Betty, the change in her was extraordinary—from the starched, repressed, efficient Ward Sister to this laughing creature who had never seen a new pig or a baby chicken and who confessed unashamed that she was afraid of cows.

"Fairly often," Martin said, "if one wants to save the whole litter. They'll be valuable one day."

"For pork," Betty put in wickedly, and Anne hugged her grotesque infant the tighter and made him choke, and they all laughed again.

They fed the other pig and packed them into their basket for the night. Anne offered quite seriously to sit up with them, but Martin would have none of it.

"I shall take them up to my room. They'll want another bottle presently."

Anne simply shouted at the idea of him solemnly preparing a bottle for a baby pig in the middle of the night. "You'll never wake up!" she teased.

"Oh yes I shall. I'm used to this sort of thing," he told her soberly, and, when she wrinkled up her nose at him, exerted himself to add, "You just wait! I'll come and thunder on your door every time I turn them over!"

He went off with the basket, and Betty and Anne put out the lamps and raced up after him hand in hand. At the top, Betty flung her arms round Anne's neck, and Anne held on to her for a minute as though she would hold on to this happiness and never let it go.

As she undressed, she thought how absurdly fond of Betty she had grown, perhaps because Betty had been so completely dependent on her during her illness. She simply hated the idea of leaving the girl behind. Tony was coming for the weekend on the following day, and on the Monday the two of them would go back to town together. Anne felt a hollow dismay at the prospect of returning to Princess Ida's.

She slept fitfully that night. Once she thought she heard footsteps outside her door, and waited for Martin's thunder. But it did not come, and when she opened the door to look there was nothing but darkness and silence.

In the morning, she found that a mood of melancholy had descended upon her. She could not catch up the threads of talk which Martin tossed to her, only look at

261

him stupidly and say yes and no. She found him watching her once, curiously, and although she smiled she felt almost irresistibly that she must cry.

"Hating the idea of going back to work?" he asked her presently, after a silence. She nodded, grateful for his understanding. So many people presumed a personal reason for any change in one's mood.

"Simply loathing it."

Martin said, "Um," and took out his pipe as though he must have something to fidget with. "You'll soon get used to it again."

"I suppose I shall. You can't think how I've enjoyed this. You've all been so frightfully decent to me."

He opened his eyes. "What rubbish! It's you who've been decent to us! Giving up your whole holiday to us!"

She could not, somehow, explain how dull her holiday would have been if she had gone home. She remembered to ask about the pigs.

"Oh, they went back to mummy this morning. They'll be all right now," he said.

When she had seen to Betty's breakfast, she went out by herself. She made her way to the old step-tree, for she had a mind to see what it felt like to sit high among its bobbing tassels. Mrs. Batty's boy, hidden behind a tree-trunk, gaped at the sight of the staid grown woman carefully testing each foothold as she scrambled up.

Anne settled herself as high as she could climb, on a flat branch with an elbow, rubbed smooth by the seats of many restless Thorns. The cherry blossom tapped her cheeks and her hands, and all round her was its faint, intoxicating scent of almonds. She could not see the grass below her. Above, clouds sailed in the blue, faint reflections of the white masses of bloom. In this fairyland, detached from earth, Anne knew that she could do that which she had come out to do. She could think out her problems clearly and decide, once for all, about her future, while she was still a free, live person before she went back into her shell.

It did not occur to her to seek help by talking to anyone. She had settled her own affairs for so long, so long maintained a quiet reserve even from her sisters. Besides, all the people she might have talked to—Betty, Martin, Tony—were too intimately concerned to give her good advice. Belsize would never understand. Angela she could not reach, and Edith and Violet were impossible.

First, she thought about herself, tried to see herself from outside. "Tony's Anne," at the Thorns' house and at the farm, was undoubtedly an attractive person; friendly, entertaining, efficient, perhaps even charming. The Thorns at any rate seemed to find her so. One of the most difficult things in the world is to become a friend to a person who has done you a good turn; only if the friendship is already there, in fact or in potential, is gratitude anything but an embarrassment to it. But the Thorns looked on her as a friend without a doubt. Yes, the self of the present time could be approved of; but there was also the self who was "Sister Jack Horner" to be taken into account. She was a different person altogether. In a few years she would be, at best, a Sister Southcliffe, at worst, a cranky, sarcastic Martinette. She could see herself as either. And Sister Southcliffe was sweet, but she was narrow, starched, ignorant; a spinster, not a wife for a young man.

She would not consider Tony yet. There was Betty to think of; dear charming, loyal, dependable Betty. She had not known it was possible to love anyone as she loved Betty; she was such a comrade and yet such a child. Anne felt that there was something maternal in her love for Betty. If they could have lived together for the rest of their lives, she would always be glad to wait on the girl, to guide her, to bully her gently, to be teased by her; in short, to manage her, just as a mother must imagine fondly that she will live with her young daughter.

Having cleared her mind about her affection for Betty, she deliberately let Tony into her thoughts. She loved Betty. She loved Tony more than Betty, more fiercely, more possessively. But it was the same sort of love, the downward sort. She remembered how proud he was of her, how he threw up his head at passers-by in frank ridiculous triumph when they looked at her happy face. Then, how he talked! And she, as always, listened and laughed and edged in little comments. Life was an affair of froth, still, with Tony. Yet she knew that there was a serious Tony underneath, who could discuss all sorts of abstract things intelligently, and who had a rigid standard of conduct which must always be adhered to. She felt that she knew nothing about that serious Tony, really, and nothing about the rules by which his life was governed. She knew that he would be tolerant if she did not conform to his rules; but would she be tolerant, after two more years of immersion in little things, if he did not conform to hers? Wouldn't she be rigid, unchangeable, un-understanding, then?

She could not even help him whisk his froth, as Betty could. She could only applaud him when he anticked, be a sort of guardian to him rather than a comrade. He was younger and weaker than she was, would always be weaker, even when the years had smoothed out the difference in their ages.

It wasn't that she was going to give him up to Betty because Betty wanted him and Betty was her friend; it was just that she knew she would spoil his life, as it might have been, to make her own, if she married him. She was sure of that.

She sat with her hands in her lap, her mind a blank. There trickled into it dreams of the time when she and Tony would live together. It would be such fun, to mother Tony, to depend on him a little as one would a grown-up son. She would always be happy, doing so, and it was a relationship which she could not imagine coming to an end, at least on her side.

Her honesty forced her on. And on Tony's side? Would he be happy, being mothered? Did a man want to be mothered, when he was grown up? A woman did not, she knew very well.

She watched a cloud like a lizard slide across her patch of sky. As it vanished, she knew that her earlier doubts had been right. She could not go on with this lovely, delicate, upside-down relationship with Tony. Because her charity had not yet dried up, because it had budded and flowered in this country setting, she must force it back into prison—for good.

She began to make plans, quite calmly now. She would go back to Princess Ida's and make Jack Horner ward the best ward for children in the whole of London. Perhaps it would not be long before the little Assistant Matron retired—she was getting old—and she would move up another step towards being Matron herself. Even now she was no longer the most junior Sister. When she was Matron not only Jack Horner ward, but the whole hospital, should be the best of its kind, not only in London but in the whole of England. Why, it wasn't so bad an outlook when you faced it squarely. A few months ago she would have been thrilled by it, if she had dared to think of it at all. Even the nastiness of the other Sisters would not be able to hurt her any more. Nothing would be able to hurt her any more. She was numb.

From her comfortable numbness she awoke with a start. How on earth was she going to tell Tony?

2

When Tony came, in the afternoon, she made him take her to the magic river, and there, sitting in a field spangled with buttercups, with the blue water dancing beyond the monkey-flowers, she told him.

"Tony!"

"Anne!" he mocked her, so evidently bubbling with happiness to be with her again.

"No, Tony, please. It's serious. Horribly serious. I can't

keep my promise." Her voice sank to a whisper, but she made it speak. "I can't marry you."

He glanced up at her, his laughter frozen, his boyish face suddenly white. Anne caught her breath at the whiteness, but realised more clearly than ever that she was right. It was such a very boyish face.

He asked her the usual questions. Had he done anything to spoil things? Was it that she couldn't wait so long? Was there someone else?

She shook her head. And, because she knew that Tony's intellectual honesty matched her own, she told him exactly what she thought.

"I love you more than anything, and I think, if I married you, I always should. But I'm older than you, in more than years, and I'm stronger. Yes, I am, Tony, it's not just conceit—"

"You wait! I'll beat you with a stick, if you like!" Tony's spirits were reviving at this silly line of reasoning.

She smiled. "You know quite well that you wouldn't. And if you tried to, I should run away, and that wouldn't make either of us frightfully happy, would it?"

"It's all such rubbish," he said. "I love you—just adore you, Anne, you know that—"

She looked away, because she was frightened. How could she hold out against him, if he talked like that?

"And you love me—you've just said so. And we're so happy when we're together—Oh, Anne, we've said all this before!"

"I know," she said sadly. "That's the point. Or one of the points. I've had time to think about it, and I think the same as I thought then, only more so. I was wrong ever to let myself believe you'd convinced me."

"I'll convince you again, if you give me half a chance," he grumbled. "I was silly ever to let you go away from me." But she shook her head.

"You won't. This lovely, silly sort of happiness won't last forever, it can't, it's not strong enough. I should turn into a hard old bully, and you'd either run away or get fat and flabby. Oh, Tony, I've seen people like that. I do know, really I do! I know myself!" She was half laughing, but she was deadly serious. She wanted him to convince her, but she knew he couldn't. She knew she was right. She knew it was Betty and not herself who would make him happy.

He rolled over and looked up at her.

"Anne, darling, we're most awfully good friends, aren't we?"

She met his eyes, as she always did, and smiled. "Why, yes. I think we are."

"It's simply awful, to look forward to not marrying you, Anne."

"I know," she said, so softly that he could only just hear.

"The funny part is," he went on, "that you haven't really hurt me. Wounded me, I mean. You might have, you know. I ought to be hating you for saying I'm not as strong as you are. But I'm not hating you in the least, because it's true. Only, I don't think I should mind. I'm not a bit keen on being master in my own house. D'you see? It's not the sort of thing that appeals to me. Does that make any difference?"

Anne thought, "This is worse than ever. How can I even be sure whether I'm right or wrong, if he talks like that?"

Tony was speaking again. "Let's think it over again, Anne. That last part of it, I mean. I'm afraid there's not much of the dominating male about me. When I'm a bit older I shall be quite happy trotting about in a velvet coat and saying, 'Yes dear,' to everything my wife suggests. *I* know people like that, and they get on jolly well. Perfectly content with themselves. Anne, don't be a loon. Everything's—sort of rarefied here. One wants to do noble deeds—"

So he had felt like that, too!

"P'raps it's because so many kids have grown up here," he said. "Played knight-errants and so on. Their dreams are still floating about. We can't decide here, it's not our proper setting. Wait till we get back to town. Please, Anne, be sensible."

Anne felt a shock of surprise, and more surprise at her own surprise. What was one's proper setting—the usual one, or a place where one felt completely at home, like this? She was quite, quite sure that she was right and that she was never going to marry Tony. And, watching him, she felt certain that he would in time recognise her rightness. Only she could not hurt him by forcing it upon him now.

She said reluctantly, "All right, Tony, we'll wait. Only, we must really think about it, not just drift. And you must remember you're free to—be friends with anyone else if you want to."

He just grinned.

They walked home together through the fields, not taking hands like children as they had done on the downs, but walking soberly side by side as though they had now grown up. Their faces had not quite their usual colour, and lines showed about their mouths which had not been there before. It was only the outside of the situation which was restrained and docile, and that was because they were both by nature and training reserved and disciplined. Inside, they were profoundly shaken by such a fundamental difference of opinion.

On Monday, Anne went back to town alone. Tony was not due at his new job for a few weeks, and she persuaded him to stay. The three of them saw her off, and she waved to them with the greatest affection but with no regrets. They had given her a wonderful time, and they and the country together had taught her that she could be mistress of herself. She would never again be dependent on things outside herself for happiness, whether circumstances or persons. She took off her ring and buried it, in its velvet-lined case, in her bag. Those two jewels of memory, the weekend at Glynde and this month with the Thorns, she buried deep in her mind. She had chosen her way, herself. Presently she would be able to take out her jewels and look at them without a trace of bitterness. Her one fear was that Tony might not be able to do the same. She could not bear to hurt Tony.

CHAPTER 4

BACK at Princess Ida's, with the babies squalling outside Anne's sitting-room, there was little opportunity for looking at jewels. Sister Theatre barked spitefully at her throughout supper, Sister Outpatients came up to her room and told her exactly what was the general opinion of people who grabbed holidays and left others, more tired than themselves, to do the work. And Anne found, to her disgust, that she minded their gibes just as much as ever. She bit back her retorts, looked down tolerantly at Sister Theatre and offered Sister Outpatients a chocolate. She wasn't going to model herself on them, anyway. "Happiness consists in a man's success in preserving his own being," Martin had quoted to her, one day. She was going to preserve her own composite being and hope that it would bring her happiness.

On her first free afternoon, she went to a florist, and ordered a great bunch of flowers to be sent to Mrs. Thorn. She must show, somehow, that she appreciated them so much. Then she thought she would go and see Belsize, and rang up St. Edmunds to find out if she was still there. She was doing temporary duty in one of the wards, and would be off duty in half an hour. Anne arrived before the half-hour was up, and wondered whether she could penetrate to the Matron's office to thank her for the testimonial to Princess Ida's. It was not really the Matron who was responsible for it, of course, it was dear Sister Southcliffe, and the Martinette, and all of them. She must go and see them too. Silly of her to have harboured resentment all this time because they had made Paley a Sister instead of her. She would have greater opportunities now than ever Paley would.

She recorded her official thanks, and raced upstairs to offer her more heartfelt personal ones. Sister Southcliffe patted her on the shoulder and wished her all the luck in the world. Sister Theatre, thinner and straighter than ever, very much the Martinette today, relaxed sufficiently to tell her that she had the makings of a good nurse in her if she would only learn to control herself, and made her feel like a Pro again. George thumped his polished counter in his pleasure at the sight of her, all rosy and sunburnt; prophesied a husband from among the younger Surgeons, and winked a dreadful, knowing wink when she dropped her eyes.

As she crossed the great court to the Nurses' Home, she reflected that, without the discipline, the impartial justice of St. Edmunds, she would never have had either the strength or the foresight to have given up Tony. It was just that knowledge, which St. Edmunds had forced upon her, that certain actions lead blindly and inevitably to certain definite conclusions, which had made her see what she must do.

She found Belsize, a little more florid, surely, than a month ago, changing to go out. She had not told her anything about Tony. She was glad, now, that she had not. She accepted with meekness and inward amusement the hint of condescension in the manner of prospective wife to declared spinster.

Belsize chattered about her house and her furniture. She was going, now, to the house, to make up her mind about the colour of some chintz. Lee must come with her and see it. And then she was going to tea with her fiancé's people and Jack himself might rush in at about five, he did sometimes. Yes, Lee must certainly come too and see them all. They were only too pleased to welcome her friends. And now, what had Lee been doing all this time?

They set out on a bus for Clapham Common, and Anne told her about her holiday and the nursing of Betty Thorn. Belsize, who was even more town-bred than Anne, called her a saint and cackled at the idea of her buried in the country.

"Though I must say you look as if it agreed with you," she said, slewing round to look at her companion. "You're lovelier than ever! I can't think why you don't get married! Don't go about it in the proper way, I expect. Too darned independent. They like you a bit timid, you know. Dewy and clinging. Like to feel top-dog."

If she had been less fascinated by her own flow of talk, she would have seen the quirk at the corner of Anne's curly mouth. Tony, top-dog, with something dewy and clinging! No, Belsize didn't know everything, not by a long way.

Belsize was giving her good advice. "You mustn't let that affair with young Dalloway put you off trying again. They're not all like that. He's done jolly well for himself, did you know? Got off with Sir Charles Terrington's daughter. Did you know he'd been knighted—Terrington? I forget why. So young Ronald'll get his ambitions, a rich

273

wife and a house in Harley Street. He got his Fellowship last year and he's Surgical Registrar now. Gets a lot of private work with Sir Charles, too. He'll be on the Staff before long. He's got such a way with him. But, as I was saying, you mustn't be put off because your first shot missed. I tried my hand at half a dozen Residents before I met Jack—"

But she laughed as she said it. She was too good-natured and too happy herself, to sneer.

Anne asked about Paley, and Belsize exploded into loud laughter. "She's simply awful! My goodness, they did themselves a bad turn over her! Everyone knew they did except Matron's office! She teaches even the oldest Sisters their jobs and everyone loathes her. I think they'll make her Matron of the Convalescent Home at St. Leonards— that's the farthest away of them—before long, just to get rid of her! So"—with a grin—"don't be jealous if she's a Matron before you are, it won't be a reward of merit! I say, look"—Belsize peered over the side of the bus, which was careering through Stockwell—"that's awfully like Jack! That big one, with the curly hair! Of course, Jack's better looking."

Anne followed her pointing finger to a bull-necked young man, hatless, red-faced, who looked as though he ought to have been pushing a fruit-barrow. He felt their eyes on him and looked up and grinned, and Belsize waved to him.

"*Is* it him?" Anne asked incredulously, and she giggled. "Goodness, no. But I'm so happy I couldn't help it. I shall never set eyes on him again, anyway. And I'm not in uniform."

The house was one of those small, pretty new ones, part of a group built round a close with trees on the grass. Anne tried to imagine herself and Tony living in it, and failed. She could see herself, bustling about the little efficient kitchen. But Tony did not fill the role of the shirt-sleeved person who dug in the garden and tinkered with the wireless and the sash-lines. She chuckled at herself. Why should he, after all? He wasn't going to be a City clerk, and a G.P. was more likely to tinker with his car than with gardens. She turned to listen to Belsize, who was telling her exactly where each piece of furniture was going to stand.

It did not take long to decide about the chintz. Belsize locked the door importantly with her own key. "We'd better get on the Tube, now. It's more direct than the bus."

"Are you sure you'd like me to come?" Anne demurred, suddenly shy. She did not feel drawn towards the people of someone who had the look of that bull-necked young man.

"Of *course* you must come! They like to meet my friends!" Belsize assured her. She went on to explain, "His father's an old dear. Likes his own way, but still. His mother's—well, she's been a bit of a gay one in her day, I should say. But you can't have everything, there's always a snag somewhere. And Jack's all right. I can manage him. And I shan't see much of her, I shall take care of that—"

Anne found them much as she had expected, in a house full of wealth and empty of taste; Mother, stout and

275

blustering, in rich blue satin, pearls and yellow hair; Father, thin and nervous, but ready to lay down the law; the daughter, who had been Belsize's patient, still languid and a little inclined to patronise; a younger brother who frankly admired Belsize's red and white comeliness and began at once to roll an eye at Anne; and a tomboy of a girl who attended the local High School. They all talked, all the time; Mother about furniture and linen, in which her likings disagreed totally, it seemed, with Belsize's; Father, when he could get a word in, prophesying great things for the Labour Party, which had just come into power. The boy tried to impress with recitals of the dances he had been to, and the girl squatted engagingly at Anne's side and chattered about hockey matches and music exams. It was their idea of entertaining their guests, who had to do nothing but listen.

Tea was nearly over when Jack came in. He was very much indeed like the young man whom they had seen from the bus. He threw an arm round Belsize's neck— Anne realised with surprise that she had never known her name was Rose—and lifted her on to his knee, and the talk went on, with humorous additions from the engaged pair. They were all perfectly pleased with themselves.

Anne left them soon, protesting that she ought to have stayed for the evening, and travelled back to town by herself. Surely Belsize was noisier, less well-mannered than she had been in the old St. Edmunds days. Or had Anne grown more fastidious? The two of them, then, had been equally ignorant, equally cut off from civilising influences, to all appearance much alike. And yet, Belsize had been attracted to these pleasant, vulgar people, and had adopted their ways and their half-educated catchwords without a thought; and Anne, to the gentle, clever Thorns and to Tony, who had no catchwords and recognised truth and untruth when they saw them. And Belsize was successful and happy, and Anne made boss-shots and could not think why she was not very unhappy indeed. There's always a snag somewhere, Belsize said. Anne wondered if she was flying too high, expecting perfection; if she was being silly and high-falutin in giving up Tony just because he was such a boy; if, presently, she would settle down happily with some such uncritical half-loaf as Belsize's Jack, and knew that she would not; wondered what Angela's husband was like; and finally, with an effort, visualised herself, cool and starched, running, first, Jack Horner ward, and presently the hospital itself, as no hospital had ever been run before; soothing anxious relatives, blushing a little under their gratitude, fulfilling on a different plane her old ambition of having a ward of her own at St. Edmunds. It was a vision almost refreshing, after the opulent household at Wimbledon.

Mr. Salter, the Senior Surgeon, had shown his appreciation of Anne's good work by saying both to her and to the Matron how glad he was to see her back. Sister Theatre had given notice in a fit of pique which Anne suspected had been provoked on purpose by the Matron, and behaved like a demon to Anne for the few weeks before she left. The nurse from St. Edmunds who had done Anne's holiday duty had applied for and been appointed in Sister Theatre's place.

Tony wrote to her from the farm, the same affectionate, excited letters as usual. Anne was uncertain at first whether to answer them or not. She decided that it would be idiotic and unfair not to, since they were such good friends. She wanted so much to stay good friends with Tony. She couldn't bear not to. She began by telling him that she had not changed her mind and did not expect she ever would, and wrote to him as often as he did to her.

Mr. Salter took to dropping into Jack Horner after his round to ask her opinion about this case or that. Anne liked the ambitious, enthusiastic little man. She also realised that he would be a useful aid in the fulfilling of her ambitions. She found her time very fully taken up and full of interest.

She found herself thinking less often of Tony and the Thorns, more constantly of her work. Her mind resumed its former preoccupation with ward linen, ward clothes, ward funds, ward decoration, the keeping within bounds the ward indentures for dressings, the treatment of wounds and of relatives, the training of probationers. With the ward's bad tradition behind her and Mr. Salter's praise in front, she found that she was almost happy; or rather not happy, for she had known happiness now, but content. The enmity of the other Sisters (less active now, with the little Welsh Theatre Sister's departure) ceased gradually to trouble her.

Then came the day when Tony came rushing back to town to see her and she realised, with a shock, how much, in a few weeks, the gap between them had widened. She had grown older, with all these responsibilities, and his holidays had made him more of a boy than ever; the dearest, most lovable boy, who left a hole in her heart when he went away from her; but more than ever, to her, like a son or a young brother. She thanked Heaven for the clear sight which had made her able to see it before it was too late. For even as he chattered of the farm and of the Thorns, her thoughts were straying back to her ward (would the Staff-nurse dress Henry's leg without hurting him?) and to her nurses (had Nurse Rees really understood why one used catgut and not silk?).

Sitting in her room that night, she looked back on the afternoon with amazement. How had it happened that he had not claimed her whole attention? He had always done so before. How had she not been more enthralled by his stories of her friends?

She understood, presently, that she was exercising her instinct of self-preservation. He did not claim her whole attention because, if she let him, she would go mad. She could not be interested in the Thorns, in the lovely old farm, because, after today, she would see neither Tony nor the Thorns nor the farm any more. And a ward Sister had no time for grieving. She had got on without friends before, she must do so again.

She pulled pen and paper towards her and began—"Darling Tony—"

Luckily her room faced the opposite way from the Assistant Matron's, or a Night-nurse might have been sent to ask if she was ill, her light was on so late.

Lucky, too, that there was a troublesome baby in Jack

Horner ward that night, whose wails drowned the muffled sobs which were boxed up in Sister's room. No one expected to hear sobs from Sister's room, so no one heard them.

INTERLUDE

1

TONY ASHE glanced out of the window as the train slowed down at Wroughton. He decided that he would not get out but go on to Piney Wood and walk back through the forest. That would give him time to think.

It was early afternoon, and very hot. From the stuffy, gritty little train he stepped into sunshine which glittered and seemed to dry the very sweat upon his face; and thence, across a lane, into the cooling shadow of the great oak trees.

All the morning, as he worked, he had resolutely dragged his thoughts away from Anne's letter. He had done so quite consciously, because it was not possible to work and to worry at the same time. He realised that he had been turning them away, less consciously, from the conversation which he had had with her in the Kentish fields, ever since the conversation had taken place. Only that had been easy, because he had simply told himself that Anne was talking rubbish and had put the matter behind his back, where it had stayed, an indeterminate shadow of which he only caught a glimpse when he turned unawares. This time he couldn't do that. Anne did mean what she said, and what she said had to be faced and dealt with.

He walked on through the trees, whose spring yellow was giving place to the deeper green of summer, until he came to a clearing. This time he welcomed the sunshine and strode across the open space in it, a small, absorbed, clumsily graceful figure beside the great watching oaks. He sat down, in a patch of shade on the edge of the hill, looking out over the shimmering leaves of the trees in the valley. The forest stretched as far as he could see. There was no sign at all that he was in a civilised land.

Tony himself was, however, so completely civilised that he could not even bring himself to be angry with Anne. He was the youngest of his family and had, as such, been well squashed. He knew very well that hollow feeling which came when, having wanted something very much, he had seen it go to someone else who hardly wanted it at all. It was a feeling very much like that which he had now. After it, one pulled oneself together and said that it didn't matter, that no one should know one was the least bit hurt, and that one would jolly well get it or something better next time. All his life he had missed things by inches. At school, he had wanted to be Captain of his form, then Captain of cricket, then Head Prefect; and had just failed to be any of them because his gentle personality and his puppyish clumsiness had failed to impress. He had always, because of his good brain and his charm, been a distinguished member of the rank and file; later, had made an excellent secretary and vice-captain. He knew the feeling so well. He had had it less often lately, because hospital life did not call for leadership so much as competence, which he had. But here it was again. Once more he was being dismissed with a certificate of merit instead of the prize. And never had the prize seemed so nearly in his grasp.

He asked himself whether he had really, seriously hoped to grasp it. He had been very much surprised when Anne had said she loved him.

He was surprised now, because his dominant sensation was one of freedom. He had thought himself at anchor, and now he must turn about and make ready for another voyage. And, instead of being angry and hurt and frightened, he was full of a sense of adventure.

He loved Anne. He loved her beauty, her slimness, her length of limb, her quickness of understanding, her Northern downrightness which frightened some people, the kind, inquiring look in her brown eyes. He had always thought it would be wonderfully restful, to live with Anne, to come back to her from the worries of life outside.

The trees below him were tossing in the wind. Did one want rest, at twenty-three? Didn't one want excitement, exploration, ecstasy, for a little longer?

He tried to reconstruct Anne's point of view. She had reiterated that she was too old for him, that she would not be able to help dominating him, that he would rebel and be unhappy. Did people really think like that, when they were in love, even women? For Anne persisted that she loved him. Such altruism, even in Anne, was unbelievable.

Doubt crept in among his thoughts. That couldn't be the reason she had given him up. There must be something else, someone else. Why couldn't she be honest and say so? Did she think him such a child, despise him so, that she must try to spare him? He was almost angry then. He kicked the pebbles at his feet and they rolled with little tapping sounds down the hill into the dark hollow. He pulled his thoughts up sharply. "I must take it decently," he told himself he had so often told himself that before— "Anne's been so awfully decent, all along."

Did people think like that, even women, when they were in love? Anne had always been so starkly direct and true. If she said she thought like that, she did. Well, then, was she in love?

Slowly the kernel of the matter was laid bare before him. Anne loved him—but she was not in love with him. That was to say, if to be in love was to want him passionately, painfully, to think of nothing else but him, to be almost unable to wait for him. And—he turned on the other elbow the better to consider this strange truth— he loved Anne, but he wasn't in love with her, either. He loved her delicately, spiritually almost. He did not want anything of her. He was happy when he was near her, with a calm, quiet happiness. He was happy when she touched him, but it was more because her touch showed him she thought well of him than that the touch itself thrilled. He had asked her to marry him because it seemed the obvious thing to do, and having asked her, had acquiesced without further thought. Being the sort of person he was, no other course had suggested itself. To live with her as a mistress was not what he wanted at all. Even during that weekend, he knew that it was not entirely out of consideration for her that he had slept in the neighbouring cottage. It was partly that he had been afraid, not so much of failing, as of spoiling the magic relation which existed between them. He remembered being told, by an elderly man, that first love, in a certain type of man, was hardly of the body at all, but more a misty, intangible affair of mind and spirit, which was as likely as not to vanish when the body obtruded itself, as it would in time. He had not understood, then, having had no experience of either. Now he did, and he thought it was true. It would have been wonderful, to have slept with Anne. But it would have laid the magic in fragments round them. If he did not marry Anne, he would, perhaps, go on loving her, in this high, golden fashion, for a very long time. If he did marry her, perhaps his love would vanish at a touch and he did not know what would come instead.

Anne was perfectly right. She was not being a ridiculous altruist. Tony wondered if she had analysed it all, as he had, or whether it was just instinct which had warned her. He liked to think that it was instinct, that the thinking out had been left for him. Anyway, she had said, "I can't marry you because, if I did, we should only be happy for a very short time." And what she had said was true.

Tony felt as if he had come up, strong and glowing, after a cold plunge. It had been so cold that no one who was not very strong could have come up as he had done. Some would have never come up at all, and some would have come up blue and shivering and with no thought but that life was cruel and everyone an enemy. He was suddenly enormously pleased with himself. He stood up and puffed out his chest. He wanted to go to Anne and hug her and tell her she was a perfect darling. And he could. If he did, she would understand perfectly.

2

He had wondered whether he would tell Betty about it or not. But when, entering the Thorns' garden by the gate from the forest, he came upon her sprawling in a hammock, he found he could not help it, and blurted out, "I say, Bet, Anne's chucked me."

Betty's face, crinkled into a smile of welcome, froze and went white under her sunburn. She swung her legs over the side of the hammock and laid her book down carefully.

"*What* did you say?" she asked.

He sat down on the grass, some little way off so that he could see her. "Anne's decided that she can't marry me."

"Why?" Betty inquired at once. Her colour had come back and she was sitting with her legs dangling, looking at him.

"She's been uneasy about it for some time. Since she was down here, with time to think. She says we shouldn't be happy any longer than our honeymoon. She's a darling, Betty."

Betty looked startled, trying vainly to reconcile Tony's news with the content on his face. "You still think that?"

"Rather. Of course. Don't you?"

"I? Think Anne's a darling? Of course I do. But then, there's no reason why I shouldn't."

He tried to tell her of his conclusions. "You see, she's

286

always been—somehow on a pedestal, for me. One does think of a Sister on a pedestal, doesn't one? Rather remote and starched and unattainable. Even when she behaves like an ordinary person, the original impression is still there, colouring one's idea of her. She says she would always be top-dog. She would, and I don't think I should mind. I might, one can't tell. But she says she would mind, herself. And—this is the odd part—I believe I'd rather have her on that pedestal than closer. I simply should hate her to find me dull and ordinary and boring and mean—you know how one does find people. She thought of me, at first, as a bit of a tin god, because I was a doctor. Then I turned into a dear little boy. But I wasn't, ever, just an ordinary man, to her; just as she wasn't ever just an ordinary woman to me. D'you see? We started out on a false basis, and she thinks it wouldn't stand the strain of close quarters. At least, that's what I gather. D'you see?"

Betty nodded. "Rather. I feel just like that about Anne myself. As if she was a perfectly charming and rare and darling Aunt. Not one who had been forced on me, as Aunts usually are, but whom I'd chosen for myself."

Tony agreed. "And, you know, no one could be happy forever with even the dearest of aunts. There would always be a restraining hand. I wonder—"

"I don't know," Betty said. "I don't see why that sort of love—yours and hers—shouldn't lead to a successful marriage. A happy one, I mean. As long as you both realised the relationship and accepted it."

He caught her up. "That's just it, I think. Anne wouldn't accept it. She's too generous. She'd go into it with a conflict. She hasn't enough imagination to see that it isn't everyone who wants to lead. She's been stewing about it all the time, beginning with the fact that she's older than I am. Someone—one of those hags—called her a baby-snatcher, and there was just enough truth in it to start her thinking. No, it's the sort of relationship you've got to go into either blindfold—you may miss the difficulties altogether then—or, as you said, with your eyes wide open, foreseeing them and accepting them."

Betty was looking away towards the forest, her forehead wrinkled. "I'm so *sorry* for Anne," she said. "I think I'll have to rush off and see her. Tonight. Now."

Tony said irritably, "Why?" He did not want Betty to go dashing off now, even for Anne.

Betty brought her eyes to his, inscrutably. "You're not a bad sort of possession to be throwing away for a principle," she said, and whisked out of the hammock and into the house.

Tony followed her, slowly. If she really was going off to see Anne, he might as well walk to the station with her.

Betty called to him as she came out. "I say, Tony! That holiday the twins have planned, with the yacht, in August—you'll be able to come, now, won't you?"

Tony's face brightened. He had decided that he would not be able to join the Thorns, as he usually did, for their holidays, this year, if he was going to save up, first for his Fellowship and then to get married. "Jingo, so I shall! At least, I don't see any reason to not, do you?"

Betty plunged into the project. They were going to sail up the west coast, to see the Highlands from the sea, to get right up to the Hebrides if they could. Tony glowed. It was just the sort of adventure he loved. They had had one boating holiday, the four of them, on the Thames, and another year had done some cruising for a day at a time along the south coast. This was much more ambitious. As they walked, he could see the bare patch of hillside where he had sat during the afternoon and watched the tossing trees. Betty—and the twins, of course—were topping people to share adventures with. He could not, somehow, imagine Anne on a wild, wet, boating holiday.

It came to him, suddenly, that Anne had funked an adventure with him. And then, with a flush which he hoped Betty would not see, he remembered how he had funked an adventure with Anne.

CHAPTER 5

1

A CRISIS was taking place in Jack Horner ward. Anne had been back over a month and everything running smoothly. But today, first a child had been brought in run over, with both his legs badly broken; then a little girl terribly scalded; and then a baby with an intestinal stoppage to whom every hour before operation was an hour to the bad. It happened to be the new Sister Theatre's half-day off duty, and Anne, because she was the only person qualified to do so, always took charge of the Theatre when Sister Theatre was out. She enjoyed doing it, and as a rule welcomed emergencies when she was on Theatre duty. But three all at once, when the ward was already busy, needed some thinking about. Anyone less efficient would hardly have known which way to begin on a day like this.

She bustled up to the Theatre floor; flattered the Staff-nurse there by saying that of course she did not need to be told what to get ready and proceeded to tell her; raced down again and helped the new House-surgeon—a woman, pleasant and good at her work—to dress the scald, keeping a wary eye on the Staff-nurse and the Pro who were preparing the other two children for operation. Then up again, to make sure the Theatre was properly ready; and down, to be standing, primly cuffed and waiting, at the ward door when Mr. Salter arrived to see the cases.

The Senior Surgeon was in a gloomy mood. He gave an

approving nod to Anne as she bade him a professional good afternoon. She at any rate was a sight for sore eyes, her rosy face set off by her trim royal-blue dress and white apron and the little Sister Dora cap with strings tied under her chin. He obviously felt a proprietary interest in her. He shook his head over the scalded child and gave his opinion that, although the dressing was everything it should have been, the child would die of shock before the afternoon was out. The House-surgeon asked if anything more could be done and he would only insist that nothing would be any good. Anne, who knew that they had done already everything which was possible, shepherded him to the next bed. Here he was sure that the accident case would lose both legs. He thought he would probably have to amputate them that very day. Anne, looking at the little dark, thin urchin to whom the legs belonged thought he would be better dead. The baby, Mr. Salter thought he might conceivably have saved if it had been brought to the hospital in the early morning instead of in the afternoon. As it was, well, he supposed he had better give it the benefit of the doubt and operate. He would go downstairs and smoke a pipe, he said, while the Theatre was being got ready.

"Its ready now," Anne said.

He looked at her with some surprise. "I was told it was Sister Theatre's day off."

"So it is. I do the Theatre while she's away. The H.S. said the baby had an intussusception, so I got it ready at once."

He nodded appreciatively and smiled. "Splendid, Sister.

We'll go right up."

She returned to the ward and felt his eye following her. She knew that he was saying to himself that he knew a good nurse when he saw one. He always watched her, now, with that air of satisfaction. Well, she might want a good word from him soon, so it was a very good thing he was satisfied.

She stayed in the ward long enough to make sure that the scalded child was being adequately watched and kept warm. It had been given morphia and was already sleeping quietly. It should not die of shock if she could help it. She gave orders for various things to be made ready for the other two when their operations were over. That would be the worrying part of the afternoon, when the first case was done and she had to be in the Theatre with the second. It was such a critical time, when a baby was coming round from an anaesthetic. However, the Staff-nurse would be there, and Anne had trained her carefully and knew that she was reliable. She found the girl and told her shortly that the baby's life would depend on her when it came down from the Theatre, and left her, serious, and carried the baby upstairs. She herself was serious, too. She had never been more completely absorbed in her work.

Mr. Salter was a deft and gentle operator. He removed the obstruction with a swift, careful manipulation and sewed the baby up, grumbling to himself that it couldn't possibly live and asking why in the name of goodness it had not been brought there before. Anne, watching every movement so that she might hand him the right instrument just before he wanted it, knew that he was making the worst of a bad job. She had seen babies as ill as that one recover before. And now, that the Surgeon's part was done, the baby's chance of life was in the hands of the nurses, just as was the chance of the little scalded girl. She made a sign to the Nurse, and the Nurse was ready before the last stitch was tied to wrap the baby in its warm blanket and carry it down to bed.

Mr. Salter smiled at her again as he peeled off his gloves. "Quick work, Sister. It makes all the difference in the world, to have good assistants."

She smiled, too. To be one of a highly trained team was one of the most stimulating experiences she knew, every member working silently, as if by clockwork, every movement dovetailing with another. She resolved that when she was Matron, she would take the Theatre herself and train the Theatre-team. She was busy, now, clearing up, scrubbing the instruments and putting them into the steriliser. She turned to Mr. Salter and asked him whether he would want splints or plaster for the broken legs.

"Neither, if we amputate. Don't be ridiculous, Sister."

She dimpled as she went across to the Nurse and gave instructions for both plaster and splints to be brought, and with them a certain padded frame which she had seen used for a similar, though not so serious case. Mr. Salter might be a man of moods, but he would not let his mood influence him when he had the child on the table. He was a trustable man, and when he made a decision he made it in the interest of his patient and of no one else. That was why he needed good nurses, for in a serious illness the

293

nurses must not expect consideration.

He whistled behind his mask as the poor little legs were unbound.

"Horrid. Very badly smashed up. Two fractures here—see—one big nerve gone—but here's the other end, we could mend that—calf muscles frightfully torn, that's the worst part, sure to go septic—um—um—"

He straightened the limb somewhat and arranged the damaged parts. It did not look as if it could ever be called a leg again.

"What about it, Sister? It'll have to have continuous irrigation and he'll need gas for every dressing, and if it goes wrong he'll die."

"And if it doesn't?"

"He'll probably have quite a good leg. But it's very likely to go wrong, with all this tearing, and if we amputate now he'll almost certainly live."

"It won't go wrong, in Jack Horner," Anne said. If it was only a matter of fighting shock and sepsis, she could do it, if anyone could.

"All right. We'll risk it. The finest catgut, first, for this nerve—"

It took them nearly two hours to fit the damaged muscles and nerves together and cover them more or less with skin. But the child left the theatre with two legs, fastened comfortably to the frame which Anne had placed suggestively ready.

"Good idea, that frame," Mr. Salter remarked. He was in better humour, now that the worry was over for him. He and Anne wished each other pleasantly good night. He was a good person to work for, Anne reflected. It *was* stimulating, to be efficient and to be approved of.

She left the nurses to clear up, and hurried down to the ward. The scalded child was still sleeping. She was warm and her pulse was strong. She was not going to die of shock, whatever Mr. Salter might say. And the baby was beginning to wake up and look about. Anne set about restoring the boy who had just been operated upon. At the end of an hour she still had three live children on her hands instead of the three little corpses which the Surgeon had predicted.

She went into the ward kitchen to speak to the children's parents. It always surprised her, to see how much these poor people loved their children, although they nearly always had more mouths in the family than they could properly feed. She had heard the histories and characters of all three of the small patients by the time she escaped from the kitchen, and was, if that were possible, more than ever determined not to lose one of them.

She came off duty at six, very tired, but leaving the three as far as they could be on the way to recovery behind her. As she came down the stairs to see if there were any letters for her on the post-board, a porter met her.

"Gentleman waiting for you in the hall, Sister," he said with a grin.

"A gentleman, for me?" With an effort she disentangled her thoughts from the afternoon's work. She remembered that the grin meant that the people at Princess Ida's thought she was still engaged to be married and had never known to whom. She wondered if Betty could be ill again and Tony come to tell her. She had met Tony, after he had had her letter, and had a long, serious talk with him and they had parted better friends than ever. But he never came to see her, now, unless with Betty. There was no reason for him to do so. Betty had spent hours with her, that night after the letter had been sent, pleading and trying to reason with her, and then Betty, too, had seen that she was right, and now Betty, too, was more her friend than ever. Every time she thought of the Thorns, Anne was flooded by a warm thankfulness for them. She had been so terribly afraid that she would lose them when she lost Tony. And she had not lost them, or really lost Tony either. Betty, of course, might have come to see her. But she always came straight up. And—silly, the porter had said a gentleman.

She peered over the banisters, and saw a tweed coat on broad shoulders, and corn-coloured hair standing crisply on end and shading into a sunburned neck.

"Why—Martin!"

He swung round and came towards her with both hands outstretched, unconscious of the eyes which would be popping out of heads, the ears which would be strained, the shocked, averted faces.

"Why—Anne! I've never seen you in that get-up! It's rather frightening, but it does suit you, my dear!"

A nurse, who was passing by, giggled.

"What on earth are you doing here?" she asked him.

"I came to take you out to dinner. Can I? Can you get off that outfit and come?"

"Rather! I'm just off duty! Oh—" her face fell. "But I can't, Martin!" She remembered that it was Sister Theatre's half-day, and that even though she was off duty there must be someone in the hospital who could manage the Theatre if anything more came in. She explained to Martin. She was quite ridiculously disappointed, almost ready to weep with disappointment. She had not seen him since she had left the farm, and he looked so healthy and country and nice.

Then, as they were deciding that, after all, it would have to be just "how-do-you-do and goodbye" and he must go, the new, young Sister Theatre came along the corridor from the Nurses' Home. She looked at them a little shyly, hesitated, and then came and touched Anne on the arm.

"Sister—I've just heard from Nurse what a lot you've had to do. I don't mind a bit being on call if you're wanting to go out. No, I wasn't going out anyway. I've a friend coming for the evening."

Anne and Martin turned to her eagerly, both at once. It seemed to matter so much whether they went out together tonight or not.

"Are you *sure* you don't mind?" Anne said.

"Perfectly sure! And it's most unlikely there'll be anything more after all that. I should doubt if we've got a bed—"

"That's true. Well, then, Martin—?"

"It would be most awfully kind of you," Martin said, and the new Sister Theatre smiled and turned away.

"What luck!" Anne, in spite of her uniform, was the

happy young woman of the farm again. "I'll just go and change and make it all right with Matron. I'll be most awfully quick. There's a seat here—see?"

As she changed, confusing thoughts came thronging into her head. "My dear," he had said. And she had been so frightfully, so idiotically disappointed when she had thought she could not go. She thrust them away. She was going to enjoy herself. It was lovely, to see Martin again, that was all.

In a few minutes she was down again, in mufti, the Anne he knew.

"Martin—let's go to Kew. We could have some food on the way back, if you've time. It's gorgeous there just now—" She felt that some sort of country setting was right, for Martin, and Kew, with its dignified grass and trees, was better than the suburban imitation which was the alternative.

"I've got the whole evening," he told her, with the grave twinkle which she remembered. She found herself chuckling with delight at the twinkle because she liked it so much.

They set off by bus, always Anne's chariot to adventure or to pleasure. It seemed perfectly right, to be going about with Martin.

Anne expected that Betty, or the twins, or all three, would join them. They talked all the way, both of them, silent Martin and shy Anne, and by the time they arrived at the gardens Anne had realised that the rest of the Thorns were probably not coming. She mentioned them, when she and Martin had settled themselves on the grass, not too near the water's edge, but near enough to see the birds which waddled and scurried there.

"Betty? No, she's home in the garden. Twins? Oh, they're up to some play of their own, I expect."

He did not seem inclined to talk about his family. Instead, he said, "Anne. You liked the farm, didn't you? You've been talking about it as if you liked it."

"Like it? I simply loved it!" Anne declared. "Why?" She would not think, she would only enjoy this lovely minute.

"Would you like to live on a farm?"

Anne debated the point. "Yes, I think I should. It would be fun to have a clean dairy like that one to play with. As good as a Theatre. You must come and see our Theatre, Martin—oh, but of course you've seen better ones heaps of times with Tony and Betty, I forgot. Yes, I like the smells and the little young things and the rabbits and being out of doors so much. I might even get to like the cows in time. Why, though?"

She told herself that Betty must be worse again—have developed T.B., perhaps—and be thinking of retiring to the country and wanting Anne to come and take care of her. She couldn't do that, of course, even for Betty. She was going to run Mr. Salter's ward for him. She looked up at Martin, because he did not reply to her question—and found his grey eyes on her, and looked away in a hurry, her heart thumping.

When she looked up again, Martin's eyes were upon the ducks on the lake.

"You see, Anne"—the way he spoke it somehow made the commonplace little name sound beautiful—"I've known for a long time that I would like to marry. But I've never met anyone who would do. I can't imagine any of Marian's learned friends, or Evadne's flappers, as a farmer's wife, can you? And anyway I wasn't drawn to them. I thought of a farmer's daughter—there are several round about—but they're all so solid. Jolly good housekeepers, I expect, but I wanted something more than that. So I carried on as I was. And then—I came home in a panic about Betty, and saw you. You hardly noticed me, you were so taken up with her. And everyone took you so much for granted that they forgot to tell me about you. I thought you were just one of Betty's friends. I knew, that first evening, that I'd found what I wanted. You were— just right. And the more I saw of you, the righter you were. And then they told me you were 'Tony's Anne.' It was too late then, I'd let myself go—"

He paused, and Anne could see that he was living the days over again. A furrow had come in his forehead and little hurt wrinkles about his eyes and mouth. As if in a dream, Anne laid her hand on his as it clenched itself on the ground, supporting him. "I'm not 'Tony's Anne' now, Martin."

He turned towards her and the wrinkles smoothed themselves and he smiled.

"I know. I wanted to wring young Tony's neck. Always felt quite friendly to him, before—I've been wondering what was the shortest decent interval, before I could come and talk to you—"

They chuckled, meeting each other's eyes frankly at first, then drawing shyly away.

"Go on—talking—" Anne said with an effort.

"Well, when they suggested you should come down with Betty, I didn't know what to do. I tried to put them off but it wasn't any good. It seemed impossible to say no and I was terrified of saying yes. In the end I did say yes and told myself I would be so busy that I simply never saw you. I knew I could control my doings, and I thought I could control my feelings too. But—oh, Anne, it was simply awful. Everything you did made it worse, and I couldn't keep away from you. If I didn't know where you were I was restless, and if I did know I had to be there too."

"That was why you didn't thunder on my door," Anne said. "I thought it was because you thought it wouldn't be proper."

"It wouldn't have been," Martin retorted. "It would have been highly dangerous!" The wrinkles round his eyes were those of laughter now. Anne wondered inconsequently how it was that she, a rather solemn person, always made her friends laugh.

"Well, anyway—"

Anne wanted to stop him. Then she didn't want to. Then she couldn't.

"Anyway, Anne—will you marry me? Will you come and live on the farm?"

Anne sat still, lips parted, eyes shining as she looked out over the lake. That dear old house—how lovely she would make it. And she could manage the dairy so much better than those men did. And sick small animals would be as good as small children to fuss after. And there would be children—her own children—playing Red Indians in the orchards and climbing the old step-tree. And then, Martin himself—dear, strong, quiet, sunburnt Martin, with whom she had always felt so curiously at home. There was no question of who would be top-dog, with Martin. They would be companions, and if he wanted his own way, well, it was inconceivable that it should not be her way too. And even if it was not, he should have it. And with Martin she could always be herself. She would never need a shell, to protect her and to smother her.

Her hand was still lying on his, and his hand stirred and made her conscious of the contact between them. Something she had never felt before shot up her arm, all over her, making her tremble, stealing their usual steadiness from her lips.

Martin pulled his hand out and took hers in a grasp which was horny and strong and very gentle. Astonishment at its strength and its gentleness filtered in among her turmoil of feelings. He said, in a voice which struck her as curious in its humility, "Well, Anne?"

She forced herself to look at him. He seemed to give out health and serenity, so that it made her happy simply to be with him. She drew her hand away and sat with it in her lap.

"It's just this," she said. "I was hasty about Tony. If I'd stopped and thought, I should never have let it go as far as it did, and I shouldn't have hurt him so much. I don't want to be hasty about this and then find I've made a mistake and hurt you. May I go away and think about it?"

"Of course," he said at once.

They sat still with their own thoughts.

When Anne moved, Martin said, "What about some food? Will you come and have some?"

Anne said, "Yes, let's," and stretched out a hand shyly and gripped Martin's and let it fall again. Martin smiled at her, and then they were talking again, as though the conversation by the lake had never been. But their eyes would keep straying to each other's face and they would smile again, or sigh with content. On the bus their shoulders bumped together, and Anne was conscious of every touch and knew that Martin was, too. She had never been conscious of Tony like that. She realised how little passion had played a part with her and Tony, how much it might with her and Martin. And it wasn't only passion. There was so much more in it, too. She liked him so much, as well as loving him. As they dined, opposite each other, she could not take her eyes off him.

When at last he left her at the Hospital steps, he said, "I shall ring you up at nine tomorrow, to see if you've done enough thinking. If you haven't, you can just say so. But I shall be on pins till I know."

"I shan't be able to say much," she objected, twinkling at him. "The telephone's in the passage, by the ward door, and I can't possibly cause more of a scandal than I've done already."

"Say yes or no or I'm not sure yet," Martin grinned at her. "And we'll make a plan when to see each other again."

She ran up the steps from him in a hurry.

2

The Staff-nurse was lurking in the passage by Anne's door. Anne would have passed without even seeing her, but she stepped out and called: "Sister!"

Anne stopped.

"I thought you'd be longing to know about those kids. They're all quite fit. The baby's had a feed. Isn't it splendid?"

Anne stared at her. Kids? What kids? The afternoon's work flooded back to her thoughts. Why, she had forgotten all about them. How could she possibly have forgotten about them? She smiled at the nurse. "That *is* splendid: I'm so glad. Nice of you to wait and tell me," she said.

In her room, she tried to think about the treatment which the children would need tomorrow. But she could only think of Martin's crisp upstanding hair. She tried to think about her Theatre and how she would train her nurses for it. But she could only think of the touch of Martin's shoulder against hers. She gave up trying to think at all, told herself sternly that she had been through a tiring day, and prepared for bed.

She did not even try to sleep. Presently her mind became more orderly and the two alternatives before her stood out clearly. She had to choose, calmly and sensibly, which of them she would take. She was not a child, to be taken in by passion, nor yet a bitter, unsuccessful spinster to whom marriage was an escape or a mystery. She was choosing, she told herself, simply between two careers; the one she knew, which she was trained for, which would lead her to independence, experience, respect; which would make her a queen in her own small but not unimportant world; the other, of which she knew nothing, which had difficulties and dangers all its own, which would give her Martin. The one assured, the other a gamble.

She thought for a long time of Martin. Every time she visualised him, her muscles tightened up in ecstasy. She loved every single bit of Martin—his looks, his strength, his kindness, his little everyday habits and mannerisms, his settled convictions which would never change. She loved him because he was slow and sure and because he knew his own job so well and did not pretend to any cleverness outside it. She loved him for his likeness to Betty and for his difference from her. She loved the life he had chosen, his hardworking life which was full of real things, not shams, of which the results were in his own hands and God's, not dependent on other men.

She almost loved Ronald Dalloway and Tony, then, because they had led her, as it were, by slow degrees, to Martin. She saw that people would say she had thrown Tony over for Martin, that she was fickle, that she had preferred a man whose career was made to a boy on the threshold of his. She shook her head and stretched her bare arms in careless denial. She had never thought of Martin except as Betty's delightful brother until that very day. She had given up Tony because it was the only thing to do, feeling about him as she had done. She tried to remember the agony of the night when she had finally written to him, and found that she could not recall it. The gladness which enveloped her had blotted it out.

She wondered how she could possibly wait until the morning to tell Martin which she had chosen.

Also published by
Greyladies

DOCTOR'S CHILDREN
By Josephine Elder

When Barbara's husband deserts her, she uproots her
family of four children to London where she resumes her
career as a doctor. Written at the time of the launch of
the National Health Service, and written by a practising
G. P., this presents an interesting picture of how a single
parent who is also a professional woman copes with the
prevailing ethos that a woman's place, and certainly a
married woman's place, is in the home.

THE ENCIRCLED HEART
by Josephine Elder

'Josephine Elder', in real life Dr. Olive Potter, a GP in Surrey, here writes with first-hand knowledge of the experiences of a woman doctor in the 1930s and 40s.

Marion Blake is a young doctor with a growing practice living with her pathologist friend, Philippa. She is totally and happily absorbed in her work – of which we are given fascinating descriptions – until she meets and marries Paul Shepherd, a university lecturer and aspiring playwright.

Inevitably conflicts arise when Paul, an indulged only son with his little boy smile, wants "to love you and work for you and have you for myself alone," but Marion, calm and competent, steadfastly self-reliant, "can't give the practice up. It's my child, I made it!" and Dr. Blake has to take precedence over Paul's wife.

The introduction includes the text of a talk Dr. Potter gave to the Women's Institute on her medical training at Girton and the London Hospital in Whitechapel.